Friends
with
Benefits

Friends with Benefits

Lawrence Ross

KENSINGTON PUBLISHING CORP.
http://www.kensingtonbooks.com

DAFINA BOOKS are published by

Kensington Publishing Corp.
850 Third Avenue
New York, NY 10022

All Kensington titles, imprints and distributed lines are available at special quantity discounts for bulk purchases for sales promotion, premiums, fund-raising, educational or institutional use.

Special book excerpts or customized printings can also be created to fit specific needs. For details, write or phone the office of the Kensington Special Sales Manager: Kensington Publishing Corp., 850 Third Avenue, New York, NY 10022. Attn. Special Sales Department. Phone: 1-800-221-2647.

Dafina Books and the Dafina logo Reg. U.S. Pat. & TM Off.

ISBN 0-7582-1065-5

First Kensington Trade Paperback Printing: September 2005
10 9 8 7 6 5 4 3 2 1

Printed in the United States of America

Friends
with
Benefits

CHAPTER 1

At first it had been cool, but now it was beginning to piss Jason off. Not because of what it was, but because of what it represented. Every Friday night, no matter how late he got home from the law office, he knew a warm dish of beef Stroganoff was waiting for him. It didn't come from his mother or from a girlfriend. It was a weekly bowl of sympathy made by Mrs. Olga Petroff, an older Russian woman who lived in his apartment building.

"Every man should have a woman cook for him at least one meal a week," Mrs. Petroff had exclaimed two years ago. "That is an old Russian proverb. What woman cooks for you, Jason?" Even after thirty years in this country, her English was still lightly accented with Russian.

This was not a discussion Jason had anticipated having with Mrs. Petroff. In fact, he'd only talked to her that day because he'd run out of milk and he didn't feel like going to the store. He knew she was always home, so he'd knocked on her door in order to save time. But there he was, standing in front of an old woman trying to explain that he was going through a dry spell on the dating scene.

"I don't have a girlfriend right now, in fact I haven't had one for a while, but I'm hoping that changes soon. I'm just sort of, well, waiting for the right woman. So I guess I don't have that woman in my life that cooks for me," he answered.

"Oh, yes you do! Me!" she exclaimed eagerly.

She grabbed Jason by the arm, pulled him into her apartment, and suddenly he was sitting in an impeccably outfitted kitchen. Shiny brass pots hung from the ceiling, fine china was displayed in the cabinets and a fresh cherry pie was cooling on the counter. This was the kitchen of someone who took cooking seriously. Mrs. Petroff bent down and pulled out a green-and-white cookbook that looked like it had been passed directly from Russian czars to her. It had little slips of paper stuff throughout, as though she'd created addendums to the original recipe. She had.

"In this country, I don't understand. Men and women work, work, work, and don't take care of each other. When you find a woman who will cook for you, you should keep her," she commented, flipping through the cookbook. "Until then, I will cook for you. What is your favorite meal?"

"Well, I like—"

"Do you like beef?"

"Yes, and I like—"

"Until you get a girlfriend, I will make you beef Stroganoff every Friday," she said, pointing to a page in her book. "Beef Stroganoff is the dish of Russian kings, and it will keep you strong. Plus, it will bring you good luck."

"Okay," Jason said, who wanted to back out of her apartment as soon as possible. "Thank you very much, Mrs. Petroff."

"You're going to find a good woman and she's going to make a great man of you," she said as they slowly walked to her front door.

Then, as she opened her door to let him go, Mrs. Petroff suddenly turned around, her face full of concern.

"You're not a homosexual, are you, Jason?" she asked.

"No ma'am," Jason stuttered, startled that this old woman was now asking if he liked men. Did he project that? he wondered. "I'm just on sort of a dry streak when it comes to women."

"A dry streak?" she said, not really understanding.

"I just haven't had a lot of luck with women lately."

"Oh, don't worry, you'll find one!" she said, pinching his cheeks a little too hard. "But I did want to make sure you weren't a homosexual. I don't have anything against homosexuals, but the

Stroganoff wouldn't help you there. It will only bring you luck if you are looking for a woman."

And with that, she started preparing Jason's first batch of beef Stroganoff.

So it came as no surprise when Mrs. Petroff greeted him on this particular Friday with the same question she'd asked for the past two years.

"Have you found that woman yet?"

Jason literally had his key in the door, and Mrs. Petroff had come bursting out of her apartment with the energy of a forty-year-old and not the sixty-year-old she truly was.

"No Mrs. Petroff, no woman again."

"Don't worry, she'll come. And when she comes, you'll know it because she'll be the right one." She then handed him his weekly dish of beef Stroganoff.

"Thank you, ma'am."

And there it was. A Jason Richards Friday night punctuated by a steaming dish of beef Stroganoff, handed to him by an elderly woman obsessed with his love life. There had to be a better way.

"What's up, y'all? You have now reached Jason Richards's residence. Please leave a message and I'll holla back at ya when I get the time."

Jason pressed the pound sign on his phone to retrieve his messages.

"You have no new messages," the computer voice said.

Jason heard those words, and it reminded him about how lonely his life truly had suddenly become.

Not even bill collectors are calling my house, he thought. Is this all worth it? Is the end result worth what I'm giving up?

He wearily sat down in his leather chair and turned on his television. Jason had never gotten used to the silence of being alone, and the television created enough white noise to help cut it. It may be only white noise, but it is noise all the same.

And so he sat there, thinking. He was Jason Richards, a twenty-eight-year-old rising star at the Ketchings & Martin law firm, and targeted for success from the minute he walked into the office two years ago. Peter Ketchings had even taken him into his office during his first week at the firm to tell him so.

"Jason, we're really happy to have you on board," Peter Ketchings had said. Peter Ketchings was a quiet intimidator. He'd made his money as a trial lawyer against corporations, and continued to make his money by attacking everything from lead paint to restaurants serving too-hot coffee. He didn't lose often, and didn't hire losing lawyers. "Over the past five years, we've been trying to diversify our firm with excellent lawyers from every background, and I think that if you work hard, you can go far here. We're always looking for stars at this firm, and you have the potential to be one. But you have to work hard and be willing to give up a lot to win. I only want winners here at my firm."

"Sir, I thank you for the compliment," Jason said, confident in his skills. He looked Ketchings directly in the eye. "I want you to know from the start that no one outworks me. I can guarantee that. Before you get into the office, I'll be here. And after you leave the office, I'll still be here."

"I wish we could transplant your attitude into some of the lawyers we have," Ketchings said, smiling. He handed Jason a manila folder. "I'm putting you on the Burger World lawsuit. Steven Cox was on it, but I'm taking him off of it. He'll brief you. Good luck, Jason."

Jason had walked out of Ketchings's office determined to prove himself. Jason had graduated at the top of his class in law school, so he knew he was good. But he also had a sneaking suspicion that the firm needed a black lawyer to "color up" the firm, and he'd fit the bill perfectly. If they were manipulating him, that was fine with Jason. But then he was going to manipulate them by advancing as far as he could, as fast as he could. He wanted to be a partner in the firm, and nothing was going to stop him.

"This case is a hellhole," Steven Cox told Jason as he transferred a box of files to him. "I think they give cases like this to new lawyers just to test them. They take a lot of time and there's little reward at the end."

"How long did you work on the case?" Jason asked, opening some of the folders.

"Six fucking months. And that was six fucking months too damn long."

Steven Cox was the other black lawyer at the firm, although he was so light skinned, Jason doubted that many of the white lawyers even knew he was black. He dressed impeccably, with tailored suits that looked ripped from the pages of *Esquire* magazine. He'd arrived at the firm about a year before Jason, and had represented Ketchings & Martin when Berkeley had invited law firms to recruit their students. Everything about him had impressed Jason, from his dress and the way he carried himself, and his example was a deciding factor in choosing Ketchings & Martin over everyone else. But when Jason got to the firm, it was clear that Steven was struggling to make a mark, and the Burger World case was one of the reasons. Steven looked at the Burger World lawsuit as an albatross around his career, and was happy to get rid of it.

"This shit was cutting into pussy time, if you know what I mean," Steven said, smiling.

"Yeah," Jason said, still shuffling through the papers.

Steven leaned back in his chair and studied Jason.

"You really believe that shit Ketchings and the others talk about, don't you?"

"What do you mean?"

"About being a star at this firm, and shit like that? You actually believe that shit, don't you?"

Jason stopped shuffling through the papers and looked up.

"Yeah, I believe in it. I believe that if I knock out something like this Burger World case, then I can move up. I'm not satisfied with being an associate. I got into law because I want to be a partner. And I don't care what I have to sacrifice to get it."

Steven smirked at Jason as though he'd seen and heard this all before.

"Ah, you're one of those ambitious Negroes I keep hearing about!" Steven laughed. "You're going to work your ass off for eighty hours a week, week after week, month after month, year after year, in order to prove to these white folks that they didn't make a mistake when they hired a black lawyer. I can see it in your eyes."

"I don't know what you're all about Steven, but I know what I want out of being a lawyer," Jason said, annoyed. "I didn't come here to fuck around, but to do the best I can. So I guess I am one of those ambitious Negroes you heard about. So as long as you don't fuck with what I'm trying to do, then we won't have any problems. We understand each other?"

Steven ran his fingers through his hair. He took the final pile of papers and dropped them on Jason's desk.

"Whatever you say, brother," he said sarcastically. "If you turn this bullshit into something, I'll be the first to kiss your ass. Don't hold your breath."

Jason turned away.

"Hey look, cat," Steven said, grinning. "If you want to be Johnnie Cochran up in here, I ain't gonna stop you. I just want to get my check and roll, myself. But the fact is that there are only two brothers in this bitch, you and me, so we should have each other's back. You cool?"

As Jason looked up from his desk, Steven offered his hand. He didn't dislike Steven, and he didn't trust him either. But he was the only other brother at the firm.

"Cool," he said, shaking Steven's hand. "Now tell me about this Burger World lawsuit."

"Do you really want to know?" he asked.

"Yep."

Steven popped open a Red Bull and took a sip.

"Okay, here it is," Steven started. "An Australian guy brings his family to California for a little vacation. It's winter in Australia during our summer, and he figures they could get a little sun and see the sights. You know, take the kids to Disneyland and the whole nine."

"Right."

"So everything's going well. The kids are happy because they've gone to Disneyland and got some Mickey Mouse ears, while the wife's happy because she's walked down Rodeo Drive and shopped in the same place Nicole Kidman shopped. And of course the dad is happy because the kids and the wife are out of his hair."

"Okay, so what's the problem?"

Steven smiles.

"The dad is kicking it poolside, checking out women not his wife, when he gets a text message on his Blackberry. It's from his best friend Ainsley, who's back in Melbourne. He tells our Aussie friend that no matter what he does, he's got to stop at Burger World and get a Burger World big all-beef burger with extra beef.

He says that he's never tasted anything like it and it has to be experienced to be appreciated."

"I love those damn things," Jason said. "Had one last night."

"Well, you might not love them after I finish telling you the story," Steven laughed. "The idea sounds good, plus he loves hamburgers, so he takes his family to get one. He goes to the one right next to Graumann's Chinese Theater in Hollywood so he can kill two birds with one stone."

"The kids and the wife could check out Clark Gable's footprints at Graumann, and he could get some grub."

"Exactly," Steven said, taking another sip of his Red Bull. "Right after he finds out that he has the same shoe size as Gary Cooper, he takes the family across the street to Burger World and orders a Burger World big all-beef burger with extra beef. And damned if it doesn't taste good to him. He eats half of it, and then takes the rest to the hotel to finish later. But that's when the problems begin. He's sitting in his hotel room when his head begins swelling to the size of Shaquille O'Neal's."

"Damn," Jason said, enthralled.

"Yeah, and that's what the wife said. I suppose if she had her druthers, she would have picked something else to swell as large as Shaq's beside her husband's head, but I digress."

"So what happens? Did the dude die?"

"Nah, he didn't die. But they take him to the emergency room where the doctor asks the wife whether her husband is allergic to anything. They go over the usual things, medicines, penicillin, all that shit. She's saying no to everything the doctor asks until she remembers that her husband was allergic to one thing."

"And that was?"

"Hold for it," Steven said, giggling. "Kangaroo meat. Isn't that funny? An Australian allergic to kangaroo meat! She remembered that when they were first married, they'd gone on a trip to the Australian outback and stayed at a hotel where kangaroo meat was served. The husband, trying to impress his new wife, ordered it and damn near had the same reaction. But where had the man eaten kangaroo meat in California?"

"At Burger World?"

"Bingo, my ambitious Negro lawyer," Steven said. "It turns out that the Burger World big all-beef burger with extra beef ain't made of beef. So after the swelling goes down, the Aussie comes to us and we file a lawsuit on his behalf."

"How come Burger World didn't just make it go away?" Jason asked, reading a paper from the files. "It says here that we started negotiations for a settlement, but things broke off."

"Yep, I almost got them to settle. But Country Bob Briggs owns Burger World, and he's a stubborn bastard. His lawyers told him they could make the lawsuit go away, but he feels that Burger World hasn't done anything wrong. So we're at loggerheads. And that's why you have the case. Ketchings & Martin wants to win this case badly because they think this isn't a one-off thing. They think folks have been eating kangaroo meat for years."

"So they've given it to a green lawyer looking to make a reputation?" Jason asked.

"Who better?" Steven said. "More experienced lawyers were already handling cases, so they gave it to me. And now I give it to you. Good luck, 'cause you're going to need it."

That had been two years ago. Jason now sat on his couch, exhausted from working eighty hours a week, month after month, just as Steven had predicted. That was the deal with the devil he'd made. But as a result, relationships of all kinds got kicked to the side. Friends, women, family, all came in second place behind his career ambitions as a lawyer. But he now realized that he needed some balance in his life other than law torts, beef Stroganoff, and ESPN.

Jason's cell phone rang and he checked the caller ID. It was Steven.

"Jason, it's Steven. Are we still on for G. Garvin's with the girls?"

"Yeah," Jason answered.

"Good, I need my wingman for Carole."

"You're going after Carole?"

"You damn right. I know you've known her for a while, but damn, have you seen that ass? I've got to keep trying to hit it."

"Only you would interpret one hundred straight rejections by the same woman as interest," Jason said.

"That's why I'm me and you're you, baby. I never give up."

"See you in a couple of hours."

"Later."

Jason went into the bedroom and pulled out some clothes. Tonight, Jason and Steven were meeting with two friends, Marcia Cambridge and Carole Brantford at G. Garvin's, the hot new spot in Beverly Hills. But before that, Jason had a call to make.

"Hello, Vanessa, Jason calling. Hey, we met about a month ago and I was wondering if you would like to go out for drinks? I'm free next Saturday, so give me a call at 323-555-4525 and we can hook things up. All right, I'll talk to you later."

Jason met Vanessa at the Conga Room last month. The firm met there to celebrate Peter Ketchings's birthday when Jason saw her sitting at the bar, stirring her drink and looking damn sexy. A milk-chocolate sister and built just how Jason liked his women, Vanessa was about five-foot five, with a large chest and perky ass, not too big, not too small. Her purple blouse was cut low, as was her white skirt. When Jason approached her, it wasn't without confidence. It's just that damn dry streak that kept getting in his way.

"Can I get a Jack and Coke," Jason asked the bartender. He was now standing right next to her, and she hadn't noticed him. So he pressed. "What's your name?"

Jason held out his hand for her to shake.

She looked up slowly and stared at Jason's face, as though searching for a secret message.

"Vanessa," she said. She shook his hand with only the tips of her fingers touching the tips of his fingers, as though she'd calculated that this was the absolute minimum she had to do in order to interact with him.

"Hello, Vanessa, my name is Jason. Do you come here often?"

Vanessa looked down at her drink and took a sip. The bartender smiled as though amused at what he was seeing.

"Look, Jason—that was your name, right?" she said.

"Yeah."

"I don't think you're my type. So why don't you just try talking to someone else."

Jason was stunned. He hadn't even really started trying and he was already getting rejected.

"Damn, sister, am I that hideous?"

"No, you're actually pretty good-looking, but you have some loose ends that you need to take care of before trying to talk to someone of my caliber." When Vanessa said *caliber,* she ran her hand down the length of her body. Here was a woman who knew she looked good.

"Okay, then enlighten me. Let me know what I need to do to get a woman of your caliber."

"Buy me a drink and I'll tell you," she said, looking into his eyes.

"What are you drinking?"

"Bartender," she said, leaning over the bar. When she did, her low-cut blouse became even lower cut. "Please fix me an apple martini. Put it on Jason's tab."

The bartender fixed the drink and Jason gave him his American Express Platinum.

"Now that's not a bad start," she said, pointing to his Platinum card. She took the martini, licked the edge of the glass, and then took a sip that just crossed her pursed lips.

"You have potential but you're about ten pounds overweight and while that's not fat, it tells me you don't care about your body. Do you work out?" she asked.

"No, I don't. I never thought I needed to." Jason did a mental Special K pinch check of his waist. She was right. He could stand to lose a few pounds.

"Uh-huh. Since you are already in your late twenties, it's probably flab city from here," she said. "That's if you don't start working out. You remind me of the cute skinny kid who hasn't come to terms with not being skinny anymore. You're not fat, but you aren't toned."

Jason began thinking that maybe he didn't really want to know all of this. He took a big gulp of his Jack and Coke and braced for more.

"And then there is your style of clothing."

"What's wrong with my style of clothes?" Jason said, looking at his outfit. "These are new clothes."

"Well that's it, you don't have any style. You're wearing tan chinos and a blue shirt," she said, eyeing him from head to toe. "Boring. I bet you bought those clothes at the Gap or maybe the Men's Warehouse because they told you it was a great look for both the office and after work."

Okay, now Jason was beginning to hate her. His gear *was* from the Men's Warehouse and the salesman had said those exact words to him.

Now this is a look that works well at both the office and after work, the Men's Warehouse salesman had said while mentally trying to calculate his commission. He was a sixty-year-old white man who would have sold Jason pink-and-black-checked Sans-o-belt slacks from the 1970s if he knew Jason was going to purchase something worth more than $100.

Why in the world did I follow his advice, Jason thought at this moment.

"Your attitude and your clothes, everything points to being an extremely plain and safe young man," she continued, long after Jason had hoped she'd stop. "You have no sense of adventure, or spontaneity about you.

"I bet you've never done an impulsive thing in your life."

She paused for a second, staring at him. She stared at him for a good thirty seconds, bringing her face directly in front of his, almost touching his nose.

"What?" he asked, getting nervous.

She moved her face and sat back in her chair.

"See, if you were daring and dangerous, you would have taken me by the face, kissed me with the most passionate kiss you've ever given a woman, and then told me 'how's that about spontaneity?' "

She got up from the bar and gave him one last piece of advice. "But you didn't, and so you missed out, darling. See, you have to understand that I, and every other woman on this planet, get safe and plain everywhere else in my life. I don't want it in a lover or even a boyfriend."

She finished her martini and placed it on the bar. She reached into her purse, pulled out a piece of paper and wrote down her number.

"So what is my final piece of advice to you? Go get you some money, or look like you have some money, and then get yourself some style. You're probably smart as all hell, but women don't look for smart at the start. We look at looks, which of course means that we are as superficial as you guys. Look me up when you've got your stuff together. I'll still be here."

And just like that, she smiled and left, with her number on the bar. And it was at that moment that Jason knew things had to change. Before Vanessa, he would have settled for a Friday night of beef Stroganoff and television. But not tonight, not after that reality check. No, this Friday was going to be different. He was getting dressed to go to G. Garvin's. And he was looking for a woman.

CHAPTER 2

"Jason!"

The gang was already seated when Jason arrived at G. Garvin's, and their enthusiastic greeting told Jason that they'd already started drinking. This get-together was supposed to be a surprise for the birthday girl Marcia, but he guessed he'd either missed the surprise moment or the gig was up.

"What's up, y'all?" Jason said, grabbing a chair.

The restaurant was packed tonight, and it was a tight squeeze to sit four folks together at a table.

"Jason, what are you drinking?" Steven asked. "The waiter has already taken our orders."

"Um, make it a Heinie for now."

"Heinie it is. Brother, we've got to make you more adventurous with your drink selection."

Jason had invited Steven to a party a while back and he soon became part of his regular circle of friends. Obnoxious and chauvinistic, Jason sort of tolerated him outside of the office. But pretty women gravitated to him, so Jason didn't mind too much. It gave him a chance to get at the ones Steven didn't want.

"Thanks for getting here on time," Carole said sarcastically. "I said meet us at six, not seven."

Carole Brantford was a classic beauty, with sharp facial features and a deep dark black skin that echoed her Nigerian roots. At nearly six feet tall and thin, she was often mistaken as a runway model, and because she wore haute couture every day, it wasn't a huge leap. Her parents were both professors, and she was used to a certain lifestyle, a lifestyle of privilege and wealth. That privilege sometimes made it seem like she was uptight about even the most minute things, such as arriving on time for a surprise party.

"Good to see you too, Carole," Jason said, taking his seat. "How about this? I've had a pretty fucked-up week and month, so how about cutting me a little bit of slack for once. Rome didn't fall because I'm late, and one billion Chinese don't give a fuck. So get off my ass."

Carole cut a look at Jason, while Steven brought back the beers.

"You two getting into it again," Steven chimed in.

"Of course," Marcia said.

"Nah, we're not getting into it, just clarifying," Jason said calmly, taking a long sip of his beer. "And by the way, happy birthday, Marcia!"

"Thank you, darling," she responded with a flourish. "I know you knuckleheads were trying to make this a surprise party, but as I told them before, I don't like surprises. I'm not good with surprises. I don't want a surprise. So of course I decided to surprise you all by figuring it out about two weeks ago. But thanks for the gesture."

A waiter noticed Jason had joined the table.

"Would you like a dinner menu?" she asked.

Jason held up his hand. "I already know what I want. I'll take an order of beef short rib ravioli with leeks. Thank you."

The waiter left and Jason leaned over and gave Marcia a kiss on the cheek. "I needed to get out of the office. Hey, where's that guy you were talking about a month ago? Are you still with him?"

"Chile, let me tell you." Marcia laughed.

If Jason, or anyone within fifty feet of her, had to describe Marcia Cambridge, they would instantly describe her as blunt, loud, gregarious and sometimes a bit crude. And that's the perfect demeanor for a black gossip magazine publisher, which she was. She published *Baldwin Hills,* the magazine that dished the dirt on black high society in Los Angeles. Whether they worked in the entertainment industry or were simply famous black people, both clamored to be featured in her magazine and to stay out of it, and she knew it. A wonderful person, but someone who didn't hold anything back, sometimes to the embarrassment of others, she's what black folks call a big-boned girl. She was about a size fourteen, but at six feet tall, she wore her size well. But as long as Jason had known her, she'd *never* had any problems getting or keeping a man. Plus, she had so-called good hair, and for some brothers, that did it for them. But in order to get with Marcia, you had to keep up with Marcia. She didn't suffer fools.

"I hadn't even gotten wet before that Negro started grunting and then stopped," Marcia said loudly. "I was like, that's it? I put on my good lingerie and panties for that? So I threw his ass out of the bed. I told him that if he couldn't go longer than ten strokes, then I don't need him. I can find a ten-stroke man anywhere in L.A. Isn't that right, Carole? You've been complaining about all of the ten-stroke men you've been fucking for damn near a year."

Marcia stared at Carole expectantly, as though Carole had agreed to share this knowledge with Jason and Steven. It was evident that Carole hadn't made that decision, but since the bell had been rung, she now had to respond. Plus, Steven was damn near drooling at the mouth. Any information about Carole's sex life titillated him.

"Uh, well I wouldn't say that I've had a lot of ten-stroke men, but I can say—"

"Now don't front on me, girl, just because these men are here. You're always complaining that all of your men need to do Kegel exercises because once they get into your pussy, they lose control!"

"Damn girl, you got it like that?" Steven asked. He kept getting closer to Carole, and she kept leaning away. "Why don't you let me have a try at it?

"And you know," he whispered to Carole lasciviously, "I'm into Tantric sex, just like Sting, so I can go for hours, or even days. I'm one of the few people on this planet who has successfully turned his body into a total love machine."

"Okay Marcia, you can stop now. That's too much information," Carole replied, holding up her hand at Steven, blocking him out dismissively. "When I tell you something in private, I mean for it to stay in private."

"Uh-huh, that makes sense," Marcia said, finishing her Long Island Iced Tea with a loud gulp. She started chewing on ice. "Telling the publisher of a gossip magazine something in secret and not expect her to say something? Yep, that makes a lot of sense!"

Marcia, Steven, and Jason all laughed. Carole got up to leave.

"You know, I don't have to take this," she said. "I thought you were my best friend, and there you go again, embarrassing me for your own amusement."

Jason put his hand on her purse.

"Stop being melodramatic," Jason said. "I swear, every time we go out, you're always getting upset about something or other. We aren't out to get you, and we ain't that interested in your sex life."

"Uh, I am," Steven said, smiling at her.

Jason took a sip of his Heineken. "Maybe if you figured out how to keep a man, then you wouldn't have to keep getting offended when somebody jokes about your love life."

"Damn!" Marcia said.

"He went there," Steven said, laughing.

Carole stopped and shot Jason a stare that could have chilled a daiquiri.

These two had a history and it wasn't all good. At Berkeley, they'd gone out casually for about a couple of months during their senior year. For some reason, which Jason didn't really understand at the time, they hadn't had sex during that period, even though Jason tried his best. Carole was trying to take things slow, and not letting sex mess up the relationship. But she was on the verge of having sex with Jason when Erica happened.

Jason hadn't intended on cheating on Carole, but Erica sort of just happened. It was after a stepshow, he was drunk, she was, too, and they ended up in her bed where Carole found them, lying naked, asleep in each other's arms. The combination of seeing one's boyfriend and sorority sister in bed together meant that the break-up would be bitter. And until recently, that had been the last time Carole had spoken to Jason. In fact, Jason and Carole were only at this table because they'd unexpectedly been brought together.

Ketchings & Martin required all its lawyers to do pro bono work in the inner city, so Jason picked a community center at random from a list when he joined the firm. It was only when he walked into Mama's House, a community center in Inglewood that helped single mothers, that he knew there might be a conflict.

"Jason." She'd greeted him with a frown. "What the hell are you doing here?"

"Uh, I'm assigned to Mama's House for pro bono," he said nervously. "What are you doing here?"

"I'm the director," she replied.

They stared at each other in uneasy silence, each recounting the last moment they'd seen each other.

"Look, I can go back to the firm and get a change," Jason said, turning to go.

"Why would you do that?" Carole asked. "I need a lawyer, and I don't want to wait another six months to get assigned one."

"But wouldn't you find it a tad bit awkward?"

"I don't understand."

"I mean," Jason started, "we used to be, you know, together."

Carole laughed. "If you think that I'm still hurt by something you did when we were twenty-one, then you're being silly. Just do your job and we won't have any problems."

Jason still felt a bit uneasy, but agreed. And for months, there'd been an uneasy détente between the two, until now.

"What the fuck do you know? I mean, at least I have a love life," Carole said, taking his hand off her purse.

Carole looked positively pissed. But then her face softened—not in a good way, but in an 'I've got you by the balls' way.

"And by the way, have you talked to Erica lately?" she quipped.

"Double damn," Marcia said. "Let me sit back and enjoy this!"

Right then, the waitress came with the food.

"Bitch," Jason said under his breath. The waitress put his plate before him and he began playing with his ravioli.

"What was that, Jason?" Carole said, sitting back down and taking her plate from the waiter. "Are you getting upset when someone jokes about your love life?"

"Who is Erica?" Steven asked, digging into his fried chicken. "I don't remember you mentioning her."

"Erica was the sorority sister Jason had slept with," Marcia said, cutting into her stuffed pork chop. "It didn't work out too well, though."

If karma's a bitch, then Jason was bitch-slapped when he got involved with Erica. After the trauma of having Carole find them in
bed, Erica and Jason still thought that they could make a go at it.

"She's my soror, but remember that not every soror is my friend
and not every friend is my soror," Erica cooed in his ear. "It was
destiny that we got together and she'll get over it. I'm yours now,
you can trust me."

And Jason bought it hook, line and sinker. Whereas Carole had
grown up rich and privileged, and acted like it, Erica was fun and
loose. She laughed easily, and Jason felt comfortable around her.
Jason had bought her flowers on her birthday, called her once a
day, and sent her those funny e-mails with dancing bears. Things
were good. So when Valentine's Day approached, Jason had it all
planned out.

The plan was to dress up as a chef, buy some food from Café
Panzo in Berkeley, and then bring the food along with some roses
to Erica's dorm room as a Valentine's Day surprise.

"I want to order your roasted chicken with penne pasta and baby
carrots, along with an expensive French white wine," Jason had ordered over the phone.

He had been looking forward to Valentine's Day. He wanted to
take this relationship with Erica to the next level, so what day was
more perfect than the day of love?

On the big day, he arrived at the Clark Kerr dorm, grabbed the
food and ran to the dorm's front door. A friend of his, Sean Carter,
was waiting to let him in, and it seemed like the whole dorm
stopped to look at this young black man dressed like Chef
Boyardee.

"Ah, isn't that sweet," all the women sighed as he walked down
the hallway.

As he got closer to Erica's door, he saw about five people sitting
on the floor right across from her room. They were talking to
themselves, but seemed to be surreptitiously listening to something.

"Yo cat, I wouldn't go in there if I were you," one guy said to
Jason, pointing to Erica's door. "The sign is out."

"What sign?" he asked.

"That sign." On the bulletin board next to her door was a
stuffed animal turned upside down.

"How do they say it on those bumper stickers?" he smiled. "If the van is a rockin', then don't come a knockin'? Well on this floor, if you see an upside-down teddy bear, it means the same thing."

Right at that time, Jason heard something that made his skin crawl.

"More, baby, more!" And then there was a loud moan.

Jason took a step back to see if he was at the right dorm room, but in his heart, he already knew the answer. It was Erica's place, and since she didn't have a roommate, it had to be her moaning. Plus, lover's moans are like fingerprints. They're unique and distinctive.

Jason stood there, listening to Erica get screwed. He was panicky and delirious, and yet frozen like an ice cube in front of her door.

"Don't stop, baby, don't stop!" she yelled.

"Damn, she is getting tagged!" one of the guys on the floor remarked.

With that, Jason lost it. He started banging on the door, dropping both the food and flowers to the floor.

"Erica! Erica!"

The noise in the room stopped and he could hear feet scrambling.

"Open up this goddamn door," he screamed. "Before I break this muthafucka down!"

The guys on the floor stood up and a group of students started congregating down the hall, watching the scene. Finally, after what seemed like an eternity to Jason, the door opened a crack. Jason burst in to see Erica standing in front of him with only her sorority robe on, and Rouvaun Muir, star running back at Cal, the nickname for Berkeley, lying on her bed, completely naked.

"What are you doing here, Jason?" Erica asked. She had a slightly panicked look in her eyes, as though she didn't know how this was going to turn out. Rouvaun, on the other hand, looked completely nonchalant, as though this whole affair had nothing to do with him.

"What the fuck do you mean what am I doing here? What the fuck is this muthafucka doing here," Jason said, pointing to Rouvaun.

"Better slow your roll, son," Rouvaun said. He started to get off the bed and Jason made a move toward him.

"Shut up, Rouvaun!" Erica screamed.

Now there was a huge crowd outside her dorm room.

"Get the fuck out," Jason yelled at Rouvaun.

"Nigga, I ain't going nowhere. You get the fuck out."

"Fuck you," Jason said, and then he took a swing at Rouvaun. Rouvaun partially blocked the punch, but still got hit in the lip.

"Son of a bitch!" he said, using his fingers to check for blood.

Rouvaun hit Jason in the chest and then in the jaw. It took Jason's breath away, and he could only begin swinging wildly at Rouvaun. Erica began screaming at the top of her lungs, and soon Rouvaun and Jason were wrestling on the ground.

"What the hell is going on, Erica?" Clark Kerr resident assistant Tony Lyons said, running into the room. Tony began separating Rouvaun and Jason, and it was easy to see that both had given as good as they'd gotten.

"Fuck it," Jason said, straightening his shirt. "I always said that I wouldn't fight over some woman and here I am doing just that. What I just want to know is, why? Why the fuck are you doing this?"

Erica was now leaning against her wall, staring at the whole scene in disbelief.

"You know how I got with you, so why in the world would you think this wouldn't happen?" she asked. Jason stared at her, and then silently walked out of the room, making his way through the crowd.

"Yo dude, can I have this food?" a voice in the crowd said. The crowd began laughing as Jason walked out of Clark Kerr. What he didn't see was Carole, who'd watched the whole thing from another dorm room.

"That's what you get when you sleep with dogs," she said to herself. "You tend to get fleas."

So Erica was still a sore topic, even after all these years, with Jason.

"But you recovered, Jason," Marcia said. "And if it makes you feel better, I saw Erica about six months ago. She's a mess. So Rouvaun actually saved you. You should be grateful."

"Yeah, I'll start thinking about it that way. That should make me feel better," he said, finishing his beer.

"Dude, I didn't know you had it in you," Steven said, leaning back in his chair. "You stole on that fool and fucked up his face?"

"Yeah, but I vowed that that would be the last time I fought a brother over a woman," Jason said. "If she wants somebody else, then she can have them."

"Oh, don't have that attitude, Jason," Marcia said. "If you really love a woman, you better be down to go toe to toe."

"Never again, Marcia," Jason replied. "Never again."

"I hope you're satisfied," Jason whispered to Carole. "You pretty much fucked up my Friday night. I hadn't thought about Erica in years."

Carole finished the last of her white wine.

"Funny, but I think of it a lot."

CHAPTER 3

Pete Ketchings and Jim Martin scared the shit out of the associate lawyers at Ketchings & Martin, and it wasn't because they shouted or intimidated their attorneys; in fact they did quite the opposite. The two partners were outwardly caring and interested in their lives. But it was like they had gone to a seminar on "how to connect with your employees without dirtying yourself in the process" and had taken the lessons to heart. The partners' interaction with their underlings was distinctly insincere. A typical conversation with them was short, sweet, and definitely one-sided. And nothing exhibited this more than their weekly Monday walk through the office.

"Hey, Peyton, how about those Raiders!"

"Steven, how's your golf game?"

"Mary, how's your son?"

On the surface, the walk seemed like a simple enough act, but that was an illusion. It was an act fraught with tension for each and every underling at Ketchings & Martin. Each wondered if there was a secret message in what the partners asked. As Ketchings and Martin walked and asked questions in rapid fire, they would sometimes dole out an additional shake of the hand, a touch of a shoulder, or a quick smile for a select few associates, but they never, *ever* stopped walking to their offices.

"The Raiders won, sir!" Peyton replied.

"Shot a seventy-six at Pebble Beach!" Steven said.

"They're eating me out of house and home!" Mary responded.

And the partners always said the same thing, no matter what their associates said: "Great!"

It was obvious that Ketchings and Martin weren't too interested in the replies. But after making that weekly walk, Ketchings and Martin disappeared into their office, plotting how to fuck with their associates' lives. The nicety of the walk was only a tactic designed to take the associates' minds off how much they really didn't actually care for them; didn't actually love them; and actually didn't give a shit about whether the Raiders won, how their golf games had progressed, or whether their kids were on crack. The associates only meant something when it was related to their master plan of making Ketchings & Martin the best law firm in Los Angeles. Everything else was pure subterfuge to them. It was a fact Jason would always remember.

On this particular Monday, Jason watched the weekly procession with one eye, and his computer with the other. Burger World was proving to be a bitch and he was not looking forward to preparing depositions for the upcoming trial. And since this was Monday, he had the added pressure of stopping by Mama's House for pro bono work. After Friday's fiasco with Carole, it was not something he was looking forward to.

"What's up, dude?" Steven said, eating a Krispy Kreme donut. He had a box on his desk. "Want one?"

"Nah, I'm trying to cut back. Tryin' to lose a few pounds."

"Getting in shape, eh?" Steven said. "Man, you should come down to my Bally's in Hollywood. Honeys all up in the seven o'clock hour, asses all moving in unison while on the treadmill. I just sit on the life cycle, watching them move. I can't tell you how many sisters I've pulled in the last year."

"That assumes a brother can get out of this bitch at seven," Jason said, shuffling some paper. "I can't remember the last time I rolled out of here earlier than nine. I know the Mexican cleaning lady by name."

"Oh yeah, I forgot you're still trying to make partner." Steven laughed. "Can't say that I didn't tell you way back, that that working late shit's for the white boys in this office. If you'd followed my advice . . ."

Jason's phone rang, interrupting Steven. Jason pressed his speakerphone.

"Yes," Jason answered.

"Jason, Mr. Ketchings would like to see you in his office."

"I'll be right there, Rebecca," Jason said.

When Rebecca Banks, Mr. Ketchings's executive assistant called you, you jumped. It didn't matter if she was asking you to fill the copier with paper, you got off your ass and filled that damn copier. And when she said meet Mr. Ketchings, you met Mr. Ketchings.

But hearing this request made both Jason and Steven freeze in their seats. Besides their initial welcome meeting, neither had been asked to meet either Ketchings or Martin privately. When a partner wants you to come into his office, Jason figured it could only mean two things: good news or bad news. There's no gray area. These are the possible scenarios:

"You're fired!"

"You're doing great!"

Partners don't have casual conversations with associates. Even if they invited an associate to spend a day on the golf course or join them for a drink after work, it was just as much an illusion of cordiality as their weekly walk-through each Monday morning. So Jason knew that something important must be up.

Still, he felt pretty good about his chances of surviving this meeting. Maybe he had done something wrong, but perhaps it was a small mistake? Maybe he needed to improve something? Hell, he was only twenty-eight years old, so he was bound to make mistakes. They'd trusted him on the Burger World kangaroo meat class lawsuit, and he was working sixty—no, eighty—hours a week to see it through. But he knew he was not perfect by any means.

"Dude, do you think I did something wrong?" Jason asked nervously. "They never talk to me, an associate, without a good reason."

Jason sat at his desk, afraid to get up and face his future. He was freaking himself out, probably unnecessarily. But Steven was taking great delight in seeing him sweat. Steven calmly bit into another donut.

"When you go in there, make sure to strike a balance between casually assured and frantically terrified," Steven told Jason as so-called helpful advice. "It always works for me."

"Thanks, that's really helpful," Jason told him sarcastically. "You've never gotten this call, but I appreciate your concern."

"What are friends for? I'll get a box so you can make a dignified exit when you clear out your desk," he said, and laughed.

The phone rang again. It was Rebecca again.

"Jason, Mr. Ketchings is waiting."

"On my way," Jason replied. "I just had to finish something."

Jason slowly rose from his chair, as Steven kept nibbling on his donut.

"Well, time to take my medicine," Jason muttered.

As Jason started the hundred-foot trek to Mr. Ketchings's office, he could hear Steven humming "Taps." That got Jason paranoid again, and he tried to build himself up before going into Ketchings's office.

Be yourself.

Act confident.

Be genial.

Don't kiss ass.

When Jason opened the door, Mr. Ketchings was on the phone. He motioned for Jason to sit down, while he continued talking on the phone.

"Yes, he's here now. I'll call you when we're through," he said into the phone.

That can't be good, Jason thought. That really can't be good if he's talking to someone else about me.

Finally Mr. Ketchings got off the phone. He shuffled some papers on his desk and then focused on Jason.

"Jason, you've been with us since you graduated from Boalt Hall law school, haven't you?" he said, leaning back in his chair.

"Yes, sir."

"And I'll be the first to say that I think you've been doing a fine job here at Ketchings & Martin, a fine job indeed. Others have told me that you don't leave here until nine o'clock on most nights, working on the Burger World case. I just want to tell you that we appreciate it."

Okay, so far, so good, Jason thought. He liked my work. But where was the "but"?

Mr. Ketchings got up and walked to the front of his desk and sat on its edge.

"How's the Burger World lawsuit going, by the way?"

"Fine, sir, we're about to start depositions and then go straight to trial. I think we can make a great case."

Mr. Ketchings folded his arms. He had something to say, but he was taking his damn good time to say it.

"I got a call this morning that I think you should hear about," Mr. Ketchings said. "Country Bob Briggs was voted out by his board yesterday. Burger World is close to being taken over by Tri-Food International, and they wanted to clean their slate. All old baggage was to go, and Country Bob was definitely old baggage."

That was great news to Jason. He hated Country Bob Briggs and his ornery ass with a purple passion. But why hadn't Mr. Ketchings just sent him an e-mail to let him know? Why had he summoned him into the office?

"But that's not all they said," Mr. Ketchings said, smiling. "They want to settle the kangaroo lawsuit. We settled on a sixty-million-dollar figure with no admission of guilt from them. Now while I would have liked to have pinned them to the wall over feeding kangaroo meat to an unknowing public, I can't be happier today. Son, you just made this firm over twenty million dollars. . . ."

Wow! He was genuinely a star now, Jason thought. Maybe he could get an office with a view and a sign. . . .

". . . and that means you are going to get four million dollars for your work on the case," Mr. Ketchings continued.

Or a new desk, and what about a secretary? Hey, what the hell did he just say?

"Excuse me, sir?"

Mr. Ketchings was beaming and Jason was stunned. "Jason, you just earned yourself four million dollars. Congratulations!"

He stuck out his hand and Jason fainted. His legs gave out as though he'd been shot and he actually fainted like he'd seen a ghost. When he came to, Mr. Ketchings was looking down on him, holding half a glass of water and a towel. He'd dumped some of the water on Jason's face and Jason was now soaked.

"Oh my God. Oh my God!" Jason kept mumbling.

He'd completely lost his cool. He, Jason Richards, was a million-aire. No, he wasn't a millionaire, he was a multimillionaire!

"Great work, Jason. You deserve it!" Mr. Ketchings said, still look-ing down at him.

Mr. Ketchings helped Jason to his feet and handed Jason the towel.

"Now Jason, this money is going to change your life. I would ap-preciate it if you kept the amount you made from the settlement mainly to yourself. We'll let everyone in the office know that you settled, and you'll get the credit for your hard work. But we want to keep figures close to the vest. That helps to keep the inner office rivalries among associates to a minimum. Every associate gets his chance for a big case. You just got yours a little sooner than most of the others."

"Understood, sir."

"Also, as a condition of this Burger World settlement, the terms will not be disclosed to the public. We're going to put out a gen-eral statement, you know, that they settled for an undisclosed amount and don't admit guilt. So don't go to the newspapers with this news, or give any interviews."

"Gotcha."

Mr. Ketchings looked at Jason as though he were looking at a protégé who'd made good.

"Keep up the good work, Jason, and you just may make part-ner!" he said, patting Jason on the back as he left Ketchings's of-fice.

Jason physically walked out of Mr. Ketchings's office but men-tally floated back to his desk.

"So what happened? Why are you wet?" Steven asked, looking at Jason's soaked shirt. "I know that it was stressful, but damn, you sweat that much? I told you to be cool."

"Man, they settled the Burger World lawsuit for sixty mil," Jason whispered, obviously disregarding Mr. Ketchings's advice. "That means the firm just made twenty mil, and I just made four million for my part in the lawsuit."

"You've got to be shitting me," Steven said incredulously. "You have got to be shitting me! They never told me that was the reward at the end of this case. I just thought we got the damn thing won and moved on. You have got to be shitting me. Four million just like that?"

Steven was both happy for him and not a little bit jealous. Jason was now the star of the office, at least until the next big case. Steven had dismissed the Burger World case as a dead end and had passed it to Jason, and now he was finding out that the dead end had actually led Jason to a fortune.

"Fuck that," Jason said, smiling. "That's payment for all those damn hours I worked and my lack of a real life. So with two years of that, I think that's just about right. But don't tell anyone, Steven. I promised Ketchings that I wouldn't say anything."

"Gotcha. These bloodsuckers around here would try to sabotage a brother if they knew he was making more than their white asses. So I've got your back," Steven said. "What are you going to do with the cash?"

"Man, I don't even know. I don't even know when I get the money," Jason said. "But I do know that this allows me to make some decisions. I've been pretty conservative with my salary, you know, savings, IRA and everything, but now that I've put in the work, I want some fun. But right now I've got to go to Mama's House for my pro bono, so I'm going to spend all day thinking about what four million dollars can do for a brother," Jason said, gathering his briefcase.

"Damn, you're going to see Carole today? After how she killed you off on Friday?" Steven said. "I still don't know why you don't let me take you out of your torture and switch pro bono assignments. I want to bone Carole, and you can't stand her. It would be a perfect switch."

"I must be a masochist, I think," Jason said, picking up his briefcase and coat. "But I can say that right now, with four mil on the way, Carole could curse me out and I wouldn't give a fuck. It's been a beautiful Monday."

"Well, if you need someone to help you spend your new money . . ."

"I sure won't be calling you." Jason laughed.

"See you later, millionaire!" he sang out.

"Dorothy, is Jason here yet?" Carole asked. The day had started badly, as most Mondays did. She had ten new cases for the week,

and she still had five holdovers from the past week. It was like that
at Mama's House, and although Carole had been director for over
five years, she still hadn't gotten used to it.

"No, he hasn't made it in yet," Dorothy said, standing in the doorway of Carole's office. "Do you want me to call him on his cell?"

Dorothy was Carole's right-hand woman. She was a retired teacher
who'd found her second career as head counselor at Mama's House,
and she handled everything in Mama's House that Carole couldn't
get to, and more. Mother figure and general badass, no one in the
center messed with Dorothy, including Carole.

"No, I'll wait. Just let me know when he gets here and send him
to my office."

"Will do," Dorothy said. She left, and Carole stared at her computer.

Friday night had gone badly between her and Jason. She hadn't
known she still felt resentment over Jason and Erica, but she still
did. For some reason, it had been sitting deep in her psyche and
had come out unexpectedly. Now, she had to do some repairs in
order to make sure having Jason at the center wouldn't be hell.
Carole prided herself on being professional, and this was a time to
demonstrate that.

"Carole, Jason is here," Dorothy said, buzzing Carole's intercom.
"Do you want me to send him in?"

"Yes, please send him in."

When Jason arrived, he was still feeling the high of being an in-
stant millionaire. As a result, he wasn't tripping off of the Friday
night conflict with Carole anymore. It was amazing how four million dollars cleared one's mind.

"You wanted to see me?" Jason said, walking into Carole's office.

"Yeah, take a seat," she said. Carole stood up and walked over to
the door and closed it. She returned to her desk, walking in a regal
way that showed she'd been trained during countless balls and
cotillions.

"I wanted to bring you in here today in order to make sure we
don't have a problem," she said.

"Why would we have a problem?" Jason asked, squinting at
Carole.

"Well, we did have some words at G. Garvin's and I thought that we should make sure that our personal animus didn't taint our professional relationship. I'm willing to leave whatever personal issues I have with you behind for the best of the center."

"I told you on Friday that I never thought of Erica until you brought it up, and I doubt that I will think of her or our relationship in the future. So you don't have a thing to worry about," Jason replied. "And you can believe that of all days, today I'm not thinking anything about last Friday."

Carole appeared to be a bit uncomfortable. In some ways, she welcomed another confrontation so that they could get all of their personal issues on the table. But she had underestimated him. Jason wasn't biting.

"So," Jason said. "Is that it?"

"Yes, I guess that's it."

Jason stood up. "Great. I'll see you later."

Carole's phone buzzed.

"Carole, could you please come to the Harriet Tubman room? Caterina is here and she needs your help."

"I'll be right there, Dorothy," Carole said. She turned to Jason. "Could you come see this case, because I think you can help her."

"Okay, let's go."

Caterina was sitting in a black leather chair that seemed to engulf her. She was a delicate-looking teenager who couldn't have been more than nineteen years old. She'd been crying and Dorothy was consoling her. In the corner, a little toddler was playing with some toys.

"Hello, Caterina. How are you doing?" Carole asked as they walked in. "This is Jason Richards and I brought him in because he's a lawyer and he might be able to help your case.

The young girl's tear-streaked face looked up at Carole and Jason.

"He took everything I had . . ."

"Who did?" Carole asked.

"My boyfriend Jacob. He said that he bought everything so it was all his. He cleaned my apartment out and took all of my money while I was at the county, getting my check."

"Did you call the police?" Jason asked, writing her story down in a notebook.

"Yes."

She started crying again.

"They told me to fill out a report, but that doesn't help me right now. He took everything, and the landlord has told us that we have forty-eight hours to get out of the apartment. We are behind on the rent."

The young woman started crying again, and Carole started to console her. She looked up at Jason.

"I'm going to send her to the Ida B. Wells shelter because she doesn't have any family out here. After that, we can get her a bus ticket to take her back to Texas. Is there anything you can do legally to prevent the landlord from evicting them?"

"Unfortunately, there's not much," Jason said. "California gives landlords a lot of power when it comes to dealing with their renters. How many months are you behind?"

"Three, at eight hundred dollars each."

"Is there nothing you can do, Jason, to prevent her from being evicted?" Carole asked. "Can we get some sort of injunction?"

Jason thought a bit and turned away from Caterina. He looked at the toddler, and then at Carole.

"Let me talk to you privately," he said to Carole.

The two walked out of the room and into the hallway.

"Look, I can't do this for everyone who comes in here, but that sister touched me. Here's a check for five thousand dollars," Jason said, writing out a check. "I'll make it out in the name of Mama's House. Pay the back rent, get some cheap furniture, and get her some groceries for the next month or so. This should keep her going for at least three months. I don't want to see that girl and boy in a homeless shelter."

Carole looked at Jason with a surprised look on her face.

"Jason, you can't do this," Carole said, holding up her hand. "Although this is a sweet gesture, it isn't your problem. And you can't solve the problems of every sister that comes through these doors."

Jason finished writing the check and held it out for her to take.

"I'm not doing this for her. I'm doing this for me. I want to give back some of the money I earn. I have enough and now it's time to give to a person who needs it more than me."

Carole took the check and looked to Jason. She was genuinely touched by his gesture, but didn't want to show it. She had grown up rich, and had been trying to develop the social consciousness she hadn't had as a child by working with the less fortunate as an adult. Consequently, when someone with privileges did the same, she understood where they were coming from.

"Jason, I never expected this from you. It seemed like you only showed up here because Ketchings and Martin made you do it, not because you had any passion for our work. But this is one of the kindest things someone has done for us.

"I won't forget this," she said, looking at the check.

She started walking out of the room when Jason stopped her.

"I forgot to tell you that there's one condition to this check."

Carole looked at Jason with a new dose of skepticism. It was like she knew this was all too good to be true.

"And that condition would be?" she asked. Her hand was now on her hip, ready to retort anything outrageous.

"You can't tell her where you got the money. Make up a name, any name. Say it's from the Mama's House emergency fund. Any name but my name. I don't want the credit."

Carole's skepticism lifted. Jason could see she was pleasantly surprised.

"Done."

Carole walked back into the room while Jason stayed in the hall, but he watched as she told Caterina the news. Caterina grabbed Carole's legs and hugged them, she was so grateful. Her life, at least for a few months, had been saved. Carole led her to a back room where she could rest and take a nap with her son.

When Jason got back to his office, all of the staff started looking at him. They knew there wasn't a Mama House emergency fund, and they'd figured out Jason had given the money. Dorothy approached him first.

"Baby, I just wanted to say thank you! That was the nicest thing I've seen in my five years here."

She gave Jason a hug and then the rest of the staff came over and congratulated him. The jig was up, so there was no reason to deny it. But Carole had been right. At Mama's House, Jason was pretty much a jack of all trades attorney. He tried to help single mothers through divorce, custody issues, husband, and/or boyfriend in jail. He did what he could. But what paid the bills was his work at the law firm, and in the end, Ketchings & Martin didn't care if he saved souls in the inner city, but they did care if he successfully adjudicated his cases. So that was the attitude Jason brought to the community center.

"It was the least I could do, and all of you would have done the same," he remarked modestly.

Out of the corner of his eye, he could see Carole watching the scene with a slight smile. Perhaps Mondays weren't so bad after all, Jason thought as he went back to his office. Not bad at all.

CHAPTER 4

"Yes, that's what he did," Carole said on her cell phone. "He just wrote a check for five thousand dollars and gave it to me. I don't know his angle, but it really was nice." Sean was supposed to be at her apartment in an hour, so she had to move quickly. It was turn on the shower, clean up the living room while the water got warm, lay out her clothes, do her makeup, and if she had time, check her e-mail. But when your best friend is the publisher of a gossip magazine, well, you tended to gossip.

"Look I know Jason, and he doesn't really have angles," Marcia said. "He's pretty genuine in what he does. And on that note, I think you should really stop tripping off that Erica madness. That was in college and this is now. Get over it already."

Carole pulled the phone from her ear. Sometimes Marcia was too truthful for a friend.

"Who said that I'm fixated on that Erica deal? I don't even think about it."

"You're lying and you know it," Marcia said.

"Look, I've got a man, and I don't need to trip over some college fling I had with Jason. That was damn near a decade ago. I even called him into my office today just to make sure it didn't get in the way of our professional relationship, and he was perfectly cool. I think you completely misread the situation."

"Maybe, but I doubt it. But we'll see," Marcia said. "You know my saying, I believe that Negroes ultimately tell on themselves, so we'll eventually see if you believe that or not."

"Whatever, girl," Carole said dismissively. "Anyway, I've got to go. Sean is on his way over and my apartment is a mess."

"Handle your business, girl," Marcia said. "I'll catch you later."

Marcia had it all wrong about her and Jason, Carole thought as she showered. It wasn't that deep. She gave Jason hell, but in her heart, she still liked him. Not in a boyfriend way of course. In her eyes, Jason's fatal flaw was that he was a work-in-progress type of guy. She didn't have time to get him ready for prime time, because she wanted to settle down and find that right man. She was twenty-eight, and getting pressure from her parents to get married, and Sean was marriage material. They'd met at a conference for non-profit organizations. He was an executive with the Green Agency, which promoted organic farming in poor communities, and they'd hit it off immediately. He was funny, smart, full of ambition, and most importantly, he was Nigerian, which definitely met her parents' approval. She was determined to make this relationship work.

As she was putting on her makeup, the doorbell rang.

Shit, she thought. He's early.

"Just a second," Carole yelled. She had two streaks of concealor under her eyes and she rushed to smooth them out with her fingers. She grabbed her blouse and put it on as she strode to the door. As she looked through the peephole, she began to smile.

"Hello, baby!" she said, flinging the door open. "How I've been waiting to see you!"

As Sean walked into the apartment, Carole tried to hug him around his neck, but she felt Sean pull back.

"What, my breath that bad?" she said laughing. "Or does my makeup frighten you?"

"No, that's not it." Sean sat down on the couch and Carole noticed that he never looked at her—not once since he'd come into the room.

Carole closed the door. What was this all about?

"Carole, we have to talk."

Sean walked to the edge of the room as though he was looking for a quick escape. He was obviously not going to dinner with her. Carole tried to compose herself and not give away her trepidations. She sat down on the couch to wait for his speech. But it felt like someone was about to hit her in the jaw and she could see the punch coming.

"What is it?" she said. "What's so serious that we need to talk about?"

Sean kept his eyes down.

"I have some bad news, Carole," he said. "I'm getting transferred to Ghana for at least two years."

Carole was shocked. She expected him to tell her that he wanted to break up. Whew, that was a relief. She started thinking about how much she was going to have to spend on tickets to Ghana. She'd been to Nigeria, Benin, and Togo, but somehow had missed making a trip to Ghana. She was so glad that she'd get a chance to go to Accra and shop. . . .

Then he dropped the bomb.

"When I get there, I'm going to get back with my ex-girlfriend. She lives in Lagos, and we've been talking for a while about getting back together."

Carole was incredulous. This Negro had come to her house to tell her that he was leaving her for his ex-girlfriend? Was he kidding?

"You're getting back with your what?" she said, raising her voice slightly. Maintain control, she thought. Maintain control.

"Carole, you've been great, but after these months together, I know now that I still love my ex-girlfriend."

Carole crumbled inside.

"You know, you have some nerve coming to my house to tell me this!" Carole said angrily. "What the hell did I do wrong that caused you to fall back into the arms of your ex-girlfriend, a woman by the way that you once told me was a bad mixture of Lil' Kim and Allen Iverson's mama, loud and obnoxious! What the hell was wrong with me?"

"Nothing, darling," Sean said in a calm voice that was absolutely infuriating to Carole. It was like he was talking to a petulant child, and she was definitely not a child. "And that's why I wanted to come here and tell you instead of calling you with a message. I just think we wanted two different things."

"Oh, thank you for your consideration," she spat at him. "What do you mean, wanted two different things? Sean, you have to be more specific than that."

Sean looked a little uncomfortable.

"Ever since we got together, you've been talking about getting married. Well, I don't want to get married. I just want to kick it and have some fun. And my ex allows me to do that."

Carole didn't say anything. A single tear streamed down her cheek, and her mascara began to run. But she refused to get too emotional over Sean. All of a sudden, his flaws, flaws she'd willed herself to ignore, instantly began popping up in her mind. He was a flaky, cheap, son of a bitch that certainly didn't deserve a woman like herself.

"Well, I guess you should leave, then," she said, walking to the door.

"Yes, I guess so."

Carole opened the door and Sean took a step toward it. But before he left, Sean turned once more toward Carole.

"If you don't mind, could I give you a word of advice?"

Carole didn't really want to hear anything more from Sean, but what the hell?

"Sure," she sighed.

"Relax. In your next relationship, just relax. If the sex is good, then just love it for the sex. If the conversation is good, then just enjoy it for the conversation. Don't put anything else into it and I think you'll be fine. And when you gradually begin to enjoy more and more of that person, you'll then find the person you want to marry."

"Thanks. Now get the fuck out of my life."

Sean smiled, and to Carole's consternation, looked too damn relieved to go.

"Bye, Carole. I wish you luck," he said and walked out.

With that, Carole closed the door.

When Sean left, Carole slowly took her clothes off, wiped off her makeup and curled up in her bed and cried. She was making emotional investments in men and those investments weren't paying off. She kept getting disappointed by one man after another.

Yes, Carole was a modern woman, and she wouldn't object if

people called her a feminist. She believed that women could, should and always had been able to stand on their own, with or without a man in their lives. But unlike sisters she knew who'd completely given up hope of finding the right man and getting married, Carole still had a strong desire to find that right man and get married. She wasn't getting any younger, and she'd read all of the magazines that said that once you get into your thirties and forties, it was easier for a black woman to get struck by lightning than to get married. Time was running out for her, but nothing in her relationships was working out, and she didn't know why. And when that happened, it was time to call Marcia. And after a good cry, call Marcia to come over is just what she did.

"Marcia, do you want to have a relationship with me?" Carole said, handing her a dish of ice cream. "No man seems to want me, so I might as well explore the other side. I mean, I can't chase a woman away, can I? So what do you think? We could have all the benefits of the orgasm, without the dirty drawers! Both of us could cook, so that's a benefit. And if and when you decided to leave me, at least I'd know it was for a man and not another woman like Sean. So what do you say? Let's shack up!"

"Girl, let me tell you something. I don't shower at the Y, and you can be damn certain I don't eat at the Y. I'm a woman that is on a strict nine-inch-dick diet!" laughed Marcia as she took the bowl of ice cream. "And if you don't have that between your legs, then we might as well end this discussion!"

"See, I can't even be a lesbian!" laughed Carole between bites. "I get rejected by both men and women! Help me, Marcia, help me!"

"Ah, but you wouldn't be a lesbian with just one woman-to-woman experience," laughed Marcia. "At least, that's what my college roommate told me! But that, of course, *that* was a different time and a different day and I was drunk at the time and she looked pretty good in my drunken haze. . . ."

Both laughed hard. Marcia was just what Carole needed at this time. Like always, she'd come over to share a bowl of Ben & Jerry's one sweet whirl ice cream, and to commiserate over yet another Carole breakup, and old reliable Marcia was there to provide both comfort and blunt advice.

Carole took another bite of ice cream and thought hard.

"Is it actually old-fashioned to want to get married?" Carole asked.

Marcia took a bite of ice cream, twirled her spoon, and thought about it.

"Darling, I don't know if it's old-fashioned," Marcia replied. "Some women get married because they simply want the dick on a regular basis, and others want to get taken care of. A lot of people just get married because it seems like it is the thing to do. Others, surprisingly, marry for love. You want to get married because your parents think you should be married. That's some African shit that I can't get my head around," said Marcia, laughing again.

"You know I can't do that. I can't just go for the dick and leave the rest of the man alone. I need a whole man and a whole relationship."

"Well I hate to say this, and I certainly know that you don't want to hear this, but maybe Sean did have a little bit of good advice. Do like he said and just take the next relationship as it comes and then analyze where you want it to go later. You can get back some of the control in your life, and maybe you can find out about yourself instead of having others tell you about who you are."

Marcia stopped eating for a second.

"Look Carole, you are a beautiful and smart girl. You have your own life, your own career, and your own sense of self. Why don't you just relax for a bit? What could it hurt?"

Carole licked the back of her spoon.

"I think I'll do that. I'll do just that. I'm going to relax. And you know what else?"

"What?"

"I was thinking I may try the celibate thing for a month or so. I read about it in *Divas*. A whole bunch of black women from around the country were regaining their sexuality by going celibate. If I do go celibate, I can then clear my head of men."

"Whoa darling, I said relax. I didn't say go crazy!" laughed Marcia. "I don't give up sex for anything. Even when things are bad, sex is always, always good. And nothing is a substitute. Take, for example, this ice cream. Now you know I like this ice cream, but it ain't no way a substitute for a good long dick with a man who knows how to use it."

"Well I may need to try a bunch of ice cream flavors because I'm officially giving up the dick," Carole said, standing up while holding her spoon in the air. "I figure if I go celibate, then the next guy I meet will know that I'm more interested in him than in the sex. But you know that I can be celibate from a human dick, but there's always the good old standby Mr. Chocolate. I used to only use him in an emergency, but he's good in the pinch if I'm abstaining. I just need to get some double D batteries and I'm all good!"

"Hey, but if you use Mr. Chocolate for your own"—Marcia coughed twice—"let's call it self-gratification for lack of a better term, isn't that cheating? I mean celibacy officially means no sex, and isn't using Mr. Chocolate sort of like having sex, even though it's not attached to anything?"

"Well, I'm not going to be a strict celibate like those vegans that don't eat milk, butter, or sit on leather. That's crazy. No, I'm going for the non-strict vegetarian style celibacy, where eggs, milk, and Mr. Chocolate are always allowed. So Mr. Chocolate is in. I do want to clear my mind, but come on, I need some electrical impulses throughout the rest of my body!"

"And that we can agree on!" Marcia exclaimed.

Marcia lifted her spoon.

"Here's to your newfound and long-lost virginity! May celibacy clear your mind, enhance your soul, and get you off via Mr. Chocolate, the ten-inch dick that doesn't care if you are clingy, emotional, or want to get married!"

"Thanks, I think!" They clicked spoons in a toast.

"Okay, now answer one last question for me," Marcia said, dipping more ice cream in her bowl.

"What?"

"Was Sean a ten-stroke man?"

"Nope," Carole said, smiling. "He was five strokes, if that. That's why it was so damn easy to let his trifling ass walk away. He's some skank from Lagos's problem now."

Marcia put down the spoon and let out the loudest laugh of the night.

"Then you didn't lose anything, darling!"

On that, they both could agree.

CHAPTER 5

Hello Jason, I just wanted to let you know that your settlement money will be deposited into your account on Friday. If you have any questions, feel free to contact me at accounting@ketmar.com. Thanks!

—Lisa Myers, Ketchings & Martin Accounting

That's the e-mail that officially made Jason a millionaire, and he sat back in his chair to revel in his new status. It had been over a week since the big news and every day, Steven had badgered him with the same questions.

"So what's it going to be, buddy boy? What are you going to buy with your newfound wealth?" Steven asked. He was trying hard to not be jealous of Jason, but it wasn't working. The fact hadn't changed that Jason had about four million dollars more than him, and junior lawyers trying to make their mark in a law firm tend to keep track of things like that. Right now, Jason was the man in the firm, and Steven was simply another lawyer. And that ate at Steven's very core.

This bastard doesn't deserve this money, Steven thought.

Jason looked up from his computer and thought for a second.

"Well, I think I'll take some of the money and put it in an annuity, and then see about buying some property, because I think that's . . ."

Steven rolled his eyes and almost screamed in frustration.

"Man, come on!"

Steven rolled his chair into Jason's cubicle and looked Jason dead in the eyes. He was not going to allow this money to be wasted.

"Annuities?" he asked. "Property? Man, you are twenty-eight years old with about four million in the bank, and you're concerned about annuities and property? Man, that stuff will take care of itself. Find a house, buy it, and then get a broker to handle your investments. Okay, that's taken care of. Now, what are you going to get for yourself? What have you always wanted?"

Jason looked back at Steven as though he'd never considered the question. The fact was that he *hadn't* considered it. He'd been brought up to deal with the practical and let the other people have fun. But now was his time to have fun.

"I've always wanted a new motorcycle," he said, almost apologetically. "I was thinking about getting a Honda because I saw—"

"Boring," Steven interrupted.

"What about a Ducati?" Jason asked.

"Looks nice, but gets smoked by the bike I'm thinking about."

"Okay, Racer X, what do you think I should get?"

"Two words," Steven said, gripping Jason's chair. "Suzuki Hayabusa."

"Haya what?"

Steven felt like he was teaching a first grader how to read. How could he not know about the Suzuki Hayabusa?

"The Suzuki Hayabusa, my friend, is simply the best motorcycle you could possibly ever think about getting," Steven said. "There simply is no equal. Nothing is faster, and nothing matches it."

"A Hayabusa, Steven? I don't know. I just wanted a little motorcycle that got me from here to here."

"To hell with that," Steven exclaimed. "Get some balls and get a real motorcycle."

Steven reached into his pocket and pulled out his wallet.

"Here," said Steven, pulling out a card. "This is the number at Marina Suzuki. They sell Hayabusas and they'll set you up. Tell them Steven sent you because I've got a 'busa on order."

Jason looked at the card closely.

"And my friend," Steven whispered, "chicks dig guys on Hayabusas."

Jason looked up from the card and a faint hint of a smile came on his face. He needed some chicks to dig him.

"I'll check them out after work," Jason said. "I could use a few looks my way."

"Now you're talking, my man," Steven said. "Now you're talking."

He crept up to Jason so no one else in the office could hear. He obviously had something significant to say. "The Hayabusa is simply the first step, my man, simply the first step. Now that you have money, you have a power you never even realized," he whispered. "You can be this."

With a dramatic flourish, he put the July issue of *Titan* magazine on Jason's desk.

"You can now be a *Titan* man."

"What the hell is a *Titan* man?" Jason asked. "I'm not a subscriber to the magazine and I don't buy it, so enlighten me."

"What the hell is a *Titan* man? What the hell is a *Titan* man? You've got to be kidding me, man!" Steven was truly astonished that he'd never heard of the term. It took him a minute to compose himself.

"A *Titan* man is simply one that can have as many women as he wants, live the lifestyle he desires, and ultimately lives a lifestyle that he's only fantasized about or seen in the movies," Steven said, getting more animated as he spoke. "It is the lifestyle of your dreams, man! The *Titan* lifestyle is about power and how as a man, you can regain a power that has been taken from you by all those dumbass people that think you have to be 'open' and 'care' about the women you date, when in reality, all you want to do is fuck them. And you know in your heart, that's all you really want to do.

"Now some people, like myself, can fake the *Titan* lifestyle, but you my friend, with your newly acquired four million, can actually *live* it, man!"

Jason picked up the magazine and began reading off the cover.

"Throw the ultimate cop-baiting, goat-in-the-limo, *never* tell your new wife bachelor party!"

"Okay," Jason said.

"Mariah Carey, we charm the pants off her!"

Now that one he liked.

"Girlfriend training and how to make a roadkill coat!" Jason read.

"Whoa, this *Titan* life seems just special! Who wouldn't want a roadkill coat in their wardrobe?" Jason said, laughing. He handed Steven his magazine back. "No thank you. I think I'll stick with living the Jason lifestyle."

Steven took the magazine and thumbed through it.

"And what lifestyle is that? A lifestyle that doesn't include women?" he said, not looking up from the magazine.

Jason started to stutter a bit. He got a little touchy when people talked about his lack of a girlfriend.

"I'm simply on a dry spell," Jason said, with not a small bit of attitude.

Again, Steven got in close. He had a faint smile on his face, like he'd heard this from someone else.

"Okay, listen to me for a hot second. Let's say that you get off this so-called dry spell with women. What type of women will you have to choose from, anyway? At best, they'll rate as sixes or maybe sevens if you're lucky."

"You're probably right. But what's wrong with sixes and sevens?" Jason asked.

"Fool, don't you know that you are now in the eleven range because you have money? That's like moving from dating the winner of *America's Next Top Model* and going straight to Tyra. Fuck that. It's like dating Tyra in L.A. and Naomi Campbell in London, at the same time, and both being cool with it."

Steven had gotten a bit hysterical about the whole *Titan* lifestyle. His whole attitude was like he was trying to tell Jason where the Holy Grail was located and Jason just didn't care.

He leaned back in his chair.

"Let me ask you another question," he continued. "Do you think money gets women?"

"Well, money and looks," Jason responded, wondering when this conversation would end.

"Bullshit man, bullshit!" Steven said, pointing his finger at Jason's chest.

He was now all up in Jason's grill, banging the magazine against the desk. Jason started to wonder if Steven didn't have some real work to do.

"Only money and *power* gets women, my brother. Only money and power. Everything else is just a distraction, and looks ain't even the same universe. Does Bill Clinton get his dick blown if he's not the president? Okay, scratch that. He got it as an Arkansas governor, so he doesn't count. Or maybe it does count. Even a governor has power.

"But think about this. Look at Jay-Z and Beyonce. Do you really think Beyonce, as fine as she is, is even going to look at Jay-Z twice if he's not a rapper and a multimillionaire? I mean, look at Jay-Z! The brother's talented but he ain't the most handsome man in the pack. There are a thousand Jay-Z look-alikes flipping burgers right now, who couldn't get even within one hundred feet of Beyonce, and yet Jay-Z is taxin' that ass."

He continued because he wasn't sure Jason was convinced.

"I can see it in your eyes that you don't believe me yet," Steven said grinning. "Let me give you another example. How about Puffy and Jennifer Lopez. Hell, Ben Affleck and Jennifer Lopez! What makes Ben any different than you or me? He's just some white boy from Boston who was lucky to be in a hit movie with Matt Damon.

"And if you're not convinced yet, I have the ultimate ugly slash beauty coupling. . . ." Steven paused for effect.

"Jermaine Dupri and Janet Jackson. *Jermaine Fucking Dupri* of all people was able to get Janet Jackson, one of the finest women in the world! Have you seen Jermaine's teeth? They're so fucked up it looks like they're kickboxing against each other. Man, Jermaine Dupri shouldn't be able to pull a chicken head from the Fox Hills Mall, and yet since he is a hip hop mogul, he has the power to pull a Janet Jackson. Now if that doesn't convince you, then nothing will."

"Okay, you've got my attention," Jason said. "Go ahead about this *Titan* lifestyle."

"I've got your attention, but I haven't convinced you yet," Steven said smugly.

"Look, I didn't mind dating fine-ass women, but why are you so interested in having me become a *Titan* man?" Jason asked. "What do you get out of it?"

Steven smiled. He was always smiling like he was Sylvester the cat and he'd finally swallowed Tweety Bird.

"Overflow, my friend. I want some of your overflow."

Jason sat with his mouth open in mock surprise.

"You mean to tell me that your ever-faithful wingman," Jason said, using air quotes to emphasize *wingman,* "is now the attraction? All of a sudden, you need help from *moi?*"

Steven again sat back in his desk chair and tapped his fingers against his chair.

"Impossible to believe, I know, but Steven Cox, who is God's gift to women, is willing to take a backseat to you. This is all because I see the potential of a Steven and Jason partnership. You see you have the power of money that I don't have, and I have the power of the pull, which you don't have. Together, we can make a great team. Think about it. The *Titan* lifestyle means that whatever lifestyle you've ever dreamed about, you can now have it. It's just whether or not you want it."

Steven reached for the *Titan* again and put it in Jason's briefcase.

"Take this back home and read it. I want you to think about doing everything they say they've done and think about whether you'd like to have a taste of their lifestyle. I think you'll like it."

Jason took the magazine and studied it closely.

"Okay, I'll read it after work."

Jason walked back into his apartment and picked up his phone.

"You have no new messages."

Same shit, different day, Jason thought as he tossed his phone. He went to his refrigerator and took out a plate of Stroganoff. Stretching out on his couch, waiting for his food to heat up in the microwave and bored to tears, he thought about calling the one person who was never bored.

"Marcia, where the hell are you?" Jason asked. "I can hear the bourgeoisieness through the phone."

"I'm up in Ladera," Marcia whispered into her cell. It sounded like a cocktail party was going on in the background, and it was. "Bradley Fuller is hosting his annual black art and black authors confab. Do you want to come through? I can get you in."

"Nah, Bradley is too damn stuffy for me. I went two years ago and he wouldn't let people put their drinks down for fear of fucking up his cherrywood tables."

"Why do you think I'm whispering now?" she said. "He confiscated everyone's cell phones so that the artists wouldn't be disturbed as they painted new works of art. I hid mine in my bra."

Jason smiled. That was his girl.

"Let's hook up next week," he said.

"Will do. Holla!"

The Stroganoff was ready and Jason began eating. It really was a good Stroganoff, despite what it represented. He thought about giving Carole a call, but they really didn't have that type of relationship. He scrolled through his Blackberry, and checked off the people he hadn't talked to in over a year. These were his friends, but he'd been so consumed by Burger World, that they'd taken the hint when he stopped calling them back. Now it was going to be awkward calling them, and he didn't feel like being awkward tonight. So he was pretty much alone. Even Mrs. Petroff wasn't home. He'd tried to return her casserole dish, but she'd gone with her Russian and Ukrainian friends to a charity affair in West Hollywood.

Jason opened his briefcase and pulled out the *Titan* magazine.

There's nothing better to do, he thought, reading the first article. It was entitled, "The Art of Control."

> *One way to control your girlfriend is to lie. But don't squander this opportunity with a small, insignificant lie, go for a whopper. Think global. The lie needs to be so extraordinary and blatant, that the woman has to believe it because no one would ever make up a lie so stupid. An example: Honey, I didn't come home last night because I was in Afghanistan on a secret mission hunting for Osama bin Laden. I couldn't call because I'm on restriction, nor can I tell you about whether or not we found him. Please love me.*

Jason laughed. Is this the type of advice that Steven was saying he should follow? But it was entertaining, with its articles "How to Get the Perfect Blowjob" and "Dating Your Best Friend's Mom . . . With His Permission." Not a bad read, he thought, closing the magazine and tossing it on his table, as entertainment. But this advice constituted some sort of serious lifestyle? What was Steven really talking about?

As it turned out, Jason didn't have long to find out.

His door buzzed.

Who the hell is that, he thought.

"Hello?"

"Hey Jason, it's Steven. Let me up."

In the two years they'd known each other, neither Jason nor Steven had visited the other's home. It wasn't by plan, it just happened that way. So it was very unexpected to Jason that Steven had made his way to his apartment.

"So this is where you live?" Steven said, walking into the apartment. He gingerly moved some socks off a chair. "Are these clean?" he frowned while holding up one of the socks to his nose. "Man, I see why you don't get girlfriends. Someone should have told you, my friend, but you live in a dump."

"Uh, I don't come over your place and insult it, so I would appreciate it if you didn't denigrate mine."

Jason took the sock and threw it to the side. He moved a bunch of clothes to the hamper and tried to do an impromptu cleanup. It didn't help.

"Sorry, man, I didn't mean to insult you. I just thought you already knew."

Steven looked around, still taking everything in.

"All right. Why are you here, Steven?" Jason asked.

It was funny. Although Jason didn't have a whole bunch of visitors rolling through his apartment, and he did lament that sometimes, although he also liked his privacy. And right now, Steven was messing with his privacy.

"I forgot to give you this," Steven said, tossing another *Titan* to him. It fell on the floor and landed at Jason's feet.

"More *Titan*. Look, I just finished reading the mag you gave me. What's different about this *Titan* than the one you gave me earlier today?" Jason asked, picking it up.

"Check out the first article." Steven grinned.

Jason looked at the cover and the headline: HOW TO LIVE THE *TITAN* LIFESTYLE . . . IN EIGHT EASY STEPS!

"So this is the famous *Titan* lifestyle that I'm supposed to live," Jason asked, giving it back to him.

"Exactly," he said.

Steven took the magazine and waved it in the air like a scroll.

"This is exactly what you are supposed to do to live the *Titan* life, and my friend, it will change your life."

Steven opened the magazine and started reading.

"Look, damn it," Jason said, taking the magazine from Steven and throwing it down. "Enough with this goddamn *Titan* life! Who said I wanted some drastic change from the life I have now? I like my life. It's not perfect, but it keeps me balanced and on target."

"And that's the beauty. You don't have to change that part of your life," Steven said. "I know, you worked your ass off to get where you are. Congratulations. Your family is proud of you, your friends are proud of you, and black folks around the world are proud of you. And believe me, we're all saying, 'Keep up the good work, Jason.' But think about it. Is that all there is to life? Is that all you want, work and then this?" he said, looking around the apartment. "Or is it annuities, torts, and back to annuities? How about a few beautiful women in your life? What about fucking living your life, for God's sake? But fuck it, if you aren't interested, I won't push."

Steven started to walk out, when Jason looked around his apartment, noticing the emptiness. He ran over to stop him from leaving.

"All right, so you say that I can keep my current life, not fuck up my goals, and still have a *Titan* life of supermodels and super parties?" Jason said, grabbing Steven's arm.

"Not only can you have it, it only helps you, baby. It only helps you!" Steven said, walking back into the living room. "If you let me, I can transform your life the *Titan* way."

"Let's say, and don't take this as gospel, that I wanted to live this *Titan* lifestyle? What steps would I take?" Jason asked, wondering what type of catch-22 was coming.

Steven knew he had Jason on the hook now and was going to do his best to reel him in.

"Next week I'm going to have a party at my place. I want you to come and check it out. After that, I promise you that you'll be a convert. But until then, read up on the ten rules in this issue. Read it closely and you'll see what it takes to be a true *Titan* man."

"All right Steven. All right. If it means that much to you that I live this lifestyle, I'll come to the party and see what it's all about. I make no promises, but I'll come. By the way, what time does it start?"

"Get there at nine. I'll e-mail you my directions. Man, you don't even know the possibilities!" He acted like *he'd* received four million dollars.

"Yeah, I'm guessing I'm going to find out soon."

"Check you later, man."

It was all moving so fast for Jason. He had four million going into the bank soon, and now he had the potential for dating super-models. Was it as easy as Steven made it seem? Jason popped open a cold Heineken, kicked his feet up and began reading "HOW TO LIVE THE *TITAN* LIFESTYLE . . . IN EIGHT EASY STEPS!"

> *Step One:*
> *In order to live the* Titan *lifestyle, you need to live in a place that exudes the* Titan *lifestyle. So that means no more run-of-the-mill apartment for our* Titan *man. No, you need something that awes the women without overwhelming them. And the only thing that does that is . . . a downtown loft. And it doesn't matter where you live. Downtown Omaha or downtown Miami, a downtown loft puts you in the center of everything a* Titan *man needs. Plus, a loft is easy to clean and easy to accessorize. A loft tells a woman you might have money, but she can't pinpoint how much money. That's good, because you want to keep your money in your account and not hers.*

> *Step Two:*
> *Drive something fast. If you are looking at a car, don't go for one of those liberal leaning, eco-terrorist-driving, bubblemobiles that get 200 miles to the gallon. No, you're a* Titan *man! You don't give a damn whether or not the oil runs out or whether the polar caps melt via global warming. Just keep the gas flowing and the pedal to the metal. With cars, you have a few choices: Ferrari, Lamborghini, Viper, or Corvette Z06 all fit the bill of a* Titan *lifestyle. Who gives a flying fuck that they don't carry much*

more than you and a grocery bag? Your girlfriend shouldn't weigh more than that anyway. But best of all is a motorcycle. Get off your ass, and live a little. A Titan *man needs a motorcycle either as their secondary vehicle, or if you're really badass, their primary vehicle. Tell your babe to either ride or walk. Our recommendations? Only one, really: the Suzuki Hayabusa. Fastest bike on earth and the Japanese writing on its side says "badass," we think.*

"Jesus," Jason muttered. In the magazine was a full-page spread of Jennifer Lopez and Beyonce sitting on two silver Hayabusas. It was the sexiest matching of women and machine Jason had ever seen. He read on.

Step Three:
   Get a new wardrobe. Our advice at Titan*? Find a designer and stick with it. And yes, we said get a designer. There's nothing worse than a man wearing a hodgepodge of clothes that don't go together. And we at* Titan *figure that most men, or most real men, don't have a clue as to what to wear. So remember what you did when you were a kid. Matching apple T-shirts with apple shorts guided us then, let Perry Ellis and Claiborne guide you now. Go to your local department store, find a designer you like, and buy everything with their name on it. Do that, and we guarantee that you'll instantly improve your look, which is critical for a* Titan *lifestyle.*

That seemed simple enough, Jason thought. This *Titan* lifestyle seemed more like common sense than anything extraordinary.

Step Four:
   The Two Girlfriend Theory: Every Titan *man living the* Titan *lifestyle needs to have at least two girlfriends living no more than fifty miles from him, but no more than five hundred miles away. The fifty-mile rule helps the* Titan *avoid unexpected visits, or surprise trips to your city. While the five-hundred-mile run means that she's only an hour away by plane, reducing the costs of seeing her on a semiregular basis. The two of course will never meet, unless you follow Step Five. . . .*

Step Five:

    Have at least one ménage à trios per year. Titan believes that a ménage à trios helps clear the mind and soul, while of course helping you get your freak on. But ménage à trioses also do more than that. They permanently expand your pool of casual sex partners, giving your black book more definition. Your Titan lifestyle will now consist of girlfriends, freaks, and extra freaky women. Each night, you'll be able to pick and choose which category you'd like to delve in. That's the Titan lifestyle personified.

Ménage à trioses? Jason thought. It had always been his fantasy. Just like every one of his boys, he'd *almost* been a part of one in college. His fraternity had been having a party when some sorority members from Stanford had come through. His brothers had never met them before, but after a little jungle juice, everyone was ready to couple up. Everyone except two women, who both fancied Jason. So while everyone else left, these two women had stayed with Jason. He'd gotten them into the room, was all ready to get his fantasy on, when the jungle juice took effect and he ended up vomiting on the floor. Not the best atmosphere for three intertwined bodies, and his ménage à trios remained elusive. He'd like to have that chance back.

Step Six:

    Throw parties at your loft on a monthly basis. Parties keep you in contact with beautiful women and their friends, and that is what the Titan lifestyle is all about. Keeping you in the right circles. Also, when you throw parties, you're invited to parties, thereby expanding your pool.

Step Seven:

    Learn how to drink like a real Titan man. Just like the Los Angeles Lakers don't recognize the Los Angeles Clippers, Titan men don't recognize anything good about lite beer. If you're going to drink a beer, then drink a Guinness. If you're going to drink hard alcohol, then go with Maker's Mark bourbon, or Jack Daniel's, over the rocks. Mixed drinks? Martini, and none

*of those apple or chocolate ones, you bastard. If the drink comes
with an umbrella or funny name, like Sex in the City, give it
to the chick next to you.*

Step Eight:
    *This last step: be cool. If you follow everything we tell you,
then cool will come. The art of being cool is not forcing it. Allow
it to envelope you by your Titan lifestyle actions, and you'll be
recognized for the cool person you are. And gentlemen, that's
what makes a Titan man and the Titan lifestyle.*

That was a lot to ingest. Jason put down the magazine and contemplated what he'd just read. They also advocated six months of
reading and following the directions of *Titan* magazine. If you listened to their advice faithfully, in the end, the reader should be a
Titan man.

Jesus, what time is it? Jason thought. It was one in the morning
and he'd read the whole magazine. Jason was sleepy as hell, so
maybe he wasn't thinking straight, but as he looked around his
nondescript apartment and thought about what he had to look
forward to in his life, he suddenly figured out that the *Titan* life
couldn't be less exciting than his current nonlife. And what the
hell, the *Titan* life wouldn't hurt anyone anyway. It is all about having fun. And Jason needed some fun in his life.

That's it, I'm going to give it a try. If I like it, I'll buy into it. If
not, I'll just do what I was going to do anyway, he decided.

And with that, he fell asleep.

CHAPTER 6

"So what has to go?" Marcia asked. Carole sat in the middle of her apartment Indian style, surrounded by boxes and, well, stuff. Week one of Carole's new celibate life required change, and so Carole had gone through her apartment and piled anything that smacked of relationships or men, right in the middle of her living room.

"All of this," Carole replied, pulling out a stack of magazines. "*Divas, Cosmo, Glamour, Marie Claire, Essence.* You've all served me well over the years, but it's time to go." She handed the magazines to Marcia.

"What Guys Are *Really* Looking For," Marcia read, throwing each magazine in the trash can. " 'His Body: A User's Manual.' Are you sure you want to get rid of all these magazines? Sounds like good advice to me."

"Feel free to take them if you'd like, but I don't have any use for them. I'm off the get-a-man, keep-a-man, rat race. Look at this," she said, pointing to the magazines. "I bet I've spent over a thousand dollars on women's magazines this year alone. And why don't we women throw them out?"

"Because we're pack rats?" Marcia laughed.

"Well, I am that," Carole grinned. "But there's something else. Women don't throw these magazines out because we always think that the answer to our relationship problems lie in each month's issue, and if we throw it out, even if we've read it thousands of times, then we might throw out a future solution. And God help us if we have to think for ourselves in order to solve our problems. That just wouldn't do."

"Girl, I think you are overanalyzing," Marcia said. "When I put *Baldwin Hills* to bed each month, we're simply looking for stories that attract readership. If we did a story on giraffes and their sex lives, and it moved issues, then you bet your titties that we'd do a monthly column on giraffes and their sex lives. For women's magazines, it's all about getting a man."

"Then I don't need to be manipulated," Carole said, putting the rest of the magazines in the trash.

Carole grabbed her books and a cardboard box.

"Oh no, you're not going to throw these in the trash," Marcia said.

"Not the trash, I never throw away books," Carole said, thumbing through her books. "But I will give them away to either Mama's House or the library. But they've got to go too."

"*Making Bad Relationships Good . . . in 30 Days!*" Carole said, reading the cover. "You're out of here. *Getting to Yes,* I say no!" Carole tossed book after book into the cardboard box. Marcia reached into the box and pulled a book out.

"Let me have this one, girl," she said. "*Black Women's Erotica.* It sounds good."

Carole grabbed the book from Marcia.

"Oh, did I throw this one in the box?" Carole said, smiling, putting the book back on the shelf. "That was definitely a mistake. If Mr. Chocolate is going to be my date for the next few months, then I need to have my mind in order. This will help me get in the mood."

As Carole put the last book in the box, she closed the box and put it next to her door. She put her foot on the box and stared at Marcia.

"There," she said determinedly, "I'm going to break my man addiction."

Marcia pulled out a cigarette and lit it. She opened the window to let out the smoke.

"As any addict will tell you, the best way to kick one addiction is to substitute it with another," Marcia said as she took a long pull from her cigarette. "And since you don't smoke or do drugs, what are you going to do as a substitute?"

"What we do best, baby," Carole said, picking up her purse. "We're going shopping!"

Marcia smoked the last of her cigarette, and then flicked it out of the window.

"Let's go get our shop on, baby," she said, putting on her coat.

They walked out of Carole's apartment and into the street. Marcia's car was parked directly in front of Carole's building.

"So, where do you want to go?" Marcia asked as she pulled out into the street. "We could cruise Crenshaw first, and see all of the guys on bikes, oops!"

"Oops what?" Carole said.

"Oops, as in oops I forgot you aren't looking for a man," Marcia said grinning.

"Just because I'm on a diet," Carole started, "doesn't mean that I can't look at the menu."

It was a sunny Saturday afternoon, and Crenshaw Boulevard was abuzz with activity. The brothers riding motorcycles were doing tricks by the Crenshaw mural, while music was blasting from every open car window. As Carole and Marcia passed Leimert Park, they saw that the Alphas were holding their annual Black History Month festival in the park. Children were playing in a giant jumper, while vendors were selling Jamaican patties. A singer was on stage, while dancers performed to her music. There had to be at least five hundred people enjoying the festival.

"Want to stop?" Carole asked.

"Nah, my ex is an Alpha, and I don't want to run into him," Marcia said, turning away from Leimert Park. "Plus, I want to get to the Beverly Center to buy some M.A.C."

"Cool."

As Marcia and Carole rode through Los Angeles, Carole thought about her life. Mama's House was the center of her life, and she wouldn't have it any other way. She'd decided on working with single mothers after a college internship at the Lake Merritt homeless shelter in Oakland. The vision of small children and single mothers burned in her brain, and after two weeks of working with them on their problems, she'd decided to meet with her college counselor and tell them she'd had a change of direction.

"Why are you switching from finance to women's studies?" Nate Carroll had asked. Nate had counseled Carole since she'd first walked onto the Berkeley campus. "You're basically throwing away a year in order to change majors."

Carole looked at Nate dead in the eye.

"Have you ever felt that you'd found your mission in life?" she asked him. "I'm not talking about some clichéd experience where you feel good about yourself, and then make an impromptu decision that you don't really mean. I'm talking about really finding your mission. Well I have, and it isn't sitting behind a desk at a multinational corporation, trying to make some rich shareholders happy. I realized that once I met people who didn't have anything, and yet had the potential to have everything. Those are the shareholders I want to answer to."

Nate looked over her paperwork and then looked back at Carole.

"Done," he said. And like that, Carole had found her way.

But whereas her professional life had been wonderful, her love life had been less so. Her mother had always pressed her to get married, and get married young. Her father had always demanded that her boyfriends be Nigerian. And combined with those pressures, she'd never had the chance to simply have fun, like her friend Marcia. Marcia had fun with her men, and Carole envied that. Whereas Marcia made the decision to leave her men, Carole's men left her. And she didn't really know why.

"Carole, I think you're great, but I think we're growing apart," Don had said. Don had been an engineer she'd dated for six months.

"Carole, I don't think we're having fun anymore," Kevin had said. "Plus, I'm moving to Atlanta and I'd like a fresh start." Kevin was a spoken word artist she'd gone out with for three months.

And Nolan, the brother before Sean, simply stopped returning her calls. What was she doing wrong? Carole asked, as they walked into the M.A.C. store.

"You are too damn clingy, babe," Marcia said, applying some M.A.C. makeup on her hand. "Does this shade look good on me?"

"No. What do you mean, clingy?" Carole asked. She leaned on the counter, waiting for Marcia to pick a foundation.

"As long as I've known you, you've never ever just dated a man without strings," Marcia said, testing another shade. "What about simply being with a guy because of the sex? No thoughts about the future. No thoughts about anything but the next great orgasm that man is going to give you. Could you do that?"

Carole thought for a second.

"I come from a very traditional family, and I think that's why I'm uptight about my relationships," Carole said. "Can I simply have a sexual relationship without any sense of the future? I don't know. Maybe I'll give it a try after this celibacy thing."

"I'll take this," Marcia said to the M.A.C. artist. She turned back to Carole. "Celibacy may work out for you, and if it does, then great. But if not, try just taking a dick for what it is, simply just a dick. Now let's go check out some lingerie."

Marcia and Carole strolled into Victoria's Secret and began browsing when a saleswoman approached Carole. Marcia went to one end of the store, while Carole was at the other. At first, the saleswoman didn't say anything; she just stood there watching. But as Carole picked up lingerie, the saleswoman saw her chance to make a sale.

"Getting something for the boyfriend?" she said with a smile, trying her best to be pleasant.

"No, don't have a boyfriend," Carole responded curtly, without even looking at the saleswoman.

Carole kept looking at the sheer underwear, trying to find the right piece.

"Girlfriend?"

"Excuse me?"

The saleswoman looked at Marcia and then back at Carole. Carole looked at the saleswoman with deeply penetrating eyes.

"You think I'm a lesbian?" Carole said "lesbian" with an emphasis on each syllable in lesbian. "Because I'm not buying your overpriced underwear for a man? So I'm a lesbian all of a sudden?"

"I just, uh, I'm sorry, but I didn't mean to infer that . . ." the saleswoman stuttered.

"I'm just looking for something that makes me feel good. You

know, women don't always have to buy things for men, or women
for that matter. You can buy things just for yourself. That's perfectly okay."

"Ma'am, I'm new here," the saleswoman said, shuffling her feet
nervously, "and if I offended you in any way, I apologize."

Carole fingered a pair of sheer black panties with a matching
bra, and handed them to the saleswoman. She'd overreacted, but
that was to be expected. Just like an alcoholic who gets the heebie-
jeebies, she was going to freak out from time to time when someone mentioned the words *girlfriend* and *boyfriend*.

Marcia walked over and took the panties and bra from Carole
and handed them to the saleswoman.

"It's not your fault, darling, she's just trying to kick a man
addic— Just charge it to my American Express," Marcia said.

The relieved saleswoman rang up the transaction as fast as she
could.

"This is going to be tougher than I thought," Carole said to
Marcia as they left the store.

"No one said giving up dick would be easy," said Marcia, laughing.

CHAPTER 7

Work at Ketchings & Martin had changed for Jason, and it was imperceptible to him at first.

"Man, I'm just staring at these new cases," Jason said. Steven, for once, was hard at work on a lead paint case. Fullerton Paints had been dumping their old lead paints in black neighborhoods, and now thousands of inner-city residents were feeling the effects.

"It's called motivationitis," Steven said, not looking up from his computer. He kept typing away. "When you get a large sum of money, then your motivation for coming to work as a wage slave disappears."

Steven looked up from the computer.

"It doesn't have to be, but it will sure make you figure out whether your original goals were as genuine as you thought they were."

"Well, I still want to be a partner, so I have motivation there," Jason replied. "But you know how people say that they enjoy their work so much that they'd work for free? That's sort of the dilemma I'm in. Do I enjoy the work that much? Because right now, I don't feel like I'm working for a paycheck. My bills are taken care of."

"Talk to the old man, then, if you have some issues," Steven said. "Wasn't he the one that had an open-door policy? Test it."

Steven knew that the associates avoided the firm's founders like the plague, but Jason had clout.

"Do you think I should?" Jason asked hesitantly.

"Dude, you made this firm twenty million dollars," Steven said incredulously. "Walk into that muthafucka's office and tell him you need to talk to him."

"Yeah, fuck that," Jason said, standing up. "I'm the one with the balls in this office."

"That's the spirit," Steven said, smiling.

Jason began walking toward Peter Ketchings's office, but unlike his first walk, this time he felt no sense of doom. He'd worked his ass off at the firm, and had delivered. So if he needed to talk to the partner, then fuck it, he was going to talk to the partner.

Jason knocked on Ketchings's door.

"Come in," Ketchings said.

Jason walked into the office. Ketchings was practicing his golf stroke. He had a line of golf balls he was hitting into a fake green.

"What can I do for you, Jason?" Ketchings said, never taking his eyes off his golf balls. Jason sat down at Ketchings's desk.

"Sir, for the past two weeks, I've done nothing but sit at my desk, staring at my computer screen, wondering what I was doing in the office. Could you give me another case, another client? It doesn't matter if it is mundane, or dead end, I just need something that would make my brain feel stimulated," Jason said.

"Oh, we'll talk about that later, Jason," Mr. Ketchings said, still not looking up from his putter.

"But I'm feeling a little lost here, Mr. Ketchings," Jason told him. "I need a purpose to come to work."

He was feeling more comfortable speaking to Mr. Ketchings after having done so well on the Burger World lawsuit, but Jason thought that may have been a bad thing to say to Mr. Ketchings. He looked a little concerned as he finally turned his head to look at him.

"Jason, do you mean to tell me that now that you've got money, you have no motivation to practice law?"

The tone of his voice told Jason that this was obviously a question that required an emphatic *no* from his lowly associate. He frantically tried to backtrack.

"No sir, that's not what I meant. . . ."

"Because I have a lot of money and I would still practice law for free."

As soon as those words entered the atmosphere, they both knew he was lying, but he wanted Jason to lie in order to back him up.

"Of course, sir, and I feel the same way. I was just saying that it would be nice to have another Burger World lawsuit to work on," Jason pleaded.

"All in due time, son, all in due time. You see, those types of lawsuits don't come around that often, and when they do, especially since you got so much success, the office is going to be a feeding frenzy as soon as one comes in. Everyone is going to try to get it."

"Yes, sir."

"You should still have some work to do," he continued. "Since we started this firm, we've never been at a loss for having cases. Maybe you can work on some cases with that Cox fellow until we get a client we feel you would be perfect for."

"Sir, I'm currently doing my pro bono work at Mama's House. Since I'm not assigned to any cases right now, do you mind if I spend the next month working at Mama's House?" I think I could do a great job there, and I could help a lot of people who need it."

"I think that's an excellent idea!" Ketchings said while clasping his hands together. "Work with the poor and get a perspective on what it means to have money, and not have money. Jason, I continue to be surprised by you."

And with that, Ketchings stood up and walked over to the door. He opened the door for Jason to leave.

"Jason, you are going to be all right. You just have to make sure that you stay levelheaded, and know what you really want out of life. Once you do that, you'll feel comfortable about who you are and what you want to do with life. Just remember to always be yourself and you won't go wrong."

And with a pat on the back, Jason left his office feeling a little bit better. Going to Mama's House would be a nice getaway, and he was right, a month there could keep him grounded.

"Did you get a new assignment?" Steven asked as Jason sat back down at his desk.

"Nope."

"Well, what do you care? Come here, turn on your computer, and play solitaire until they come up with something."

"I asked if I could spend more time at Mama's House while they find something for me. I want to be useful and not just sit on my money."

"Mama's House? You're going to spend your time listening to babies' mommas bitch about how their Negroes ain't worth shit?" Steven said. "You can have it. The only thing good about Mama's House is fine-ass Carole, who I will fuck, I tell you, before I die. But stop worrying about that. Are you ready for my party tonight?"

"I guess."

"Well, man, you are going to be in for a treat."

"Is anyone I know going to be there? Marcia, Carole . . ."

Steven snickered.

"Let me tell you something. Marcia and Carole aren't a part of the *Titan* lifestyle. I'm talking about women who are willing and ready to party. Those two are in a different category. Plus . . ."

Steven lowered his voice.

"Carole is my special project. After I'm finished sowing my oats, I'm going to concentrate on her."

"She's just not into you, Steven."

"I'm just the man for her. She just doesn't know it yet. And by the way, don't you ever get an idea about going after her. I've claimed her, so she's mine."

"Been there and done that, cat," Jason answered. "Been there and done that."

"But from what I've heard," Steven retorted, "never actually tapped that."

Jason shot a glare at him. "You don't know that," he said.

"All right, you're right, I don't know that," Steven said, slightly sarcastically. "But don't fuck with her."

Then, Steven tried to defuse the situation. He smiled at Jason.

"What are we talking about them for, anyway? This is a *Titan* party and not just some get-together. This is what I need you to do. Just bring yourself and an open mind and you'll have a great time."

"Will do."

Jason turned back to his desk, and with nothing else to do, he decided to give Carole a call and see if it was okay to come in for the month.

"Mama's House, Carole speaking."

"Hi Carole, this is Jason."

"Hey Jason, what's been happening? We didn't see you this week." Carole had actually missed Jason after his good deed.

"No, I had a couple of things at the firm that were keeping me busy. But that's why I'm calling. I asked my boss if I could go full time at Mama's House for a month, just to reenergize. I really liked working with that young lady and I think I could get in some good work if I at least worked at Mama's House full time, rather than just part-time. I can't solve everything, but I could make some headway with the cases you already have."

"We'd love to have you, Jason. Come in on Monday and we'll talk about the setup."

"Great."

"Hey Jason, thanks. The women will really appreciate your work, and I appreciate your help."

"No problem."

"I'll see you on Monday," Jason said.

The rest of the day had gone swiftly for Jason. Spending some time away from the law firm would let him focus and figure out what he wanted to do. In the meantime, he needed to get ready for Steven's party. And that meant new clothes.

"Now, how does that look to you?" Scott asked as Jason preened in the mirror. The salesman straightened out the wrinkles in Jason's shirt and then stood to the side.

"Nice," Jason said, staring into the mirror. "What designer is this, again?" Jason had never been into clothes much, so he couldn't tell one designer from the next.

"This is Sean John, P. Diddy's line," he said. "We can have you dressed in Sean John from head to toe."

Before he went to Steven's party, Jason had decided to follow *Titan*'s advice on clothes. And that meant a trip to Criners-On-Melrose. Criners-On-Melrose, according to *Titan*, was the hottest shop in Los Angeles. Criners-On-Melrose was casual in a cool way, not a dorky way, and was definitely on the upside of trendy. Scott was the salesman assigned to put together Jason's look.

"You know, I normally wouldn't wear this," Jason said, "but I'm trying to change my wardrobe. I'm trying to break out of a rut."

"Then you've made a good start. The black-and-white-striped pants are new from the Sean John line and they can't keep them in stock in London," Scott said.

"How much are they?"

"Five hundred and fifty dollars," he answered.

Normally, Jason would have balked at paying over fifty dollars for pants, but with four mil large in the bank, it didn't even raise his eyebrows.

"Okay, I'll take the pants, this shirt, and definitely these shoes," Jason said.

"This is special Vietnamese silk," Scott explained, as he wrapped up Jason's purchases. "The silkworms of this region produce a silk that is unmatched in the world. And these shoes are handmade and imported from northern Italy. The lining is pure sheepskin, massaged for a year by the hands of old Italian peasant women, who work night and day to get it to feel just right."

"Thanks," Jason said, taking his bag. From Criners-On-Melrose, Jason went home to prep for the party.

As he approached his apartment, Mrs. Petroff was right there with his Friday Stroganoff. "Thank you very much, Mrs. Petroff," he said, taking the hot dish.

"You're welcome, my darling," she said, pinching him on the cheek yet again.

Jason walked into his apartment, when his cell phone rang.

"Hey Jason, how've you been?"

"Fine, Marcia, what have you been up to?"

"Nothing much. I've got a foundation banquet to attend tonight, and then after that, it's working on the next issue of *Baldwin Hills*. What are you up to?"

"Oh, nothing," he lied. He didn't know why he lied. Maybe he didn't think the *Titan* lifestyle and Marcia jelled.

"Well, if you want to come with me to the banquet, you are more than invited. I could use the company and conversation. These things tend to be as boring as hell."

"No, I think I'm going to stay in tonight."

"Okay, leave me to my boredom. I now know who my true blue friends are!" she laughed.

"You know I've got your back, Marcia! Just not tonight."

"That's okay. Hey, Carole told me that you are going to be working at Mama's House for a whole month. That's great of you, and I think you really impressed Carole. And you know how hard that is. Plus, she told me about the help you gave that young woman. I almost teared up when I heard about it."

"Ah, it's no problem, but Carole has a big mouth. No one was supposed to know that I gave that sister that money. As for volunteering at the center, I needed to get out of the office anyway. This was a pretty good excuse to do some good work."

Marcia paused a bit.

"Jason, can I tell you something?"

"Sure," he said, wondering what was up.

"Carole has broken up with Sean."

"Hey, that's not surprising." said Jason, laughing. "I knew it wasn't going to last that long. Her relationships never last long."

Marcia laughed too.

"Yep, she does have difficulties with men. But I would like you to do one thing for me."

"Sure, what is that?"

"I need you to be a friend to Carole. She's wounded and doesn't believe in men right now and I think she holds you in pretty high regard, even if you guys have had issues in the past. She needs to hear from a man that isn't trying to get at her, but has good advice on what she should do in her next relationship."

"Are you sure about that? Did you see how she lashed out at me when we were at G. Garvin's? I mean, the sister tried to make it personal."

"Well you shouldn't take it personally because she's always touchy about the relationships."

Marcia paused again. "I trust you because you are a good guy among the sharks," she continued. "And she needs a good guy to talk to."

"Hey, if she asks me, then I'll be there for her. But I don't think she will."

He liked talking to Marcia, but she was making him late for the party.

"Okay. But just watch out for her, will you? If she does ask, be there for her."

"Will do."

"Okay, I'll check you later, Jason."

"Peace out."

And with that, Marcia hung up the phone.

Hmm, Carole and boyfriend number fifteen bites the dust. What a surprise. What the hell does she do to these men? Jason wondered. She's fine as hell, but her men run like a white woman being chased by OJ to get away from her.

Jason showered, and put on his new gear.

It was time to go, but he needed to do one last bachelor thing.

Okay, maybe I'll get lucky tonight, he thought, putting a condom in his wallet. *Titan* says that a man should always be prepared for sex, so here goes.

He left the apartment and ran into Mrs. Petroff, who was leaving for her weekly Russian social in West Hollywood.

"Jason, you don't look like yourself! You look, well, different."

"Yes, I thought I'd buy some new clothes. Do you like them?"

She looked at Jason up and down.

"Well, they are certainly interesting," she said. "Darling, you always look handsome. Are you going on a date?"

"No, just going to a party."

"Well have a good time. Maybe you'll find your girlfriend there."

Jason smiled.

"Well if I did that, I wouldn't get your wonderful beef Stroganoff!"

She smiled. That remark made Mrs. Petroff's day.

CHAPTER 8

Why does this Negro live downtown in the first place? Jason thought as he navigated the traffic on the Harbor Freeway. Los Angeles is unlike other American cities in that it seemed to have a downtown only because every city is mandated to have one. But in L.A., no one actually lived there. Old dilapidated buildings, long defunct art deco theaters from the 1930s, and indoor swap meets offering cheap knockoff clothing and electronics populated the Los Angeles downtown. Actual inhabitants? Well, the city had been trying for years to get folks to consider downtown as an actual place to live, giving developers cheap loans to develop abandoned warehouses into Soho-style loft space. Apparently, Steven had bought into the chamber of commerce propaganda about L.A.'s downtown being the next big thing and had gotten a spot.

My building is on 359 3rd Street. Jason read from his Blackberry. *You'll see a red star on the side of the warehouse and you can't miss it.*

Jason got off the freeway, made a left onto Hope Street, and then saw the red star. Three fifty-nine 3rd Street was a loft building, just like *Titan* magazine had instructed a potential *Titan* man to find and live in. On the side of the building, you could read a faded sign that said this building used to be the Michael Gary Art Co.

As Jason pulled in the Gary building parking lot, he noticed that it was slowly becoming full of cars. Porches, Escalades, Chrysler

300s were all filling up the spaces, and while there were men getting out of some of the cars, he noticed another thing. All of the women exiting their cars were supermodel types. Not sixes or sevens, but tens and elevens. They were absolute superstars, just like Steven had said they would be.

Jason jumped out of his car and migrated with the crowd walking toward the elevator. As they gathered, the pre-party chatter had begun. No one paid much attention to Jason. Two stunningly attractive women were already talking about Steven and his previous parties.

"Have you ever gone to one of his parties?" a pretty one said to a gorgeous one.

"Yes, and I swear I left there not knowing where my bra was," the gorgeous one responded in a low voice.

"It was like that?"

"It was like that, girl."

"Ooh, you are scandalous!"

They both laughed.

As they walked into the elevator, Jason swore that the air smelled so good that he could have bathed himself in it. The space was being lightly scented with the perfumes of eight beautiful sisters. Right then and there, Jason was already halfway to declaring himself a believer in the *Titan* way, when the elevator opened up to Steven's place. It was then that Jason knew the *Titan* lifestyle was for him. He just instantly knew.

"Welcome everyone, to my home!" Steven said, damn near looking like a black Hugh Hefner. He had this confidence that said "I'm in complete control and you all are my minions."

Steven's loft was spectacular. Not great, *spectacular.* The place was all brick and wood, with exposed silver piping running on the ceiling. It was huge, but it was not too huge so that you couldn't get a feel for the space. It felt rich.

"Ladies, you'll find a bar to your left," Steven said as everyone flowed into the loft. "Charles, our bartender, will fix you anything you'd like. Enjoy yourselves and feel free to mingle. Jason, come with me."

The ladies looked starstruck, as though Steven was a Hollywood star instead of just an associate lawyer who worked next to Jason every day. Hell, Jason was starstruck too.

"Let me give you a tour of the loft," Steven said as he took Jason by the elbow.

Steven started out by going into the living room. *Beauuuuuutiful* people, men and women, were all either in conversation or dancing. They each casually held a drink while doing their best to impress each other. Jason knew this whole scene was superficial, but it was pretty to watch.

A waiter came to them with martinis, and both took one. Jason kept surveying the place.

"Did you get this furniture at IKEA?" he asked, pointing to a couch.

Steven looked at him as though he'd told him someone had just pissed on his couch.

"Uh, no. The only thing this furniture has in common with IKEA is that they were both designed in Scandinavia. This furniture is custom made by a company called Dansk Mobel Kunst. If you want to live the *Titan* life, it requires that you don't buy where everyone else buys. You buy where only you can buy. I can't have some damn IKEA madness in my loft. Come on, Jason, be serious!"

Steven continued to take Jason on a tour: the kitchen, the bathroom, his bedroom. Jason had seen the whole place when the gorgeous girl from the street came up and gave Steven a huge kiss. This wasn't just a friendly kiss, no, this was a kiss that said "I've kissed this man before and it was in private." Steven was completely nonchalant about the whole thing. And then this super-model type, who Jason swore he'd seen in a magazine or television or somewhere, gave him another huge kiss, with the gorgeous girl standing right next to him. Gorgeous Girl didn't even flinch. Steven gave Jason a sly smile. He knew he was convincing him.

"All yours, buddy," he whispered to Jason, sweeping his hand over the scene. "All yours if you want it."

"Steven, I need to talk to you," the gorgeous girl said sexily. "Can we speak in private?"

She led Steven by the hand so that they could go into another room.

"Jason, make yourself at home and mingle, mingle!" Steven said over his shoulder as he disappeared from view.

Jason didn't know anyone here, but he thought he'd refill his

now-empty martini glass. As he made his way to the bar, that's
when he saw her. His old friend Vanessa, the woman who'd given
him all the blunt advice on how to "improve" himself a few months
back, was sitting by herself. She, like all of the women in the room,
looked beautiful. She was wearing a low-cut apple red dress that
showed off her ample breasts, just like Jason liked them, and her
milk chocolate skin was looking even more supple than before.
And he had to admit that if he wanted any woman at this party, he
wanted her. Badly.

"Well, hello," Jason said, saddling up to the bar.

"Well hello to you," she said, smiling. Her eyes didn't betray any
sense of recognition.

"Having a good time?"

"Sure, and you?"

The bartender walked over.

"Would you like another one?' he asked, pointing to Jason's
martini.

"No," he answered, thinking about the *Titan* article. This was
the time to follow its advice.

"Give me a Maker's Mark bourbon and water with just a little
ice."

Vanessa looked up when he said bourbon. Jason had passed, just
as *Titan* said, the wuss factor. "Haven't we met before?" she
probed. She fingered her drink glass seductively.

"No, I don't think so. Have you been to Steven's loft before?"

"No, this is my first time here, but I've heard that the parties can
get wild. What about you?"

"Can I get wild?"

She smiled.

"Yes, that too, silly. But have you been here before?"

"No, this is my first time here, but I do know Steven."

"Where from?"

"We both . . ."

Right at that time, Steven and the gorgeous girl came bounding
toward them and interrupted Jason.

"Hold on, let's stop the chitchat," Steven said. "Excuse me, darling, but what's your name?"

Vanessa looked a bit taken aback.

"Are you talking to me?" Vanessa asked, pointing to herself.

"Yes darling, you."

"It's Vanessa. And who are you, may I ask?"

"Great, I'm Steven and I own this place. Do you know who this young man is?"

"No, I don't think I've gotten his name yet."

"His name is Jason. He's worth four million dollars and he'd like to fuck you right now."

The gorgeous girl smiled when she heard the words *four million dollars.*

What in the world was Steven doing? Jason thought. He is going to absolutely ruin this for me.

"Now, if you fuck him, you may be on the end of a lottery," he continued. "Or it could be that you just got fucked tonight and nothing else came of it. But you've got to make a decision right now about what you want to do. If you say yes, then I have a room in the back for the both of you. If you say no, then there's no more reason for him to talk to you."

Jason downed his bourbon and water in one gulp, absolutely mortified. This woman is going to slap the shit out of Steven, Jason thought, and then leave me when I finally had a chance to finally make . . .

"Sure, that sounds good," she responded. Vanessa took a last sip of her martini, put down the glass, and looked at Jason expectantly.

"Go get what you want, girl," said the gorgeous girl.

Steven smiled.

"The room is straight to the back and then the first right. Condoms are in the top drawer. There are many to choose from, so choose the one that you feel gives you the most pleasure."

This is not happening, Jason thought. This is not happening. But it *was* happening! Vanessa, a woman who didn't give Jason the time of day only three months before, was now willing to let him fuck her simply because he had money and Steven said she should do it? What the hell is happening? What the *hell* is happening? Jason thought.

Vanessa stood up and held out her hand.

"After you, Jason," she said sexily.

When Jason took her hand, an electric current went through his body. He hoped that his nervousness didn't come through his hand, but he was sweating like a little boy in Neverland. But in one of those instances where a person weighed the morality of the situation with how good something was going to feel, Jason instantly decided that he was going to do this, no matter how scandalous it may have been. If anything, this was a once-in-a-lifetime experience and he was not going to pass it up.

As Jason and Vanessa cut through the party, the atmosphere had changed from a schmooshfest to an all-out party. The music was extremely loud, and the living room was packed with people dancing. And not one of these party people was aware of what Vanessa and Jason were about to do.

"Nice room," Jason said, trying to break the tension as he opened the door. Five candles were lit on the windowsill, and there was a low-slung bed with rose petals spread over the silk bedspread.

"Even nicer company," she responded, looking into his eyes.

She walked to the edge of the bed, and even though the room was dark, Jason's eyes soon got used to it. He could see Vanessa's silhouette, and it was beautiful. Jason slowly walked over to her and stood about three feet from her when she reached to her shoulders and pulled down the spaghetti straps that held her dress. And just like in a thousand movies he'd watched, the dress fell straight down to her feet. She was wearing nothing under the dress. No bra. No panties. No nothing. It was just beautiful, wonderful nakedness.

"Do you see anything that you like?" she asked rhetorically.

Jason moved in and began kissing her. She tasted wonderful. Things were happening so fast that he just couldn't form coherent thoughts in his brain. All he could feel was that his dick was getting harder than it had ever been in its life, and was starting to think for him.

I want pussy. Give me pussy.

That was his dick talking. His hands had other thoughts.

They were saying, *Grab her breasts.* And that's exactly what they did.

"Keep doing that," she moaned as Jason both caressed a breast with one hand, and the curve of her back with the other.

Jason wanted to jump for joy and he could have kissed Steven, on the mouth, with full tongue, and no, he wasn't part gay. It was just that he was just that happy. If this is the *Titan* lifestyle, then thank you, God, for the *Titan* lifestyle, he thought.

Vanessa reached up and kissed Jason on the neck, in that little spot between his neck and his ear, and he couldn't get out of his clothes fast enough.

Jason took his shirt off, busting his buttons, but struggled to get out of his pants, damn near stumbling.

"Slow down, Jason," Vanessa whispered. "We have a lot of time."

"But what . . . what if someone knocks on the door?" he asked breathlessly.

Vanessa smiled.

"I won't answer it if you don't."

And with that, they were on the bed. Jason began kissing her over her whole body. He started at the top, kissing her breasts, making tongue circles around her areolas, and then licked his way to her belly button. Then, his tongue flicked as he began licking her pussy. Vanessa's pussy tasted luscious, not too wet and very soft. There's no right or wrongs to pussy, Jason thought, but there's good and real good and Vanessa's was real good.

"Good, right there," she murmured. "Yes, keep, keep doing that."

Jason circled the clit with his tongue, touching it lightly. She put her hand on his head, slowly guiding his movements without being too forceful.

"Sssss," she hissed, after Jason began kissing her clit. "Sssss."

Suddenly, she put both her hands on Jason's head, as though commanding him to stop. Jason wondered if he'd done something wrong.

"Turn over on your back," she growled.

Jason laid on his back, and Vanessa began licking his balls, and then gently sucking them.

"Jesus!" he said, moaning. Why do so *many* women forget about the balls? Vanessa didn't. How long had it been since he felt like this?

Vanessa moved from Jason's balls and began giving him a slow blow job, moving slowly over the shaft of his dick and lingering on the tip. Her mouth was warm and as she moved up and down on his dick, she carefully used her teeth to provide friction.

"Keep going, keep going," he said.

But instead of continuing, she stopped. She got up from the bed, opened the top drawer and pulled out a condom. He expected her to give it to him, but instead, she tore open the wrapper and put the condom in her mouth. And then she expertly, and for a second Jason's brain clicked on and thought *too expertly,* but his dick took over again and shut the brain down, slipped it on his dick with only her mouth. Jason was impressed.

She hovered over Jason, her face only a few inches away.

"I love pleasure. Which way do you want me?"

This was all happening way too fast for Jason. He hadn't had a girlfriend for nearly two years, so his only sexual activity in that time had been the intimate relationship between his right hand and a nudie magazine. That wasn't the same as a real live woman. Not by a long shot. Now he hadn't forgotten what to do, that wasn't the problem, but he wondered about his control. Only in the movies does a man have sex all night with a new woman without being a little short on the ol' strokes. In real life, it's a few strokes and out. He didn't want to be a ten-stroke man.

It's a risk you're going to have to take, his dick thought.

"I want you on top," Jason said, figuring he could have more control this way.

"Beautiful."

She took his dick in her hand and in a second Jason was inside her. Like an ocean wave, her body oscillated to an internal rhythm that he wanted to dance to. Jason didn't think he could ever feel this good. His hands again decided to fondle her breasts, which was okay by him. And he had control!

"Oooo, God!" she moaned, "Oooo, fucking God!"

After a few minutes of letting her do all the work, Jason was feeling a little more confident.

"Let's change positions," he said.

Vanessa got on her back and they started having sex in the missionary position.

"Give it to me, Jason," she cooed.

Jason's ego took over and he tried to give it to Vanessa as much as he could. That's when his dick said to his brain, *Okay Jason, I've had my fun. Now I'm ready to let it all go.*

But Vanessa wasn't ready for him to let it all go. She was really getting into it.

"Fuck me, I'm about to come!" she said in a deep guttural voice.

Jason was now on his knees, and Vanessa raised her head, looking at Jason's dick go in and out of her, placing her hand on Jason's stomach. He could feel her fingernails dig into his abdomen, and it got him even more excited.

He was determined to hold out until she came. For Jason, there was nothing better than making a woman orgasm. He didn't even care if the woman was faking. But in Jason's experience, when a woman told you that she's going to orgasm, you as a man inevitably began to struggle not to orgasm *yourself*. So to prevent that catastrophe, he began thinking of as many nonsexual things as possible to prevent an embarrassing premature ejaculation.

Al Roker!

Shaquille O'Neal!

Ronald Reagan!

Dennis Rodman!

Star Jones!

Halle Berry! No, don't think about Halle Berry!

"Right there, don't stop. Keep going. Oh, right there! Whatever you do, don't stop!" she whispered.

And then it began to happen. Jason could feel he was in the right spot, because Vanessa's body tensed up. He slowly moved his dick in a circular motion and then stroked deep inside her pussy. He hit her clit just right, and it seemed like Vanessa was holding her breath.

"God, God, God, God!" she repeated. Vanessa's body began to shudder, and her back arched. Her head came forward and she was watching Jason's dick again, and then her head fell back. A tiny yelp came from her mouth, then a long, deep breath seemed to wash over her.

"Yes!!!!!" she screamed. Her orgasm was intense, and Jason tried to keep it intense.

She turned her head, and then whispered into his ear: "Come for me."

Jason thrust into her, and she swayed to his rhythm.

"Oh my God!" he yelled. Jason had been considerate with his thrusting, but now that he was coming, his dick was like a jackhammer. But Vanessa rolled with it, scratching his back as his body spasmed.

And like that, it was all over. They collapsed on the silk sheets, completely sweaty and spent. All of this couldn't possibly have taken more than twenty minutes, but just like water tastes like fine wine to a parched man, this sex was a blast to a man who'd been without a woman for nearly seven hundred days, but of course, who's counting.

All of the sudden, the music from the deejay came through the door, and it seemed like the party had gone on without them. Initially Jason thought they'd been so loud that people could hear, but he didn't think so now.

Vanessa got up without a word and began to put on her dress again. She didn't wear any underwear so it only took her about five seconds to get dressed. Jason stretched out naked on the bed.

"Did you enjoy yourself?" she asked.

"Yes I did."

She didn't look up. He didn't feel there was any shame in her voice, just matter-of-factness. Jason then rushed to get his clothes on. He wanted to appear to be as nonchalant as her.

"Did you?" Jason asked hopefully.

"Uh, yeah," she smiled, looking up at him. "Didn't you notice?"

I am the man, Jason thought.

"You've changed," she said as he was putting on his shoes. He stopped and looked at her.

"What do you mean?" he asked.

"You've changed from when I first met you a few months ago. I see you took my advice to heart," she said, putting on her pumps.

"So you did remember me?'

"Of course."

Jason stopped putting on his clothes, and looked at Vanessa.

"So you mean to tell me that a change of clothes, a boatload of cash, and a bourbon and water made you get in bed with me, when the last time I couldn't even get your phone number?"

Vanessa put on her last shoe. She was sitting right next to Jason.

"In a word, yes. That, and the fact I was horny as hell. Is that cool with you?"

He paused, looking into her beautiful eyes.

"Yep, that's cool with me."

Vanessa stood up to go. He still had to put on his other shoe. Where was his other shoe?

"Look, you don't have to call me and this could just be a one-time thing. If it is, cool. But if you want more"—Vanessa pulled out a card from her purse—"then call me.

"Good-bye lover," she said. "Thanks for everything." She leaned down, gave him a kiss on the lips and then walked out the door.

He read the card: "Dr. Vanessa Petry, Ph.D., Associate Professor, University of California at Los Angeles."

Jason sat on the bed for a second, trying to take everything in. Man, oh man, what a night. He finally found his other shoe when there was a knock on the door.

Jason scurried over to the door without opening it.

"Who is it?" he asked, thinking Vanessa had left something.

"Steven."

"Oh, my new best friend!" he said.

Jason opened the door and must have had the biggest grin in Los Angeles because Steven started smiling himself.

"So I'm guessing you had a good time?"

He closed the door behind him.

"Man, whatever you did to get me here, I'm buying in."

Steven smiled again.

"That, Jason, is the *Titan* lifestyle and attitude," Steven said, spreading his hands out. "Did you notice how I took control of the situation, and got her to do everything I wanted her to do?"

"Yes, and how did you know how to do that? I thought she was going to knock the shit out of you when you made that proposition."

"But she didn't, did she?"

"Nope."

"So do you want to buy into all of this? Are you ready to follow the *Titan* lifestyle? Together, we could be unstoppable."

Jason sat down on the bed.

"Why do you need me? It seems like you've got it all worked out and the women are flowing for you. Even if I tried, I couldn't be as smooth as you."

Steven got up and walked around.

"This is all fun, but it would be even more fun to have a buddy to do it with. We could take the *Titan* lifestyle to a whole new level. So, are you in or out?"

Jason sat for a second and then made a fateful decision.

"I'm in, at least for six months. If it doesn't work, then I'll go back to my old lifestyle."

Steven laughed.

"And again, what was that lifestyle?"

He had a point, Jason mused.

"Well, whatever it is, I'll go back to it."

Steven laughed again.

"Okay, fair enough."

They both got up to leave the room.

"You staying for the party?" Steven asked.

"I'm already at the party."

Steven grinned at his friend slyly.

"One thing you need to realize is that *Titan* says that you need to have two parties. There's the one party where all the people can attend, and another one where only the special people can attend. The special party happens in about three hours. You may not want to miss that."

"I think I've had enough excitement for the night, thank you. I'm going to head home."

"Fair enough. All right, I'll check you out at work."

"No, remember, I'm going to be at Mama's House for a month."

"That's right. You're going to be working with that fine-ass Carole. Tell her I said hello. I may have to stop by Mama's House in the near future."

"To volunteer?"

"Come on, Jason!" Steven said as he opened the door for Jason to go. "I don't do community service. I do women."

And with that, Jason's first *Titan* night was over.

CHAPTER 9

"Just let the brother come to work and do some good."

Marcia had called her over the weekend and Carole had told her that Jason was coming to work at Mama's House for the month.

"Jason's a good guy," Marcia said. "In your time of celibacy, why don't you use him as a way to get to know other men better? Ask him questions, and maybe you can get an insight into why things fall apart in your relationships."

"But Marcia, Jason hasn't had a girlfriend in what, like two years? And even then, I don't remember actually seeing the girl. Didn't she go to Stanford or something?"

"She was at Stanford med school."

"Yeah, well, I don't know if he's the best person to talk about having a relationship if he can't find a woman himself."

"That's where you're wrong. He's the best person to ask. Don't you think he's had time to figure out what has gone wrong and what can go wrong in a relationship? Girl, you're getting a man who's an all-around good guy, and God forbid, is deeper than the ones you've been meeting."

"Maybe you're right."

"You damn right I'm right, and if you listen to me once in a while, you'd be better off for it."

"All right, I'll give him a try. I'm not going to force the issue, but if I see an opening, then I use it."

"That's my girl. Now let me off this phone. I've got a banquet to go to."

"Ciao!"

So Carole was going to see if Jason would listen to her, because the whole celibacy thing was driving her nuts. Take last Friday, for example.

She'd had a hard day at Mama's House. An elderly white donor, Mrs. Myers, had made a million-dollar donation the year before, but was thinking about reneging on this year's donation because she seemed to object to all of the Latina and black women who were getting assistance.

"Where are all of the white women who need help?" she'd asked as she and her representatives made a surprise visit to Mama's House.

"Ma'am, we are located in Inglewood, so the majority of the women who come in here are Latina and black women. But you can be assured that we give help to anyone of any race. We do not discriminate."

Mrs. Myers was not satisfied. It was obvious to Carole that she never bargained that her money was going to help people she didn't know or understand.

"You know, I grew up here in Inglewood during the 1950s, when things were quite different. Things have certainly changed." She looked out the window onto Crenshaw Boulevard. Across the street, a tattoo shop was playing music loudly, and it seemed as though every motorcycle club in Los Angeles had decided to get a tattoo on the same day. Andy Griffith's 1950s Mayberry, Inglewood was not.

"Inglewood used to be a very nice community, where people knew each other and said hello. That's why I sent the money to Mama's House. I regard single parenthood as being a temporary condition, and I'm not sure if the women you serve think the same way," she said.

Carole seethed. She couldn't go off on the woman because at the end of the day, she needed her money. But it burned her that she had to take such ignorance from people who did nothing but write a check.

"Inglewood is still like that, ma'am. Just a few blocks from here, you'll find families that love their neighborhoods, and do all they can to make sure that they stay nice and neat. And as for the women who come into Mama's House, I assure you that these women are looking to make this life a temporary one also," Carole said. "Now, are each and every one of these women looking to find a husband? No. But I have been here for three years, and I can honestly say that these women, although often poor, have the same wants and desires as we do."

"That may be so," Mrs. Myers said as she and her representatives made their way to the door, "but I'm not going to make a decision on whether or not I give money this year until you can prove that you're expanding the amount of people you're helping."

"Mrs. Myers, our center has won the top community service award from the City of Inglewood for five years in a row. What we provide is a service that changes lives, and if you don't want to be a part of an organization that helps these women because they aren't the race you want them to be, then I suggest you take your money elsewhere."

Mrs. Myers stood there in front of the door, unable to speak.

"I am not a bigot, dear, if that is what you are implying," she explained. "It is just that I was in these women's place nearly thirty years ago."

Now it was Carole's turn to be surprised.

"Oh yes, I was a single mother before they had things like community centers and shelters. Actually I was called an unwed mother, but that's another story. And the reason I give money to this center is because I want to help women, all women. But of course, you always want to see people who look like you receiving help. You would do the same thing if you walked into a center and noticed that no black women were receiving help."

Carole nodded.

"You'll receive your donation. Just keep me informed on the progress of the women."

"Thank you, Mrs. Myers."

"And who knows," Mrs. Myers said. She opened the door just as a motorcycle was revving up its engine. "I just may come back to the center as a volunteer."

"I think the women would love to hear your story. It would be an inspiration."

"Indeed."

And with that, she left. Fire was averted.

"Dorothy, I'm out of here," Carole had said, gathering her coat and purse.

"TGIF?" Dorothy responded.

"Oh yes, TGIF. Could you lock up?"

"No problem. Have a nice weekend."

Carole ran out of Mama's House as fast as she could because she had planned a Carole's night at home. No going out. No calling friends. And there would be no men, definitely no men. Just a night for Carole.

So there was the obligatory stop at the store for some snacks: Ben & Jerry's chocolate brownie ice cream and some Earl Grey tea. Next came the personal improvement supplies: fingernail polish and a full manicure set. Then it was on to facial products. She was now set for Carole's Pampering Evening.

Carole came home, then put the ice cream in the fridge and a teakettle on.

"What should I put on?" Carole said as she looked through her CD collection. The choice? A little Norah Jones would come first, and then some Dave Matthews Band for a sing-along.

An oatmeal facial scrub followed by a warm bath with new bath crystals from Bed Bath and Beyond, thanks to Marcia for the gift certificate, was next. She ran the bath and then spent an hour soaking, breathing in the jasmine and lilac–scented bubbles and singing to her friends Norah and Dave.

The evening was going swimmingly, and once she put on some nail polish, Carole was feeling pretty damn good about herself.

But then, the CD player played the Dave Matthews song #41, and Carole fell apart. She always fell apart when that song came on anyway, but now as she listened to the words, they became even more poignant.

I don't have anyone to come and see how well I'm doing! Carole thought as the tears began streaming down her face. Sing it, Dave! Sing it! By now, Carole was singing at the top of her lungs, with a special emphasis on "I wanted to love you!"

"Why did you leave me, Sean, Daniel, Henry, Robert, Rouvaun, Damon, Kevin, Marcus, and Michael?" Carole sobbed.

By the end of the song, Carole was a mess. All of the bad decisions of her life came crashing down on her. She realized that she didn't want to be celibate. She didn't want to be without a man. For all of this feeling of independence, Carole sure didn't feel good about herself.

Is it so wrong to want someone special in your life? Carole said to herself, lying on the bed.

CHAPTER 10

Jason walked into Carole's office, hoping to get off early. "Carole, I have to take care of some personal issues this week, and if you don't mind, I'm going to work only until noon each day this week." Mama's House had been busy on Monday morning, and as the clock moved toward noon, Jason needed to get going.

Steven's party had convinced Jason that the *Titan* lifestyle was a winner. He'd just had sex with the finest woman he'd ever met, and he could either call her, or not call her. Would he call Vanessa again? Nah. Any woman who'll have sex with a man five minutes after they meet them isn't girlfriend material, he thought. But this whole *Titan* lifestyle thing had Jason thinking about whether or not he really wanted or needed a girlfriend. Why one girlfriend when you can have a bunch of women? Didn't *Titan* magazine teach you that?

"Sure, but I would like you to work on Caterina's case. Her boyfriend's back in town and she'd like to protect herself legally," Carole said. "So concentrate on her situation this week."

"Sure, I'll be here bright and early."

Jason looked at Carole and it seemed like she had something else to say but was having a hard time saying it.

"Jason, do you mind if we go out to lunch this week? I have some things I'd like to talk to you about."

"Sure, any time," Jason replied. "Is it urgent?"

"Oh no," she said, backtracking. "It's not urgent or that important. I just need an ear about something."

"No problem, just let me know when you want to go."

Jason wrapped up his work, walked out of Mama's House, and jumped into his car. He was headed toward Beverly Hills, because he had a purchase to make, the first purchase for his *Titan* lifestyle.

As he walked through the glass doors of Beverly Hills Suzuki, a small, wiry man came bounding toward Jason.

"Don Stuart," the salesman said, extending his hand. "Welcome to Beverly Hills Suzuki. How may I help you?"

"Hello, Don," Jason said, scanning the showroom. "I want that bike right over there."

He pointed to a beautiful gunmetal gray–colored Hayabusa that was rotating on a pedestal. "You, sir, have taste," Don said, walking Jason toward the bike. "Others would have gone for the common, such as a Honda or Yamaha, but you understand that this motorcycle tells people that here is a man that knows quality and class."

They stopped right in front of the bike, watching it slowly spin.

"This is the 2005 Suzuki Hayabusa limited edition," Don said, sweeping his hand over the length of the bike. "You know that this is the fastest street bike on the market, don't you?"

"Yes, I do, and that's why I want it. It's my dream bike and I felt it was time to finally go after my dream," Jason said authoritatively.

And we at Beverly Hills Suzuki will be here for you as long as you own the bike," Don said.

"I want to go fast and look good doing it."

Do you mind if I ask your occupation?" Don asked.

Jason paused.

"You could say that I'm into kangaroo meat," he answered cryptically.

Don gave him a queer look but asked no more questions. He didn't want to risk the sale.

"Do you want to finance?" Stuart asked, leading Jason to his office.

"No, I'm paying cash."

"Well," Stuart said, and smiled. "This should take only a few seconds to complete."

Fifteen minutes later, after Jason fended off offers of extended warranties and insurance, the bike was Jason's.

"If you'd like, we can drive your car to your home and you can ride the Hayabusa out of here," Don said, tossing Jason the keys.

Jason slid into the seat of the Hayabusa and turned the key. He smiled as the engine rumbled underneath his body. "You can give my car to Goodwill. I don't need it anymore."

Jason revved the bike again and began to leave the parking lot.

"Take her easy and get used to the power," Don said. "You can be going one hundred miles per hour before you even look down at the speedometer."

"Will do," Jason said.

Jason rode gingerly at first, since he hadn't been on a bike in years. But then he gained more and more confidence, and was soon barreling down the San Diego Freeway with the motor blazing. He never knew a motorcycle could make a person feel so good, so free. It made him feel like a real man. And best of all, women in other cars turned to look as he rode by them.

"I'm a *Titan* man!" Jason screamed at the top of his lungs. He kept riding up and down the 405 Freeway, not knowing where to go. He didn't want to go home, so he turned around and decided to visit Steven. Jason knew he'd freak out when he saw that Jason had his Hayabusa before him.

"You missed out," Steven said as they kicked it in his loft.

"What else happened? I mean, my night was pretty damn exciting as it was."

Steven slid Jason a beer, and took a sip of his own.

"Well, remember how I said that *Titan* said you needed to have a second party within a party?

"Yeah, well I had that party, and man, was it wild."

"What happened?"

Steven sat back and looked at the ceiling as though he was trying to take it all in.

"Remember that girl I had on my hip?"

"Yes."

"Well, she invited a friend she brought to the party and another girl and we had a fourway. It was the bomb! You could have been there, I wouldn't have minded. Just as long as your dick didn't touch my dick."

They both laughed.

"Sorry, but two dicks in a room is one dick too many for me."

"Suit yourself. But with this new life you've started, you may find a lot of dicks around and you ain't gonna always care."

"Sorry, but I think I'll always care."

"We'll see."

Steven got up to get the remote control and turned the channel to ESPN. Sports Center was on, so they half talked to each other and half watched television.

"Here, take a look at this," Steven said, throwing Jason a copy of *L.A. Loft* magazine. "*L.A. Loft* magazine is the Bible on loft space in the city."

Steven sat back and looked at Jason.

"I can't believe you got your Hayabusa before me!" he exclaimed.

"I had cash, my man, and cash speaks," Jason responded.

"I guess bastards that need to finance get waiting lists," Steven said, laughing.

"If there was some room in this building, then I would simply say move in here, but it's completely full," Steven said. "Are you on a month-to-month or lease?"

"I'm on a six-month lease, but it's up at the end of this month," Jason said, strumming through the magazine. "So I needed to figure out if I wanted to stay anyway."

"Where do you want to live?" Steven asked.

Jason sat back in his chair, thinking about the question.

"What I really want is something in Santa Monica, you know, something on the beach. But I was intrigued with a downtown loft. They seem cool and different, slightly away from the crowd. Where I'd first thought it was crazy to live in downtown Los Angeles, it now made perfect sense."

"You'll save money moving down here. Look through the magazine, and tell me what you see," Steven said. "I'm getting a beer, you want one?"

"Nah," Jason said, looking through the magazine. "Don't want to get drunk on the 'busa and crash the first day I have it. Hey, this looks cool. It says the loft is 'New York Living in Los Angeles.' Well, I like New York, but I live in Los Angeles. So what could be better for a young stud like myself?"

"I went there. It looks and feels like a cold-water flat," Steven said, looking at the ad. "The space was narrow and if you threw a football from the front door, it would sail straight out the back end of the apartment. It was not to me and I don't think you'd like it."

"What about a dream home come true? That looks nice."

"It is if you like living right next to a homeless shelter and small oil refinery," Steven said. He took the magazine from Jason and pointed to an ad. "I almost moved here. Check it out."

Steven looked at his watch. "If you roll right now, you might be able to see it. It's only about three blocks away."

Jason took a look at the ad. It looked beautiful, with seemingly great views of the city.

"All right, I'm out."

Jason hopped on the bike and flew to the Robert Lyons building. He jumped off the bike, looked at his watch. It said six-thirty. He pressed the buzzer of a Mrs. Grier, following the ad's instructions.

"Yes?"

"Hello, I'm interested in one of your lofts. I'm sorry I'm coming so late, but is it still available to show?" Jason asked.

"Yes, just one second."

"Normally I would only show this with an appointment," Mrs. Grier said, opening the loft. Mrs. Grier was an older white woman who dressed as though going to church. "But since you're in a hurry to find another place, I'll do you this favor."

She opened the front door and Jason walked in. The loft was spectacular. Whereas Steven's loft was nice, with its brick and exposed pipes, this loft was more finished, more elegant. The kitchen had granite counters, while the floor was a combination of hardwood flooring and Spanish tiles.

"It's a two-bedroom loft with bathrooms on both floors." She walked to the far wall and pulled open the drapes. What she revealed were ceiling-to-floor windows with a spectacular view of Los Angeles. "This is what happens when you combine the thirty-second floor and downtown."

Jason stood in the middle of the living room. He was sold.

"What do I need to move in?" Jason asked.

"There's a five-thousand-dollar deposit, and as long as your credit is fine, you can move in at the end of the month."

Jason wrote a check and handed it to Mrs. Grier.

"I want to move in on the first."

"We can make that happen," Mrs. Grier said, looking at the check.

As Jason rode back to his apartment, he was feeling pretty good about all that he'd accomplished. Motorcycle and loft space purchased. He was well on his way toward the *Titan* lifestyle.

When he got back to the Gower Gulch apartments, he saw Mrs. Petroff bringing her groceries into the building.

"My goodness, Jason, what a nice motorcycle!"

"Thank you, ma'am!"

"What happened to your car? Did you get into a wreck? Are you okay?"

"No, no, ma'am. I didn't get into a wreck. I just got a bonus at work and I thought I'd reward myself."

"Well no one deserves it more than you," she said, squeezing his cheeks as she always did. "You're such a sweet boy."

"Thank you, ma'am."

"So, are you going out with anyone?"

"No, ma'am."

"Then I make your beef Stroganoff as usual on Friday."

Jason paused as he waited for her to find her keys. They were deep in her purse and she couldn't find them right away.

"Mrs. Petroff, I'm glad I found you because there is going to be a change."

"Yes?" she said, looking at Jason expectantly.

"I'm going to be moving next week."

It was like Jason had told Mrs. Petroff that someone in his family had died. Her face just crumbled. It was as if her adopted baby was about to leave, and she knew in her heart that despite all of the coming promises, he wouldn't see her regularly. What twenty-something is going to visit a woman in her sixties? They both knew that most likely it wasn't going to happen, but they went through the ritual anyway.

"Where are you moving to, Jason? Why are you moving?"

"I'm moving downtown. I just needed a bit of a change."

They were putting up her groceries when Jason suddenly realized that she looked a little older than she had five minutes before. He hadn't known that he meant that much to her.

"If you are moving, you've got to promise me that you'll visit. And if you want your Stroganoff each Friday, there's no reason to not pick it up. I'll keep making it."

"Thanks, Mrs. Petroff, and yes, I do want your wonderful beef Stroganoff. I wouldn't think of eating anything else on a Friday."

She stopped putting up her groceries and walked over to him.

"Oh, I'm going to miss my little Jason!"

"I'll miss you too, Mrs. Petroff."

Jason stood there realizing that while *Titan* was verbose on the ways of young women, they didn't have a guide to dealing with kind old ladies.

"But I was thinking that since I didn't need my current furniture, I would sell it and then donate it to the Russian fund," he said.

"Jason, you are such a wonderful boy!" she beamed as she again pinched his cheeks.

Jason sat down and surveyed his apartment, thinking about how his life was about to change drastically. This *Titan* life was an unknown. It was something he hadn't known he'd wanted only a month ago, yet he was going after it now. He was feeling a bit uncertain, but on the other hand, the feeling of having sex with Vanessa lingered with him. Jason still wanted a girlfriend, but right now, it was more important to have girlfriends plural. This period in his life was going to be all about him, Jason thought, and nothing but him. There was a knock on the door.

"You have the weakest security in apartment history," Steven said, entering Jason's apartment. He couldn't wait or call? Jason thought.

"So, did you get the loft?"

"Yes, it was great."

"Cool. Did you get it furnished, et cetera, according to *Titan?*"

"I'm about to get on the Internet and start ordering."

"Good, then I've got a proposition for you," Steven said.

"What is it?"

"We are going to inaugurate your loft with a special *Titan* party. Don't worry about anything other than finding a caterer and bartender. I'll find the rest."

"Man, that sounds like a great idea!"

And it did. Jason knew that the hardest part of this *Titan* lifestyle was finding the women when he didn't have them before he started living the lifestyle. Now women would know him.

"Good, when will your loft be finished?"

"I move into it next week, so we could schedule the party for two weeks from now."

"That'll give me enough time to get the word out. Remember, this is going to be your party, so people are going to be coming to see you, and not me. When we get this rolling, we'll have two places rolling the *Titan* lifestyle, and no one can stop us."

Steven had brought his bag and pulled out yet another issue of *Titan* and handed it to Jason.

"Any interesting articles?" Jason asked, flipping through the pages.

"Yep, there's one."

Steven took the *Titan* and thumbed through it. Finally he found the page he was looking for.

"Check out this one. It's called "Friends with Benefits." It's genius, absolute genius."

Jason put the *Titan* on his table.

"I'll check it out."

Steven got up to leave.

"Do what it says, and it'll change your life."

CHAPTER 11

"Carole, could you come in here, please?"

Jason was sitting with Caterina, chronicling her life, but things weren't going well. He didn't know if this was going to have a happy ending.

"Yes, Jason," Carole said once she got into his office.

"I've been talking to Caterina," Jason said, with Caterina sitting meekly, "and I'm trying to see if there's a solution to her problem. I don't know if there is one."

"I'd like to stay with my boyfriend and protect myself," Caterina said.

"But her boyfriend won't agree to sign any agreement that spells out who owns what in their relationship. He thinks that if he bought any of the stuff, it's automatically his. We all know that isn't correct, but there's nothing preventing him from loading up the U-Haul and leaving again with her furniture and goods," Jason said.

"I'd like Caterina to get her boyfriend to come in here so we can sign an agreement, or have him move out until these issues are resolved. And there are other issues."

"Yes, I know them," Carole said.

She sat on the edge of his desk looking at Caterina.

"We all know that he's been violent toward you in the past,"

Carole said. "Why do you keep him in your life when you know that you might have to deal with some violence in the future?"

"Because I love him," she responded. "And he's my baby's daddy."

Caterina stood up and walked to the window.

"It's hard to explain to people not in this type of relationship," she said. "When I was a junior in high school, Jacob was a senior. He showed interest in me when others didn't even give me a second glance. I wasn't pretty like the other girls, but he made me feel beautiful. So we dreamed about being together. Everything was okay until I had our baby. Then things changed. We struggled with money, because no one would hire a high school grad with no skills. So the stress changed him."

"Caterina, there's absolutely no excuse for hitting you."

Caterina looked at Carole. "You don't know what it means to be me," she said. "You find love with men who are lawyers like Jason here, and live happily ever after. Me? I'm destined to scrape through life with whoever I can find to help me live an okay life."

Caterina sat back down. "Jacob is about as good as I can get. And that means I have to take the good with the bad."

"So why are you here, Caterina?" Carole asked.

"What do you mean?"

"I mean, what are you doing here?" Carole asked again.

"Well, I'd like some help."

Carole walked over to Jason and looked at Caterina.

"No you don't. You don't want help, you want people to tell you that you can live your life in the same way you did before you walked into this office, but you don't want to make any hard decisions."

"But I do want some help," Caterina pleaded.

"Then if you want me to help you, you are going to have to change your own life," Jason interjected. "You are going to have to make hard decisions, and not only that, you are going to have to make hard decisions about who you are and what you want out of life."

He then sat down beside her.

"You're wrong about Carole and me. Just because we were fortunate to be able to go to school, we have some of the same issues that you have."

"Men beat their wives even when they have money and education," Carole piped in.

"And they have the same issues about standing up to these men as you do. But like them, you have a choice," Jason continued. "You can either take control of your life, or your can decide to keep wondering why things happen to you. And if you are afraid of Jacob and won't make changes, then there's really no reason for you to come in here, because no matter how good our advice, it won't do you any good.

It seemed like this was the first time anyone had demanded Caterina take charge of her own life.

"Well, you guys don't understand. I just can't do that. I'll lose Jacob if I confront him like that."

"What did he do just a few weeks ago anyway?" Carole asked.

Caterina was quiet.

"Stand up for yourself and for your baby. I'm not going to lie. You may lose Jacob over this. But wouldn't it be better to know that now, than when you are standing in an empty apartment with no money because Jacob decides to get out and take everything with him? At least with this, you'll be protected."

Again, Caterina was quiet.

"Okay," she said softly. "I'll ask him tonight. If he doesn't want to come in, then I'll work with you all to protect myself."

Carole walked over to Caterina and put a hand on her shoulder.

"What you do now is going to determine your future. We aren't that different, as Jason said. I still struggle with love and you just have to trust the decisions you make. Talk to him—Jacob may surprise you."

Caterina got up to leave.

"Thanks for everything you guys. I won't disappoint you."

Jason opened the door. "Don't worry about us. Just don't disappoint yourself," he said.

Caterina left and Carole and Jason were left in the office.

"We're not a bad team," he said, smiling.

"No, but I still have work to do. I've got to figure out a way to get Jacob to an anger management program, and the both of them to couples counseling. The problems never stop, but this is the path I chose."

Carole actually looked sad to Jason. He didn't know why, but all of a sudden, he was concerned about her.

"Hey, do you want to have that lunch today?" he asked.

She perked up when he said that. "I can't do lunch, but what about dinner? I could use a nice dinner. Where do you want to go? I'm feeling a little Mexican. What about El Cholo's on Western?"

Jason smiled. "Sure, I could use a dose of the famous number-two plate."

"Sounds good," she said, checking her watch. "See you at five."

"What happened to the old Jetta?" Carole asked as they stepped out of Mama's House.

"I decided to get an upgrade, and this Hayabusa seemed like a nice change. Do you like?"

Carole looked at the motorcycle and instantly thought this was way out of character for the Jason she knew. The Jason she knew drove a car because it was simply faster than getting on a bus. She never expected him to be a motorcycle guy.

He watched Carole study the Hayabusa and wondered what was going through her head.

"Hop on," he said.

"Well, I wouldn't have thought that you would get a motorcycle like this, Jason," Carole said, straddling the back of the bike. Jason liked how her arms wrapped around him. He could get used to this. As they sped along, Carole desperately tried to keep from falling off and her grip became tighter and tighter.

"Now you see why sisters don't drive motorcycles," she smiled as they pulled into El Cholo's. The wind had completely messed up her hair.

El Cholo's was one of those uniquely Los Angeles Mexican restaurants that had been open since the 1920s. It had great food, but they tone down the spices to appeal to the American tongue—read white folks. The famous menu item was the #2 platter, which contained a chile relleno, an enchilada, plus rice and beans. It was comfort food Mexican style.

Carole and Jason got a table near the back. Jason figured she might want to talk about her relationships—Marcia had warned him about that—but he had to get two things off his mind first.

The waiter brought their food.

"Carole, why don't you like the lawyers who work at Mama's House? I mean, I talked to Dorothy and she said that I may be the first lawyer you actually liked."

Carole dug her fork into the beans and rice and took a small bite before answering.

"I might, and that's no guarantee," she said smiling. "See, most of you guys only come here because you want to get over the guilt of sucking your clients dry during the day. How much do you guys charge on an hourly basis? What, four hundred, five hundred dollars an hour? That's obscene. But you shouldn't take it personally."

"No, that's where you are wrong. I really do care about the work I do at the center. That's why I decided to devote a month to working with the young women."

Carole took another bite of her food and looked at Jason pensively, as though she was trying to see if he was really genuine.

"If you care that much, then quit the firm and work for us for less money than you currently get at your big-time firm."

She had him there. Jason didn't want to work for less, but he also didn't work at Ketchings & Martin for the money. He was there because he enjoyed consumer law. Even though Jason felt gratified with his work for the single women at Mama's House, it didn't completely fulfill him like his law work.

"But I like what I do. I mean, what if I told you that your work at Mama's House wasn't as good as working for the government? We each do what we do for our own reasons, and it's unfair to put your own ideas on what I should do. I'm not motivated by money. If I was motivated by money, I would be a corporate lawyer on the other side of consumer law. I'd be defending tobacco, liquor and asbestos companies against the little guy. I want a nice lifestyle, but I want to go to work because I like the work."

Carole stopped eating and frowned.

"Yeah, nice speech, but you know you're completely full of shit. You're just like Steven, after the big payday. And like all the rest of the lawyers who came before you, you'll say sayonara to us when your pro bono obligation to the law firm is up and then we'll get someone else. And they'll say the same 'I care' speech until their time is up. It never changes."

Carole picked up her fork and played with the cheese in her enchilada. She then looked up at him.

"In the past three years, we've had six lawyers in our office doing pro bono work. How many do you think have come back to even visit after they did their time with us?"

"I have no idea."

"Then I'll tell you. None."

This was an argument Jason wasn't going to win, so he knew he had to get some sort of détente going. Plus, maybe she didn't realize that a young lawyer probably had over 100,000 dollars in law school debt. Or, maybe she didn't care. Carole was a smart sister and there was no reason for him to have this ongoing dispute with her. The only thing he could do was to try to coexist with her the best way he could.

"Look, I don't know if I can change your mind, and I don't even know if I should change your mind, but I have compassion and I do care about my pro bono work or I wouldn't be here in the first place."

Carole didn't say anything. She just kept eating. Jason nibbled on his food.

"I have another question," he said, looking at her closely.

"Yes," she said, continuing to eat.

He didn't even know this question was on his mind, and it surprised him. "Do you still hold it against me that I slept with your soror?"

Carole nearly spit out her food. "What?"

He couldn't believe that he was bringing this up.

"We've had tension since we found each other, and I just want to know if you're still mad?"

Carole giggled a little as she contemplated the question.

"Is this really important, Jason?"

Jason began feeling a little uneasy, as though he had overestimated his own importance.

"I'd just like to get it out of the way if you think it's a problem. I didn't mean to hurt you. It was something that just happened, and I always regretted it."

"I'm not going to lie," she said, her eyes downcast. "It hurt me at the time. And when you got your comeuppance that Valentine's

Day, I didn't cry many tears for you. But then again, I thought that part of it was my soror's fault."

She smiled and looked into Jason's eyes. "But I think I'm over it."

"Then why did you bring it up back at G. Garvin's?"

Carole laughed. "Just because I'm over it, darling, doesn't mean that I won't use it as a weapon. You came at me so I had to come back at you. But that's just the bitch in me, not any long-held grudge. Women are like that sometimes."

They both laughed and it cut the tension and formality that always seemed to stay between them.

"Now that I've cleared that up," she said, sipping her soda again, "maybe you can help me?"

"What's up?"

"I broke up with Sean a couple of weeks ago. Or maybe I should be more accurate and say that he left me."

"I'm sorry to hear that," Jason said.

He really was sorry to hear that, but he wasn't surprised, of course.

"Jason, you're a guy I think I can trust," she said.

"Sure," he said, sipping his soda.

For the first time, Carole looked a little vulnerable.

"From what you know about me, what do you think I'm doing wrong?"

Jason started feeling a little uncomfortable, even though Marcia had warned him about this conversation. He didn't know if he felt like playing the relationship advice guy to Carole.

"Well, Carole, from the outside, and this is just from the outside, it appears that you always want to run a relationship, and that means your potential mate runs away because he thinks you don't and won't give him room. In my opinion, you tend to smother your men."

Jason could tell that Carole wanted to object, but she bit her tongue. She was resolved to listen to him.

"But I'm just a strong black woman."

"That's not the problem. Men can handle, or should I better say, can have a relationship with a strong black woman. In fact we welcome it. But we don't like to be pressured."

"Well how do I pressure the men I go out with?"

He picked at his food a bit.

"I don't know what goes on in your relationships, but I do know that in the past two years or so, you always think that each boyfriend is going to be your lifelong mate."

"What's wrong with looking for a husband when you're dating? I mean isn't that why you date in the first place?"

"But what I think you do is make it the main point of doing everything with your boyfriend. And the boyfriend feels that pressure. What you should do is just live life."

Carole looked even more uncomfortable.

"What do you mean, just live life?"

Carole was intelligent but high maintenance, and she didn't have that natural, innate ability to see beyond herself in relationships. She saw her goals and only her goals, and that's why she continued to run into these roadblocks, thought Jason.

But as Jason gave her advice as to what she was doing wrong, he had to admit that he still found her sexy as hell. She looked like she needed a friend, and that was Jason's curse. He was the friend and never the boyfriend.

"Men just take a relationship as it comes," he continued. "If the sex is good, then they rely on that and figure out what comes next later. We men aren't on a schedule and for the most part, we don't have a lot of expectations."

Jason felt like he'd crushed her heart. She wanted a boyfriend who'd turn into a husband.

"But that doesn't mean we don't want the same things women want," he finished.

"Wait, I'm confused."

"Carole, we like marriage, babies, and all the things you like. But we just like to take our time. Here's my advice. In the next relationship, take it as it comes with no expectations, and no ambition. If he's the right guy, it will play out over time. If he's not, you'll both know it."

"I've heard that advice before," Carole said, finishing her meal. "Maybe I should take it."

CHAPTER 12

"Does this stay or go?" the movers asked.

Jason sat down in his brown Barcalounger. It enveloped him like a giant brown hand.

"You can leave it right here," Jason said. "I have someone coming to buy it."

One of the movers looked at the Barcalounger again, as though trying to understand why anyone would want a chair made of ten-year-old pleather.

"They're collectables," Jason said, answering the unasked question. "Basically, if you put something on craigslist, someone will want it."

"Whatever you say," he said, getting back to work.

Not much of his old furniture was actually going to Jason's new loft. He'd made arrangements for the West Hollywood Russian Charitable Society to get the money from his furniture, and folks had been buying things all week. Besides, Beth Allen, his new interior decorator, was on the job and she hadn't seen anything he currently owned that she wanted to take to the loft.

Jason called Beth after having remembered reading about her in a *Divas* magazine (*Divas* was a black woman's magazine, but Jason liked it anyway). Although she was based in New York, Beth had agreed to come out and decorate his place for him. She

charged about twenty-five large to do everything, but it was going
to look at lot better than what Jason could ever do on his own.

When they'd met last week, she'd dazzled Jason with swatches
and color palettes. It was all very different to a man used to plain
white apartment walls.

"I'm going to turn your loft into a postmodern interpretation of
Harlem's Dark Tower of the Harlem Renaissance," Beth said, strid-
ing through the loft. Every so often, she'd bend down and look
closely at a door handle or a cabinet pull. "It will be eclectic, yet re-
flect your taste in African art and its people."

"Okay," Jason said, confused. "But will that make my place look
good?"

"It will make your loft the envy of everyone in the city," she said,
spreading her arms. "I'll even make sure you get profiled in a magazine."

"It'll look that good?" he'd asked.

"I'm that good," she'd responded.

So Jason really only had a ton of clothes to move. That's what
happens when you buy over thirty thousand dollars of Sean John.
Titan had told him he needed to find a designer, and that's what
he'd done. The clothes had been delivered and they were piled up
in his bedrooms. The movers had been organizing and boxing
them up for over an hour.

With nothing to do, Jason picked up the *Titan* issue Stephen
had given him. Life had been so hectic over the past week, he hadn't
had a chance to read the article "Friends with Benefits" Stephen had
so enthusiastically recommended. But the more Jason read, the
more enthused he became.

> *Every* Titan *man is surrounded by hundreds of women: old*
> *college friends, professional colleagues, casual acquaintances, et*
> *cetera, and these are women who could otherwise be willing sex*
> *partners. These women often go unnoticed by most* Titan *men*
> *because we classify them as simply platonic friends. But what if*
> *you could take these women friends, especially the pretty ones,*
> *and turn them into sex partners, yet not mess with the friend-*
> *ship? Meaning that if you found the right woman, and it has to*

be the right woman, then you could make her agree to a sexual relationship, without either of you thinking that the relationship was going any farther than the pure sex. Take all of the emotion out of the sex, and just have physical pleasure. In other words, you could keep the fun "friend" part of the relationship, with the added "benefits" of having regular sex with someone on a regular basis.

That's a real good deal for most men, Jason thought, but how do you convince women, who are more likely to use emotion as the basis for each and every relationship, to take the emotion out of sex? Jason read on.

You laugh with them, confide in them, and you're there for them when other men have screwed them over. So why aren't you getting something for that? How come you can't be the sexual intermediary between boyfriend and rebound man? They need sex just like you do, so why don't you fill in as the friendly dick while they sort out the myriad ways they're going to sabotage their next real relationship? The possibilities are endless. Think about the number of women friends you can have sex with if you establish yourself as the designated dick? Women will thank you for not only listening to them, but also providing them with some sexual relief. Don't believe all of the propaganda that says women must have emotional sex and men only want physical sex. Women like screaming, back-scratching, sweaty sex just like we men. And who better to give it to them but one of their best male friends? Titan says it can be done, if you follow our rules. . . .

Jason looked up from his *Titan* to see the movers dragging a box roughly through the living room.

"Hey, be careful with that," he shouted. "I don't want to find anything damaged when I get to the loft."

"No problem," they responded, picking up the box.

Jason started reading the article again. According to *Titan*, there were certain "Friends with Benefits" rules that had to be established at the beginning of the scheme.

Rule number 1:

    Neither party can have feelings, boyfriend or girlfriend feelings for the other, or the relationship is immediately over. Feelings beyond the friendship or sex unnecessarily complicate the Friends with Benefits relationship and must be stopped.

Rule number 2:

    Neither party can expect to sleep over after sex. That's a biggie, since sleepovers make things awkward if you want to stay autonomous. While all women love physical sex, there are some clingy women who love to spoon with men and feel that sense that this guy is the one. So, ya gotta go once the sex is done.

Rule number 3:

    Neither party can become jealous in the relationship. If either friend starts having a regular boyfriend or girlfriend, but wants to keep the other as a late-night booty call, the other party either has to accept it, or end the relationship. And if your Friend with Benefits partner gets married to someone else, go to the wedding, smile, and feel sure in the knowledge that you know her as well as the groom does.

The article was genius, pure unadulterated genius, Jason thought, and he wondered why he hadn't thought of this first. It was the perfect scheme for a newly emerging *Titan* man who didn't have a lot of new women around. And he was the king of having women as friends and not girlfriends. Why not convert some to friends with benefits? But who?

Marcia? Nah, he thought, she's my girl, but there's absolutely no sexual attraction there. Was there someone at the office who fit the bill? There were a few cute women at the office but none he considered to be friends. If Jason tried the scheme on them, he could easily see them misinterpreting his intentions, wanting to make the relationship a boyfriend/girlfriend one. He needed someone who was a friend, but attractive. And there was only one person who fit the bill. Carole.

Jason would *love* to have sex with Carole because she was fine as hell, and plus he always had a nagging regret of never having sex with her. She had her boyfriend issues, but Jason thought he could turn that into his advantage. If he proposed a friends with benefits relationship, then all of the expectations would simply drop away for her. She could have her cake and eat it too.

But there was one stumbling block. Of all the things Carole was, dumb wasn't one of them. The friends with benefits scheme required the man to manipulate the woman so that she would think she was the one who had come up with the idea. Jason didn't know if that would work on Carole.

The movers dropped a vase, and there was a deadly silence. Jason stormed out of his chair.

"What the hell is going on?" Jason asked angrily.

"Sorry, sir, we'll write that up on the insurance forms and you'll get reimbursed."

"Fine," Jason said.

I'm going to spend this week trying to probe Carole to see if this article would work on her, Jason thought, closing his bedroom door. The movers were finished. It was worth a try.

"Carole is about to join the *Titan* lifestyle," he smirked. "God help her!"

Jason's loft really came together, and Beth had bought things he'd never heard of. Jason thought that you could just buy a sofa, chair, and entertainment cabinet and call it a day. But Beth introduced him to the chaise longue, something he'd never seen, and a bidet, something he'd never had before. But both certainly looked good and felt good to sit on.

"You've done a wonderful job, Beth," Jason said, and meant it. She said she'd make his loft into a postmodern interpretation of Harlem's Dark Tower, and she had, even though Jason didn't have a clue to what the original Dark Tower looked like.

"Do you mind if I make your house one of my showcase homes?" she asked.

"What does that mean?" he said, relaxing in the chaise longue.

"Well, I need a Los Angeles home for my portfolio, so I'd like a professional photographer to take some pictures of it."

"Great," he said. He was falling asleep in this chaise longue. It was really that comfortable.

"And, if a magazine wants to showcase my work, I'd like to use your home as a showcase home. It will be an example of what I can do. So a magazine might want to come take pictures of your home and interview you. I'll pay for a cleaning service to make the home spotless, so you won't have to do anything except make the loft available."

"I have no problems with that. Plus, I'm pretty sure they'd do a profile of me along with the loft. Sure, anything you want. Just give me a little heads up."

"Great! And I'll take care of the cleaning."

The doorbell rang. It was Steven.

"Oh my God, you just set this thing off!" Steven said as he looked around the loft. "A long way from the stinky socks apartment you had just a few weeks ago, eh, Jason?"

Then he saw Beth.

"Hey, what's your name?" Steven asked Beth. He just couldn't resist chatting up every woman he saw.

"Beth Allen of Beth Allen Design of New York," she said, handing him a business card. "I'm Jason's interior decorator."

"Steven," Steven said, taking her hand. "Steven Cox. And if you kiss like you decorate, I need to have you over for dinner."

Steven then kissed her hand. Beth was not at all impressed. She took her hand back and looked disdainfully at Steven.

"You can make me dinner, but only if I can bring my boyfriend," she said, smirking at his attempts to be suave.

"Hey, whatever floats your boat. If he'd like to join in, uh, have dinner, I'm cool with that too."

Beth then did the smart thing and ignored Steven.

"Jason, you've been a wonderful client and I look forward to working with you on your future homes. Steven," she paused, "it's been . . . interesting meeting you."

Jason led her to the door. Steven was now walking through the loft oohing and aahing at everything he saw.

"I want to apologize for Steven," Jason said in a low voice.

"Don't worry, I've done spaces for men just like them," she said, as Jason opened the door. "Suave pseudo playboys that think they can have it all. They can't. But he won't realize it until he's forty-five, standing at the club by himself, still living off that 'player' attitude that worked for him twenty years earlier. I'm just glad you're not like him. Stay sweet!" she said, kissing him on the cheek.

And then she was gone.

"Dude, the party is on," Steven said. "I've sent out the invites and you are now officially on the A list."

"But the A list doesn't even know who I am," Jason said, laughing.

"Sure they do. They knew who you were the minute you got four million dollars."

With that, they both laughed. Money does get the attention of folks, even people you didn't even know.

During the week, Marcia had to check out the latest happening place to see if it really was the latest happening place. It was her field research, and if it passed her tests, then she would report on the place in her magazine. Tonight's new happening place was Firefly in Studio City, and so far it was living up to the billing. Firefly wasn't new, most of the movie industry met there for cocktails, or dinner, but it was new to most of her readers, who tended to live on the other side of Los Angeles. It was going to get a positive review from Marcia, since it seemed like moneyed black Angelenos were having a ball. Carole had decided to join her for cocktails. Plus, Carole needed to get out.

"Are you still on your no-dick sex diet?" Marcia said, and laughed. Both Marcia and Carole were nursing martinis. They couldn't decide on whether to have dinner there, or somewhere else.

"Lord, yes, and it's killing me," Carole said, sipping on a chocolate martini. "I was this close to picking up my old black book and calling any one of my old boyfriends. My proposition? If any one of them would wash my dishes, they could have sex with me."

Marcia laughed and Carole smiled.

"Does that make me a whore?"

Marcia sipped on her apple martini. "Well dear, it not only makes you a whore, but a damn cheap one at that. I should be your pimp because I could get you a better deal than that. He should at least paint your apartment, fix your car, and buy you some clothes for simply a chance at the pussy!"

They both laughed.

"So there are no new men in your vision?"

"Well, I've had men approach me, but I'm trying to be good. So instead of looking at them as potential boyfriends, I've been taking it slow. I have a date with one guy I met through Mama's House."

"Whoa! You're now going for the boyfriends of the single mothers?" Marcia laughed again.

"No, fool! He works for the City of Inglewood. He's a nice brother, nothing spectacular, and I'm not putting any expectations on him."

"Good girl. Just let things go as they go. Did you ever get a chance to talk to Jason?"

"Yeah, he pretty much told me the stuff I knew. I was killing my relationships by putting pressure on the guys. It's too bad black men can't handle strong black women."

"Is that what he said?" Marcia asked, slightly surprised. "I doubt Jason would say anything like that. And if you believe that, I think you've haven't heard what we've all been telling you."

"Look, I'm trying to take things as they come but I'm starting to hear that biological clock tick," Carole said while ordering another martini.

"I don't want to be one of those women who write into *Divas* talking about how it's okay to be alone. I want the marriage, kids, the two-car garage, and the whole nine yards. Jason was saying that would all come, but I have to be patient."

"And he's right."

Carole took a long sip of the martini.

"Hey, did you know that Jason bought a Suzuki Hayabusa?" Carole asked.

"A motorcycle? Does it look nice?"

"It looks great, but that's very un-Jasonlike, isn't it? I would never have thought he would want to ride a motorcycle. I think he's going to try to get some women to ride the back of it."

"It can't hurt him. He's been on a longer drought than you."

"Thanks!"

"Well, it's true."

"And do you know something else," Carole smiled. "We went to dinner and he asked me about us breaking up back at Berkeley. Can you believe that he still thinks about that?"

"Well if you've been hurt, you tend to never forget those types of things. Anyway, I always thought that Jason still liked you."

"Hey, he cheated on me, not the other way around," Carole said, annoyed. "Besides, I never picked—"

"Ladies!" a familiar voice interrupted their conversation.

Marcia and Carole looked up. It was Steven. More accurately, it was a slightly drunk Steven. He was walking from across the room, dodging the people in conversation. He was holding two drinks in his hand and was sipping from both.

"Oh God, he's been drinking and that means he's going to be even more obnoxious than usual," Carole said.

"Hi Steven," they both said.

Marcia found Steven more amusing than harmful, but Carole absolutely couldn't stand him. He tried to hit on her each and every time they were out together. She didn't like playboys, and to her, Steven was the ultimate playboy—shallow and callow.

"How come you never call me, Carole?" Steven said, saddling up to Carole a little too close. It was like a few cocktails had not only blurred Steven's perspective, but also his sense of distance. His face was so close to Carole's that it made her bend her head to gain a little bit of personal room.

"Every time I give you my number, you never call," he said. Carole used her hand to push Steven back.

"Now an intelligent man would figure this out, Steven," Carole said. "But obviously I overestimated your capacity to understand subtle gestures. So let me be frank."

Carole now moved in close to Steven, real close.

"I don't like you, I don't want you, and I don't want you to give me your phone number. You're never going to get 'lucky' with me. I'm never going to change my mind. You have no chance, and I laugh every time you try to shoot your 'game' at me. So stop wasting your time, find another girl to be smooth, suave, and debonair with, and you might be successful. But it's not happening here."

Marcia started laughing again.

"What are you laughing at?" Steven said angrily, embarrassed that Carole had called him out.

"You!" Marcia replied loudly, still laughing.

Steven had lost his bearings.

"Well fuck you both!" he said, getting up to leave.

"Bet you wish you could," Marcia and Carole said at the same time while laughing.

Steven got up and walked to the other side of Firefly while Marcia and Carole kept laughing.

"Okay, what was I talking about before that fool came over here?" Carole asked.

"I can't remember. It was something about Jason still liking you."

"No, that was *you* putting words in my mouth," Carole said, finishing her martini. "I said he *used* to like me. There's a big difference."

"If that's what you'd like to think," Marcia said, smiling. "But I know different. When a man likes you once, he never stops liking you."

"Jason is a friend, and that's it," Carole said. "Don't read too much into it."

"Okay," Marcia said, still unconvinced.

"Okay!" Carole said emphatically.

Carole downed the last of her drink, and Marcia studied her friend.

"You know I'm going to Rio in a week," she said.

"What, do you have an assignment down there? Something like an article on the black men of Rio?" Carole laughed.

"Nope, I'm going on a nice, easy, relaxing vacation. I haven't had even a day off for the past five years, and so I'm taking ten days to recharge."

"Good for you! Hey, *Baldwin Hills* has turned into *the* magazine in Los Angeles, so you deserve the rest."

"Why don't you come with me?"

Carole thought for a second. Rio would be nice. But unfortunately, she didn't have the time.

"No, I can't," Carole said reluctantly. "I don't have anyone who could take over Mama's House for ten days. Plus, I have some cases that I really need to get done. These sisters are in bad shape."

Marcia finished her drink and stood up to go. Firefly was a hit and she had her article.

"Well, if you change your mind, let me know. Think about it . . . fine men on the beach in Ipanema! Girl, you could sow your wild oats for as long as you wanted."

"It's tempting, Marcia," Carole said, getting up to leave, "but not what I want. I want a man here, not in Brazil."

CHAPTER 13

"Come on, Jason, get your butt moving! I know you can do better than that! You're embarrassing me!"

The shouts were coming from Anderson Recaro, the head trainer at Magic Johnson's 24-Hour Fitness. Jason was sprinting back and forth on an empty basketball court, and each time he got to one end, he'd drop down and do fifty push-ups and fifty crunches. It was part of Anderson's "Fitness Boot Camp" he ran at the club. It even had Magic's personal recommendation: "No other workout gets me in great shape like the Anderson Recaro Fitness Boot Camp. I highly recommend it!"

Everyone working out on that basketball court saw a huge poster of Magic's smiling face and his quote. And everyone took it seriously because in L.A., Magic was a god, both on the basketball court and in the community. When Magic talked, you listened. And when Magic opened a business, you patronized it.

You could get your coffee on at the Magic Johnson Starbucks in the Ladera Center, along with your chicken wings at his T.G.I. Friday's right next door. After eating, you could head over to the Crenshaw Baldwin Hills mall and check out a movie in the Magic Johnson Theaters. And after all that, you could work off the movie theater popcorn, the double lattes, and the potato skins at his gyms.

Jason worked off those chicken wings because *Titan* said he needed to drop ten pounds. Plus, as Vanessa so memorably told him, he was rapidly on his way to flab city if he didn't do something about it. So he was having Anderson torture him in order to do something about it.

"Get on the ball, Jason," Anderson barked.

"I'll try to do better," Jason answered.

"No," Anderson explained, "get on that blue ball over there. I want you to sit on it and balance yourself. We're going to give you a six-pack."

Jason sat on the ball, balancing himself, when Anderson pushed his body forward.

"Use your back to stay off the ground and balance yourself. We're going to burn those ten pounds off you just like that!"

"My thighs and abs feel like they're on fire," Jason said through gritted teeth.

"Good, that means they're working. They're crying out to you. They're saying, 'Jason, why didn't you work me hard all these years?' By the time I get through with you, you'll have thighs and abs like Jamie Foxx. You know I used to train him, right?"

"No, I didn't know that," Jason said, sweat now dripping into his eyes. He was really hurting now. Finally he collapsed to the ground.

"Not bad," Anderson commented, looking at his fallen client. "Not bad for the first session. Go get showered up and I'll see you on Saturday."

> *Have you gotten a caterer for the party? I've already received an RSVP from sixty women, so you should have a ton of people at the loft. Holla at me when you stop trying to be captain save-a-ho at Mama's House. Peace out! Steven.*

Jason read the text message from his Blackberry while getting dressed after the workout. He'd been a bit anxious about the party at his loft, but Steven seemed to have it all under control. As he walked out of the gym, he thought about his friends-with-benefits plan for Carole. His plan had consisted of building up the trust factor with her each day with little things—little things designed to get Carole's mind just right for the plan.

On Monday, the plan was to let Carole know that he was "there for her."

"Hey, Carole, if you need to talk again, feel free to let me know and I'll clear some space for lunch," he said in his most caring voice. "I was thinking about some of the things you were saying last week and I was thinking that maybe I should ask you for some advice."

Carole studied him curiously. "Why, thank you, Jason," she said. "I appreciate it."

"Not a problem," he responded. "What are friends for?"

On Tuesday, the plan was to see him socially, one on one.

"What's up, Carole? Hey, Eric Jerome Dickey is having a book signing at Eso Won next week, and I thought you might want to go."

Carole brightened up.

"I love Dickey, and I didn't even know he was having a signing!"

"We can roll out there on the Hayabusa, and then maybe get something to eat?"

"Okay!"

On Wednesday, it was time to confide a bit, to give a little bit of his soul to her.

"Carole, I'm seriously thinking about my future at Ketchings and Martin," he said, sitting on her couch at the end of the day. "I don't know if I would be the right fit here, but I may want to go to a law firm that does work for the poor and disadvantaged. Something like the Southern Poverty Law Center or the NAACP. I've felt so good leaving Mama's House each day, where I don't get that feeling when I leave Ketchings and Martin. What do you think I should do?"

Carole walked over to the couch, and looked at Jason tenderly. He looked conflicted.

"I say, what do you want people to say about you when you die? That you made some money for a corporation? That you got some CEO out of trouble because of some legal trick? Or do you want people without hope to sing your hosannas long after you're dead? Thurgood Marshall is remembered, Jason; the corporate lawyers at IBM aren't."

On Thursday, the plan was to impress her with his generosity.

"Carole, I just got an end-of-the-year bonus check from Ketchings and I was wondering if I could set up a foundation that could subsidize a single mother at Mama's House."

"That's so nice, Jason," she said, giving him a kiss on the cheek. "We could really use it, especially since we have a donor who may or may not come through for us this year. Thank you very much, and I know the women will appreciate it."

And on Friday, he rested. The foundation had been set. Each day he looked at Carole's face and he could see her coming closer and closer to him. The plan was working like a charm. *Titan* said he should let his work set in for a week and that's what he fully intended on doing.

Carole's brain, Jason thought, would begin to take all of his mutterings and try to make some sense of it. Hopefully, she would come to the conclusion that he, Jason Richards, was a desirable sex partner, even as a friend.

When to spring the trap? That was easy. *Titan* said wait until the next Saturday. In the meantime, tonight, Jason was hosting his first *Titan*-style party at the loft. Life was good. Life was very good, he thought.

What had gotten into Jason? Carole thought as she washed her dishes. All of a sudden he was talking about working in nonprofit, and being fulfilled at Mama's House. What was going on? Maybe the experience was changing him? He'd never been a bad guy, and maybe she was still judging him from college.

Carole found herself thinking about Jason more and more each day. Before he started working at Mama's House, he was just Jason most of the time, and that was it. But something had changed in their relationship, and it had happened subtly. She was starting to like Jason. She was starting to see him in a new light.

It was Friday night and she found herself wanting to call Jason, just to see what he was up to. Maybe he could come over and kick it for a little bit? It wouldn't be that big of a deal, just two friends kicking it together.

Dishes done, Carole began relaxing on her couch. She did a mental inventory of her refrigerator and figured out that she had a few guy things that could attract Jason.

I've got a pizza, although it's a Wolfgang Puck goat cheese pizza, it's still a pizza. And I've got a beer or two. Guys like that. To hell with it, I'm going to call him.

Carole picked up the phone and began dialing Jason's phone number. She got to the sixth digit and then hung up the phone.

Wait, will I seem desperate if I call him? she thought, hesitating. I don't want to appear desperate.

She looked around the room, thought about how she hadn't had the touch of a man in over a month, and picked up the phone again.

Hell, I *am* desperate! she thought. She dialed his number again.

"It's been a long time since I rocked and bowled!" Jason sang in his shower. "It's been a long time since I did that crawl!"

Jason couldn't sing, nor could he remember the correct lyrics to songs, but it didn't matter to him. Tonight was the night of his first *Titan* loft party. Was he excited? Hell, yeah, if it was anything like Steven's party. Jason didn't mind mindless sex with beautiful women. It was something he could get used to.

He chose a cream-colored outfit for tonight's party, and *Titan* was absolutely right: find a designer and let them clothe you. Sean John fit to a tee, and Jason looked like a million, no make that four million, bucks.

The door buzzed.

"Yes?" he said, walking to the door.

"Caterers," came the response.

"Come on up."

With the caterers now here, Jason's job was nearly done. The only thing left was for Steven to arrive. Where was Steven, anyway?

He picked up his cell phone and tried to dial Steven's phone number, but the dial tone was beeping. Someone must have called while he was in the shower and left a message on his voice mail.

"Hi Jason, uh, this is Carole . . ."

Carole? he thought. Whoa! She's never called my house before. What's up with this?

". . . and I was wondering if you were doing anything tonight? Um, I mean I have some pizza and some beer, and I thought we could just, you know, sit around and eat pizza and drink beer. But there's no obligation, I mean if you're busy, you don't have to. . . ."

And then the message ended. There were two messages, so he clicked to hear the second one. It was Carole again.

"Ooh, I just forgot. Here's my phone number. Uh, give me a call if you can."

Jason put down the phone and just stood there in amazement. How could a magazine be so right about women? The "Friends with Benefits" article was working, Jason thought. It was already fucking working! He couldn't believe it, and yet he felt a little dirty about doing something like this. Carole was a friend. Sure, she wasn't a close friend, but she was still a friend. And here he was trying to manipulate her into having sex. But, Jason thought, it was better to have had sex with Carole now and regret it later, than to never have had sex with her in the first place.

"Are you ready for a party!" Steven said, yelling at the top of his lungs.

Steven had arrived, and as usual, he wasn't subtle. Jason decided that he wasn't going to tell him about the whole Carole thing, and just be vague about what he was doing with the *Titan* article in the first place.

"Man, I've got at least seventy-five beautiful women coming, and I do mean coming," he said slyly, as though he were the most clever person in the world, "to see you. And that's just for the party. I'm not even talking about the after-party."

"Excuse me," Steven said as he intercepted the caterer. She was on her way to the kitchen.

"Who is tending bar tonight?" he asked.

He grabbed a sprig of celery from her tray and began munching on it.

"George will be tending bar tonight. Any special requests?"

"Thanks, no special requests. I'll talk to him later."

The caterer walked back to the kitchen and Steven began instructing Jason on the ways of throwing a party.

"Now the party itself kind of takes care of itself. All you have to do is mingle, meet people and give them about a minute of your time. Even if you don't know them, give them a feeling that they are in your inner circle. Give them a feeling that they are living vicariously through you by being here. That's probably the most important thing."

At that point, Steven walked to the center of the loft and spread his arms wide open.

"Look at everything you have! People envy this! Men are going to want to be you, and women are going to want to be with you. Enjoy it!"

He was right. Everything was perfect. Jason was a bachelor that other men envied, and he hadn't done anything more than get some money and follow a magazine's advice. It was funny, Jason thought, how simple life could be when you follow instructions.

The caterers worked at a feverish pace and the room came together. It was a little weird having people he didn't know coming into his house, but it had to happen if he was to be a *Titan* man.

"Why did you ask who the bartender was?" Jason asked Steven.

"Because we are going to have a freaky party at the end of the real party, and I want to make sure that he holds on to a case of Cristal. Your bedroom is to be the center of it, so I want him to put a case on ice and have it in your closet, ready to go."

"A freaky party in my bedroom?" Jason asked. What did Steven have in mind, and just how freaky? Hell, at this point, Jason didn't care. He hadn't steered him wrong yet, so he might as well flow with it.

"Yep my friend, it's going to get really freaky tonight," Steven said with a smile.

"Cool, I'm down for whatever."

And "whatever" was about to come.

Jason excused himself and walked into his bathroom. He needed to make sure he called Carole before the party started, and he didn't want Steven to hear.

"Hello."

"Carole?"

"Hi, Jason, did you get my message? I know that it's last-minute, but I was wondering if you were free. . . ."

"Hey, I think that's a great idea, but Ketchings called me today and I have to go in and do some last-minute work on a case I was working on. But hey, can I get a rain check, say next week? I'll clear my schedule for it."

"Oh, you don't have to do that," Carole said, sounding mortified that she'd ever made the call.

"No, I'd love to, and I will. So are we on?"

"Yes, and I'll keep the pizza and beer for you," she said.

"I hope it's fresh pizza and fresh beer!" Jason said, and laughed.

"Okay, I'll see you at Mama's House on Monday."

"Take care and don't work too hard tonight."

"Don't worry, I won't."

"Good night."

"Good night."

He had her in the bag. Little did she know, but Carole was about to be Jason's first "friends with benefits" victim.

A party is good when there's an even distribution of men and women, because most parties have too many men and not enough women. But that wasn't the case with Jason's party. Steven had done a great job with the invites and these women looked like the ones who'd come to Steven's party.

For the most part, Jason tried to follow Steven's instructions by glad-handing everyone. He half expected most of them to look at him and say "Who the hell are you?", but they all seemed to know Jason, even before he introduced himself.

"Are you enjoying yourself? I hope so. My name is—"

"I know who you are," said a supermodel type to Jason. She was tall and lean, and had an air that told him she'd gone to a bunch of high-society parties in her lifetime.

"You're Jason Richards."

"How did you know who I was?"

"Everyone knows who you are," she responded, nibbling on a canapé. "You're the buzz of the town."

I am? Jason thought.

And every conversation was just like that. The women gave Jason more attention than he'd ever had.

"Two cannibals are eating a clown," Jason said to one group. "One says to the other, 'Does this taste funny to you?' "

"Apparently, one in five people in the world are Chinese," Jason said to another. "And there are five people in my family, so it must be one of them. It's either my mom or my dad or maybe my older brother Calvin or my younger brother Ho-Chin. But I'm pretty sure it's Calvin."

They laughed at his corny jokes, not just because they thought he was extraordinarily funny, but because he could tell that they wanted him to like them.

That's pretty damn powerful, and Jason was starting to feel that power. And with that power came a sense of confidence and entitlement. He felt himself moving from a feeling that he hoped these beautiful women would give him a chance to the feeling that he was going to have any one of them. It was just simply a matter of which one he wanted.

The air kisses from the women kept coming throughout the night, and Jason was having a ball. Steven kept guiding him to different women and they all seemed to find him interesting. "You see them over there?" Steven asked, as Jason had taken some time to scope the party.

"Yeah," he responded.

They were looking at three women who were sitting on his windowsill. The windowsill framed a picture window to die for, and he'd only seen city views like this in the movies. Steven's loft didn't have anything on his, he thought. But there they sat, all beautiful. Men were coming up to them, but they weren't giving them the time of day.

"They want to party with us later."

"Cool," Jason said.

"No, I don't think you understand," Steven said, putting his arm around Jason. "They want to *party* with us."

He smiled that same "cat ate the canary" smile that Jason used to think was annoying as hell, but now found pretty damn cool.

"Oh, I get what you're saying."

Steven took another sip from his drink.

"You know what I did just to make it interesting?"

All of the women at this point noticed that they were looking at them while they talked, and they all gave Steven and Jason a wave.

"I told them," he said as he took another sip, "that they could only party with us if they rejected every man at this party. If they even looked at another man at this party, then the party was off. That's why they keep brushing brothers off."

As Jason watched men try fruitlessly to talk to these three beautiful women, it dawned on Jason that power was indeed good.

"Power is a muthafucka, ain't it?" Steven said.

"It's an aphrodisiac too," Jason replied.

"No doubt, baby, no doubt," he said, laughing.

CHAPTER 14

As Jason lay naked in his bed with the sleeping sounds of strange people all around him, he wondered one thing. How had he gotten here? How had he moved from beef Stroganoff, ESPN, and then straight-to-bed Fridays, to a bunch of legs, arms, mouths and holes all constantly moaning and groaning? But let's back up a bit.

The party lasted until about three-thirty in the morning. Folks began streaming out, looking to go to the nearest after-hours spot, except for those three beautiful women who didn't move. They hadn't moved an inch for at least six hours.

The caterers cleaned up their stuff and packed up the food. They were going to try to clean the loft, but Jason and Steven wanted them out as soon as possible. Jason was tired from his first party, but not tired enough to miss the after-party Steven had set up.

"Mr. Richards, we can clean this up in about thirty minutes if you'd like," the caterer said.

"Don't worry about it, Marge, it'll give me something to do."

"Okay," she said. "Well, the food is in the fridge, and thanks for the check."

"You were wonderful and the party was great."

The caterers walked out of the loft and suddenly it was just Steven, Jason and the three beautiful women.

"Jason, I'd like to introduce you to three young ladies," Steven said, walking toward them. For the first time all night, the women stood up.

"This is Miss Blue," he said.

Miss Blue walked over to Jason and gave him a deep, luscious kiss. Miss Blue was fair-skinned, about five-foot five, with crystal-clear blue eyes. She had long, dark hair, and had small, delicate features. She was drop-dead gorgeous, and her kiss lingered with Jason.

"Hello, Jason, nice to meet you," she said. She then walked slowly, seductively, into Jason's bedroom.

Steven stood there like the host of a beauty pageant. He had the same shit-eating grin he always had as he introduced the women.

"And this is Miss Green," he continued.

Jason was a breast man, and Miss Green was dark-skinned with a large behind and extremely large breasts. He could have gotten lost in her cleavage. She walked up to Jason like she was a black Marilyn Monroe. And yes, she had green eyes. Again, it was another luscious kiss with lots and lots of tongue. After the kiss, she took her index finger and put it under Jason's chin, her manicured nail scraping against his chin only so lightly. Jason's dick was just as hard as when Vanessa had agreed to fuck him at Steven's party.

"And last but not least is Mrs. Brown," Steven said.

"Missus?" Jason asked, surprised. The missus part made him a bit nervous about who was the mister in her life.

"Yes, Missus," Steven smiled.

"Don't let that bother you, darling," Mrs. Brown said. "It's not bothering me." And with that, Mrs. Brown gave Jason a small peck on the cheek.

Mrs. Brown was model-tall, with an athletic build. She was a bit older, maybe in her early thirties, and her youthful beauty was just about to fade. However, she wore a red dress that showed her lean muscles. It wouldn't have surprised Jason to find out that Mrs. Brown worked out regularly.

"You'll get more in a few minutes," she whispered in Jason's ear.

And in little more than two minutes, three beautiful black women were waiting for Jason in his bedroom. Suddenly, he was feeling a little anxious.

"Dude, I don't know if I'm going to be able to handle three women," Jason said, wanting to have the chance of a lifetime, but also not wanting to fail.

"Oh, don't worry, you won't have to," Steven said while unbuttoning his shirt.

"Uh, you're going to be in there with me?" Jason hadn't expected that, for some reason.

Steven stopped. He looked at Jason strangely.

"Did you think I set this up all for you?" he said.

"Well, you did with Vanessa. . . ."

"Brother, I ain't your pimp," he said, taking off his pants. "I want to get with three women just like you do. So don't fuck this up."

"Man, I'm not trying to fuck it up," Jason said. "I just want to make sure we get a few things straight. I know I have a one-dick-per-room rule. So you keep your dick away from my dick and we'll be cool."

Steven laughed.

"Brother, I ain't gay or bisexual. I just love to have sex, lots of it. And don't worry, my friend, I don't even want to touch your dick, and to tell you honestly, I don't want to even see your dick. I'm freaky, but I ain't that freaky."

"Boys!" three voices softly called from the bedroom. "We're waiting!"

"Cool," Jason said uncertainly.

As Jason walked to his bedroom, he found that he had the same feeling he'd had as a kid on Christmas: crazy anticipation for what was about to come. So when he walked into his bedroom and saw three beautiful women, one with blue eyes, one with green eyes, and another with brown eyes all lying naked on his bed, it was like finding out that there really was a Santa Claus. This was a fantasy right out of a porno, and Jason wanted to make sure that his fantasy came true tonight.

"Hello everyone," Steven said, pulling out a sheaf of condoms, "let's party."

Jason tried to get out of his clothes as smoothly as possibly, but when he tried to pull his legs out of his pants he fell in a heap. Why can't I get out of my clothes without fucking up? he thought.

The three women laughed, and Steven was cracking up. At first

Jason was mortified as he lay there on his floor, but then he had to laugh. It was funny. Mrs. Brown climbed down from the bed and got between his legs. His pants were still around his ankles.

"Well, I guess it looks like I have you where I want you," she said.

She then proceeded to slowly take Jason's pants and then his underwear. His dick was hard as a rock.

"Wow, you've got it going on, darling," she said. She was impressed by his dick's size, and Jason liked that. There's nothing that boosts a man's ego more than a woman commenting on your dick size in a positive, he thought.

"I'm glad you like it," Jason said proudly.

On the bed, Steven was now completely naked and kissing Miss Blue, while fondling Miss Green's breast. It's not like he was trying to look, but Jason noticed that Steven had a tiny dick! Mr. Smooth had a small dick and he had a big one.

"Do you like this?' Mrs. Brown asked.

Mrs. Brown had expertly taken Jason's dick in her right hand and was slowly jerking it up and down.

"Ooh," Jason murmured. "You've done this before, eh?"

"That's why I'm a missus," Mrs. Brown said, smiling, still steadily stroking Jason's dick. She would stroke fast, and then suddenly slow down. If she were conducting an instructional video, she couldn't have been better.

"Your husband is a lucky man," Jason sighed.

"Pop!"

Steven opened up a bottle of Cristal and the women all giggled.

"Champagne, anyone?" he asked as the liquid spilled over his hands.

Jason walked over to the closet, got his own bottle, and then jumped on the bed. Miss Blue, with her fine-ass body, lit a few of the candles Beth Allen had set up on a candelabra, and then turned off the lights. It was a little like the room Steven had set up at the loft, only better. These candles had a scent and created a highly sexualized atmosphere.

And after that, it was all legs, arms and holes.

Jason started licking Mrs. Brown's pussy while Miss Green sucked his dick. Mrs. Brown was sitting on his face, and Miss Blue was eating Miss Green's pussy while Steven began fucking Miss Blue from behind.

"Ahhh, grrrrrrrr, ahhh," Mrs. Brown said as Jason licked her up and down.

"Fuck me harder, deeper," Miss Blue cooed. Steven was about as deep as he could go, the poor bastard.

They were one big sex chain, and the pleasure of one gave pleasure to all of them.

"Fuck me," Mrs. Brown said.

"Fuck us," Miss Green said.

And Jason did. He first decided to fuck Mrs. Brown, because he'd never fucked a married woman before. As he entered her, she immediately let out a sigh.

"Yes, yes, keep going, yes," she barked at him. She was on her stomach and Jason was fucking her from the back, taking his time. Her pussy was tight and she moaned with every stroke, arching her back. It was like her pussy pulsed, and Jason's dick was the reason. Suddenly, Jason felt a nibbling on his balls.

"Ah, ah, ah!" Mrs. Brown said. Miss Green decided to get on her back and lick his balls and lick Mrs. Brown's pussy with every stroke.

"Oh my God!" Jason screamed, as the feeling was both intense and incredible. Miss Green's tongue flicked so that it caught him on the shaft and balls, and it was a pleasure he'd never felt in his life.

In minutes, Jason was in a trancelike state. All he could hear was the sound of kissing, fucking and slurping. Bodies moved in concert, seeking and hungering for more pleasure.

"Bitch, come here," Steven shouted at someone. "Suck that muthafuckin' dick!"

Jason couldn't see who Steven was fucking, but he could hear her cries. The cries turned him on, and he wanted to make sure he got at everyone in the bed. Everyone except Steven, of course.

"Let's switch," he said, pulling out of Mrs. Brown.

He took off his condom, opened another and then laid down on his back.

"I want to spin on that dick. Are you ready for me?" Miss Blue said from the shadows.

"Yeah, I'm ready for you. Are you ready for me?" Jason answered.

"My boy!" Steven said on the other side of the bed.

Miss Blue took Jason's dick with her left hand and Jason entered her. He was too big for her pussy, but it didn't seem to matter to Miss Blue. She spun around on his dick and Jason began fucking her in the reverse cowgirl.

"Give it to me baby, give it to me," she demanded. She leaned back, so that her tiny ass slid up and down Jason's upper thigh. With one hand, Jason grabbed her left breast, and with his other hand, he rubbed her clit. It was then that Jason wanted to thank Anderson Recaro for all those abs exercises at the gym.

Mrs. Brown was now fucking Steven and Miss Green kept moving from Jason to Steven, kissing both of them. While Miss Blue was riding Jason's dick, she decided to give Miss Green some tongue. Little things were starting to envelope Jason's senses. He'd never been so turned on as when he'd had one woman on his dick and another one kissing her. And out of the corner of his eye, he could see the fuck face of Mrs. Brown, as Steven had her bent over the bed. He was fucking her doggy style. She had a beautiful fuck face. Jason reached out, pulled her face to him and began kissing it.

"I'm co . . . !" Miss Blue screamed. She couldn't get the words out. She kept turning her head from side to side, as though an invisible person was slapping her face.

Miss Green was now licking Miss Blue's clit as Jason was moved up and down. Miss Blue held Miss Green's head down as she tried to make her keep contact with her clit.

Miss Blue's pussy quivered as her body got hard and rigid.

"Yahaaaaaaaaaah!" Miss Blue screamed, coming hard on his dick. Her eyes rolled in the back of her head, and Jason kept stroking her, harder and harder.

Jason was on top of the fucking world. He felt like he could fuck all night. Miss Blue got off his dick and fell to the side of the bed. Miss Green took a towel and wiped her face. Jason took another sip of the champagne, passed it around and just let all of the sensations go over his body. This was simply great. It felt great and sounded great.

Suddenly there was a break in the action. Everyone was all sweaty from the sex and a little out of breath.

"Anyone want to do two dicks?" Steven asked as he took a swig of Cristal.

"Me," Miss Green said, raising her hand as though it was the most natural of requests. "But I need some lube."

"Got you," Steven said. He walked over to his pants and pulled out a tube of lube.

Damn, that fool thought of everything. But what's this two-dick thing? Jason thought. He thought he and Steven had an agreement. But he hadn't fucked Miss Green, and he wasn't going to let the night end without fucking all of the women.

He tossed her the K-Y jelly and she put some on her finger and then in her ass. Jason was feeling big, bad and bold.

"So since you want to take two dicks, you get the choice of where you want the dicks," he said.

Miss Green looked at Jason through the candlelight.

"I want you on the bottom because you've got the biggest dick in the room," she said.

"And Steven, you fuck me in the ass."

"He may have a bigger dick," Steven said, pulling out more condoms and passing one to Jason. "But no one knows how to fuck like me. So get your bitch ass up and let's get to fucking."

It was then that Jason gave up his "your dick near my dick" edict and just decided he was going to have to blank out any memory of Steven's dick being close. This was a once-in-a-lifetime-thing orgy, and he'd never double-penetrated a woman before. The pleasure had been so intense, that he was doing things he'd never thought he wanted to do, or even could do. But he wanted more. So, he got on his back and Miss Green got on top of him, her face inches from his. Jason's dick slid nicely in her.

"Eat me out," Miss Blue demanded, crawling over to Jason, "and I promise that I'll come again."

"Get over here, you bitch," Jason growled. Who was this person in my body? he wondered.

Miss Blue sat on Jason's face and Jason began sucking on her clit. At the same time, Miss Blue and Miss Green began kissing each other. It all turned Jason on.

Steven put on a new rubber, mounted Miss Green, and entered her ass. She let out the deepest moan Jason had *ever* heard from another person. He didn't want to think about the fact that Steven's dick was right next to his, nor did he want to think about how his dick was really pressing against Jason's dick, even though Jason was in Miss Green's pussy and he was in her ass. Jason didn't think about this because it felt so damn good.

"Fuck . . . me . . . boys . . . *faster!*" Miss Green demanded.

Steven and Jason got a rhythm going and Miss Green was holding on for dear life. Mrs. Brown kept herself busy by licking both Steven's and Jason's balls, while Jason tried to eat out Miss Blue, who was sitting on his face. It was all so much, but somehow it all worked. Jason felt like he could come any time but he was going to be damned if he was going to come before Steven.

"Oh, shit! Oh, shit!" Miss Green screamed as she came for the first time. Jason grabbed her now-stiff breasts as she came. She was done.

"Harder!" she screamed at Jason. He grabbed harder.

They kept the rhythm going for a good ten minutes, with Miss Green coming so many times that everyone lost track.

"Oh, yes! Yes, fucking yes, ahhhhh!"

"Get that dick, bitch," Steven shouted, slapping her ass.

Steven and Jason were pounding Miss Green now. Miss Blue came on Jason's face, quietly and with a sigh. She slipped down to the bed.

Suddenly Steven yelled out.

"I'm going to fucking come!"

Jason was not worried that another man was about to come only inches away from him, but he didn't want any of his come to land on him.

"Oh shit, yes!" he yelled. Even though Steven was in Miss Green's ass, Jason could feel Steven orgasm. It was a sensation he didn't want to think about again.

"There you go, baby," Miss Green said. "Come in my ass."

Steven pulled out and took off his condom. While he walked over to the side to get a towel, Jason kept fucking.

Miss Green was doing most of the work now, moving her ass up and down, and slowly sliding against Jason's dick. Mrs. Brown rubbed both Jason's body and Miss Green's breasts, while Miss Blue was still on her side, but now kissing Jason on the neck. Now it was Jason's turn to come. How he'd managed to last this long without coming, he just didn't know, but he had. But the sensations from all these places had become too much for him.

"God . . . good . . . God . . . God!" he screamed. His orgasm seemed to start at his curled-up toes, up through his leg where it finally stopped at his groin. The pleasure lingered as Miss Green just kept riding his dick.

"Oh, Jesus!" Jason's arms and legs went flailing as he came, but he didn't remember because he'd never come like that before in his life. And the next thing he knew, he'd blanked out. It was that good. But as he faded into a long sleep, Jason thought about one thing. The *Titan* life was definitely a winner.

CHAPTER 15

Jason woke up around six in the morning, with the rays of sun just breaking through his window shade. As he looked around the bedroom, he saw condom wrappers and underwear everywhere. Miss Blue and Mrs. Brown were sleeping under both of his arms, while Miss Green's head was on Steven's belly. They were a matrix of arms, legs and ass, and his brain was trying to take everything in.

What an evening, he thought as everyone snored. How did this happen?

Here he was, lying in bed with three women, and Steven, and he never would have considered this situation a possibility a little over a month ago. How did this happen, indeed?

Jason gently moved Miss Blue and Mrs. Brown's heads away from his arms and somehow got out of the bed without waking anyone. He grabbed his underwear and walked into his living room. The place was a mess, but a nice mess. After a night like that, he needed something productive to do, and that would consist of cleaning up the living room all day. But how could he get everyone out of his house?

As it turned out, it wasn't too hard. Jason made a fresh pot of coffee and the aroma must have awoken everyone. Soon, Miss Blue and Mrs. Brown walked out of his bedroom wearing only their panties and no bras. Damn they still looked sexy, he thought, and he'd fucked them both!

"Do you mind if we get a cup of coffee?" Miss Blue asked.

"Sure, how do you take it?"

"With a little sugar," Miss Blue said.

"Black," Mrs. Brown said.

Jason fixed them their coffee and then watched them. And it was funny, but within the bedroom, everything seemed to be natural, so fluid. Everyone was comfortable and relaxed in there, but now that they were simply three people drinking a simple cup of coffee, naked and seminaked, of course, things were suddenly awkward. It was the morning after a one-night stand, except with a bunch of people. All of a sudden, they became strangers again, and even though they'd done very intimate things to each other, Jason realized that they didn't even know each other's real names.

And he also started to notice a few things. The light of day was starting to expose the realities that had been obscured by the champagne, candlelight, makeup and the excitement of the moment. One, Mrs. Brown was a little older that he'd originally thought. She was still beautiful, but she had to be in her midthirties, and he could see a few wrinkles around her mouth and her eyes. Conversely, Miss Blue was a little younger than he'd thought, but still with a banging body.

Steven and Miss Green rolled out of the bedroom, with Steven wearing nothing, but Miss Green already dressed to leave.

"Oh my God, I can't believe I did this! Oh my God, I can't believe I did this," Miss Green said as she struggled to put on her shoes.

"Come on, you guys, let's go," she told Miss Blue and Mrs. Brown.

"Well, I guess my morning coffee is done. She's driving," said Miss Blue, laughing and putting down her cup.

Miss Blue and Mrs. Brown walked into Jason's bedroom and began putting their clothes back on.

"Meet me downstairs in the car!" Miss Green yelled. She said nothing to either Steven or Jason, and left the loft as fast as she could. Steven, still not wearing any underwear, attempted to sit on Jason's beloved chaise longue with his bare-naked ass.

"Yo! Yo!" Jason yelled. "Don't sit on my shit with your naked ass! Go put on some clothes!"

"Okay, okay, man," Steven said, catching himself before sitting. "I didn't think you'd mind."

"Well I do mind," Jason remarked, trying to clean things up.

"So how did you like last night?" Steven asked, still standing there stark naked.

"Dude, go put some drawers on," Jason said. "I can't talk to you with your nuts out there like that."

"Oh okay, okay," Steven said as he moved to the bedroom. Just then, Miss Blue and Mrs. Brown emerged. They were dressed and ready to go.

"Thanks for the party," Mrs. Brown said, giving Jason a kiss on the cheek.

"It was great," Miss Blue said.

"I don't think Miss Green enjoyed herself," Jason said, leading them to the door.

"Oh, she's just freaked out that she's freaky," said Miss Blue. "She'll get over it."

"Hey, let us know when you want to party again," Mrs. Brown said. "Steven will know how to get in contact with us."

And with that, they were gone.

Steven reemerged from Jason's bedroom with his underwear on.

"Okay, is this cool?"

"Yeah, much better."

"So how did you like the party?" Steven asked again.

Steven sat down on the chaise longue, taking it all in.

"Do you do that at every party?" he asked.

"No, of course not," Steven said, laughing. "Normally I only have two women."

"Naw, the party was the bomb, but I can't do this four times a week as *Titan* says," Jason said, leaning back in the longue. "I'd be worn out."

"But do you see what we could do together? Did you see how freaky Miss Green is? She took us both, dude! That's some shit!"

"Yeah, man, they were all freaky. They said that if we wanted to party again, that you'd know where to contact them."

"Yep, I got Mrs. Brown's private phone number."

The same awkward silence that enveloped Miss Blue, Mrs. Brown, and Jason, now descended on the two men. Jason realized that they'd crossed a Rubicon in their relationship, and things were definitely different. Steven was not just a fellow lawyer, friend and running mate, but now a fuck buddy. And Jason needed time to synthesize what that all meant. Jason didn't think Steven was contemplating this as much as he was, but he knew he had to get Steven out of his loft as soon as possible.

"Man, I've got to get some stuff done for Mama's House, so if you don't mind . . ." Jason said, rising to his feet.

"Say no more," said Steven. He proceeded to get up and get dressed. Somehow his clothes were strewn over the whole loft. It took him about five minutes to get everything. Finally he managed to get himself dressed.

"Man, hit me up on the phone later. We've got some more partying to do," he yelled as he left the loft.

Finally there was silence. Jason turned on the television, got his quilt, and slept all day.

That wasn't too bad, Carole thought, while hanging up her cell phone. She settled into a scoop of Ben & Jerry New York fudge ice cream. She'd taken a risk with a friend, and Jason was simply a friend, who had been really open. In fact, he sounded excited to be spending some time with her.

I think I'll order a super-stuffed pizza and a good gourmet beer for next week, she thought. He'll like that.

Why am I thinking so much about this? she thought as she nodded off to sleep.

The television droned on and Carole started drifting asleep. She started dreaming that she was falling through a hole in the sky, and her arms were flailing. As she twisted in the wind, she felt the apprehension of landing, and she was yelling at the top of her lungs. But out of the corner of her eye, she could see a man flying at the same altitude, coming closer and closer to her as she fell. Suddenly, she felt two strong hands steady her in midair. She'd closed her eyes only seconds before, but when she opened them, she saw who was saving her. It was Jason. It was a Jason that she'd never noticed before; strong, handsome and confident.

"Jason!" she said in the dream.

Carole woke up with a start. She looked at the clock. It was now four in the morning.

What the hell did that mean? she thought.

She got up and began pacing around her apartment. She didn't know if she was sleepwalking or just nervous, but that dream had disturbed her. What the hell did that dream mean?

Was she falling in love with Jason? Did she think Jason was her savior? Why was she falling in the first place?

For a person who liked to be in control, Carole was finding herself getting out of control. These were feelings she'd never had before, even when she thought she was desperately in love with her past boyfriends. Why this and why now? Was Jason the one?

Carole needed some help and she couldn't think of a place to turn. Normally, Carole would call Marcia, but it was four in the morning. And she had either thrown away or given away all her usual aids—the women's magazines and self-help books. She could try the Web, but then a lightbulb went on. There was a chance if she wanted to get information right now.

She'd thrown out all of her women's magazines, but she still hadn't canceled her *Divas* subscription. She dug around her old mail and found her latest *Divas* magazine.

Come on Divas, *help a sister out,* Carole said to herself as she scoured the table of contents for something, anything that could help her figure out what the dreams meant. And then she found it. It was the article that perfectly encompassed what she was going through. "From Friends to Lovers: How to Find Long-Lasting Love with Your Best Friend."

"Yes!" Carole exclaimed.

Carole was fully awake now and she couldn't read the article fast enough.

The author, Taigi Bryant, said that women had to get over the idea that there weren't enough men to go around.

For years, social scientists, population experts and your grand-mother have all been saying that there aren't enough men to go around. Don't believe it, sistergirl! Don't believe it! They are just trying to defeat you! Men are all around you, but you have to take a good, good look around you. You see we've eliminated brothers that are eligible. Have you taken a good look at the man who works right next to you? What about the friend, you know the one. He's the brother that listens to you mumble and grumble about how bad your boyfriends are, but gives wonderful advice? Those men are there for you, and no, they aren't all gay! You just have to put them back on the dating board. If you want to find out if your friend can also be your lover, then sit down and write out the positives and negatives. If he has more positives than negatives, and isn't behind bars, then girl, put him back on the eligible men list! You'll thank me for it later.

That's right, Carole thought. I need to put Jason on my board. She read on.

. . . and who better to have a boyfriend and potentially a husband? They already listen to you; you laugh and cry with them; and you probably have a good idea about how they are in bed, because they've critiqued how bad your previous boyfriends were. If you follow our "From Friends to Lovers" plan, you can have the best of all worlds: a best friend that you have lust for!

Carole closed the magazine and sat back in her chair.
I need some tea to help me think, Carole thought.
Tea was good for the brain cells, and Earl Grey tea was especially good. Plus, tea relaxed Carole and she needed relaxing. She read some more:

Rule number 1:
After you pick your target, begin changing your feeling toward your friend. It is necessary for a Divas woman to look at that guy friend as a sexy guy friend. Stop saying things like, "We're great friends but we could never get together." Get together! Take that chance. Men are simple creatures and will follow your lead on relationships, and male friends will be pleasantly surprised when you open up to them as a romantic possibility.

We'd been romantic in the past, Carole thought, but I don't know if Jason thinks of me in that way anymore. But if I work on it, I think I can get him back in that romantic mode as opposed to friend mode.

> *Rule number 2:*
>
> *Gradually merge your two lives into one. Men tend to be individualistic—that explains the lack of taste in their apartments and homes. They'll put up kung fu posters in their living room, hanging just above a well-worn beer keg and a pile of clothing, because they're really only thinking of themselves. A Divas woman has to figure out how to merge her togetherness with his untogetherness. It can be done, but it takes patience. If you're good, your male friend will be unaware that his space is now your space too, and changes are being made.*

I've first got to be invited to his place, she thought. It dawned on her that she had no idea where Jason lived or how he lived. He could live on his bike, for all she knew. She must get invited to his house, she thought.

> *Rule number 3:*
>
> *Allow yourself to become jealous. Jealousy means that you are taking ownership of your male friend from all those "bitches" that want him. You have an advantage. You know your male friend better than any of those women at the club, so fight them off. This is not a time to allow them, or him, to stray. But if he does stray from you, and you have concrete evidence, walk away and don't look back. Because "Friends to Lovers" is about trust and if you can't trust your male friend, who can you trust?*

This is the one area she felt shaky about, Carole thought. Jason cheated on her once, so should she give him a second time? On the one hand, that was in college with a stank soror. He wouldn't do that again because he'd grown now, hadn't he?

I'm going to go over this methodically and rationally, Carole thought. Just because I had a simple dream about Jason, and he seems to be all the things they talked about in the magazine, doesn't mean I should try to convince him to be my boyfriend. That's kind of silly.

She sipped on her tea, continuing to think things over.

"Maybe I should list out the positives and negatives of Jason," she said aloud.

Carole walked over to her computer and turned it on. With a buzz and a hum, the computer tried to come on, but it stopped suddenly.

"Come on, you damn computer!"

But the computer didn't start up. A blue screen appeared with the message MICROSOFT ERROR JIDKJF3434KMK343434KNJKNJ34234 3423434.

"Why do they bother to tell me the error message???" Carole screamed to herself. "I don't know what the fuck to do with this damn message. I just know that the computer doesn't work. The message should simply say FUCKED UP, TURN ME OFF!"

Computer on the fritz, it was time to make an old-fashioned list on a yellow pad.

"Okay," she said as she made two columns, "the positives and the negatives of Mr. Jason Richards."

The positives, she thought. *Jason has integrity. What you see is what you get with Jason,* Carole wrote. *And that's one thing I like about him. He didn't tell me what I wanted to hear; he told me what he thought was the truth. It may have hurt, but it was the truth. You've got to like that in a man.*

Jason listens to people, she continued to write. *Just last week, he called me to ask if I wanted to talk. What a sweetheart!*

He had a sexy bike, she thought. Hey, a woman can be a little superficial! His new Suzuki Hayabusa is sexy as hell and she looked good on it, Carole thought.

Okay, he probably had a lot more positives, but what are the negatives?

Well, the first thing she could find negative is that Jason could stand to lose a few pounds. But damn, that's changeable. And of course, he was a lawyer, but Carole could learn to live with that, as long as she got him to leave the law firm and work for a nonprofit. And hey, he had said he was thinking of doing that. So that may even be on the positive side.

Carole sat staring at her yellow pad and counted up the positives and the negatives. For the first time in a few months, she was clear on what she wanted and whom she wanted. She wanted Jason. Now, how to get him? She opened the *Divas* back up to see what she should do. She wouldn't get to sleep until noon. Little did Jason know it, but he was about to move from being a friend to being a lover.

CHAPTER 16

The cab was outside and the taxi driver was honking his horn. It was time for Marcia to go.

"Okay, everyone," Marcia shouted to her staff. "I'm off to Rio."

The *Baldwin Hills* magazine staff gathered to see her off. This was Marcia's first vacation in five years and she was not about to let anyone spoil it. Ten days of rest and relaxation, and hopefully Brazilian men, meant that for the first time, her managing editor and assistant were on their own. They had strict orders.

"Now what did I say about contacting me?" she said as they all laughed.

"Unless the office is burning down, *and*," they all said in unison, "some staffers are burning with it, *and* the money gets burned, *don't call me!*"

The staffers all loved Marcia, but it was going to be good to have a break from her. Marcia could get a little overbearing at times. They all needed her to go on vacation.

"You all are going to get raises for making the boss happy," she said as she walked to the door. "But if any one of you tries to contact me, you'll be fired as soon as I get back. Jordan, come here a second."

Her managing editor Jordan McCoy came over and they talked as Marcia made her way to the cab.

"I was serious about that no calling thing, but do e-mail me if you get some juicy material," Marcia said, smiling. "We need to find something new because I'm tired of publishing the same old black people. Remember, this is your issue, so I want to give you full reign to do what you think will get people talking. This is a test to see if you can handle *Baldwin Hills* without me. You think up the theme, the articles, and the people profiled. When I get back, I want to be amazed by how innovative you've been. Take some chances and even if they don't work, I'll be happy. Surprise me."

Marcia got into her cab, and rolled down the window.

"And by the way, if the office does actually burn down, please do give me a call, will you?" she smiled. "I don't want to hear that you followed my instruction too closely!"

And with a hearty laugh, Marcia turned to the cabbie. "Off to the airport, my baby, and don't look back!"

And off to Rio Marcia went.

Jordan turned to go back into the office, and thought about her new temporary position. She was a little nervous about handling the magazine while Marcia was gone, but there was a little excitement there too. She was finally going to get to take the magazine in the direction she wanted, at least until Marcia got back. For this issue, she was going to find out who were some of the new people making things happen in the city.

When Jordan walked back into the office, she saw that the staffers were already acting as though the cat was away. If she was going to keep control over the next ten days, she needed to do it now.

"Editorial meeting now," she yelled.

There was an audible groan from the staffers. They thought they'd get at least a day of messing around, but apparently Jordan wanted to actually put out the magazine and do work.

They all trudged into the conference room, taking seats around the conference table.

"Okay, what are we going to cover this month?" Jordan asked. "Give me something new and something that is happening in the city that we're missing. What's the newest club to visit? Who's throwing the best parties in town?"

There was silence as everyone on the editorial staff looked at her in silence.

"Come on, guys, where are your ideas? I know that half of you are always bitching and moaning that Marcia won't let you cover this story or that story. Well, now's your chance to cover that story. Right now, I'm the person who's okaying the stories. So give me some good stuff."

There was a little bit of stirring from the writers.

"What if we follow a member of the Lakers for a day?" one writer asked. "I can get Devean George."

"Devean George? Who wants to follow Devean? That's boring and has been done before anyway," Jordan responded. "What's next?"

"B. Smith is throwing a party at her new Hancock—"

"Who cares? Next!"

"We could profile the sister on *Access Hollywood*."

Jordan stood up. She was getting exasperated because she wanted cutting edge, and the writers were giving her mundane.

"Stop it! Don't anyone say a word until someone can give me something juicy, interesting and absolutely captivating to our readers. I'm going to get a soda. When I get back I want at least one person to have that idea."

Jordan walked out and the writers began talking among themselves. After about five minutes, the writers were ready and Jordan came back into the room.

"We came up with a concept that we think you'll like," Karla said.

Karla Smith had worked at *Baldwin Hills* magazine since its founding. She was Marcia's favorite writer.

"Okay, throw it at me," Jordan said, sipping her soda.

"We'd like to do a 'private parties' issue," she said.

"Okay, I'm listening. What's the spin on it?" Jordan said, finally feeling interested in what was being pitched.

"Barbara, tell Jordan about the party your friends went to last Friday," Karla said.

Barbara looked like she knew a secret and was dying to tell it.

"A girlfriend of mine went to a party last Friday," she started. "She didn't know whose house this was, but she said that it was held at a bomb downtown loft. A lawyer she knows named Steven Cox, a cute guy but a little too smooth if you know what I mean, invited her. It was supposed to be a housewarming party for this guy who I think worked at his firm. I think his name was Jason something. Anyway, she went there with two girlfriends."

"Now other than that your friend went downtown, and God knows why anyone lives downtown, I don't understand why this party was extraordinary," Jordan interrupted.

"I'm getting to that," Barbara said.

"So my friend at the party with her two girlfriends and Steven comes up to them and asks if they want to party with some guy worth four million dollars," Barbara said. "She's like, who's that, and he points to some ordinary guy standing by the bar. He goes, 'That's Jason something, Robertson, Richardson, or something like that. He just got four million dollars and he's looking for a woman to spend it on. But you've got to want to party after this party.'"

"Okay, so he propositioned your friend. What does that have to do with *Baldwin Hills* magazine?" Jordan asked.

"To make a long story short, my friend and her two girlfriends did take Steven up on the offer, and they had what they described as an orgy."

"That's freaky, but what does that have to do with us?"

"After the party, one of my friends talked to Steven again and he said that he had about ten friends who were throwing parties like this. Rich black men in L.A. were throwing what they called '*Titan* parties,' you know, after *Titan,* the men's magazine, where they looked for the prettiest black women and then held orgies afterward. It's the new trend, and I think there's a story there."

"So what if we do a full profile on the best private parties in Los Angeles, and then do a special exposé on black men throwing these sex parties," Jordan said. "Can you get in contact with Steven again?"

"My girlfriend can find him and probably reenact what happened at the party."

Jordan stood up and looked at her writers. She had a theme and an interesting topic. Add the element of sex, and this was going to be her signature issue. Marcia would be thrilled with sex and the rich.

"Okay, the theme of this issue will be 'L.A. house parties.' I want everyone to come up with a list of the best house parties in the city. Fan out—don't just concentrate on Ladera and Baldwin Hills. I want the downtown scene, Hollywood, and the Westside covered. There are plenty of people doing a lot of things, and we need to be there. But don't go there as a writer, go there as a guest. If the people know you're a writer, then they'll clam up. Get the scoop on everyone hosting the parties and the people attending."

Jordan was on a roll now. The staff looked like they had some confidence in her, and it wasn't about to be "substitute teacher" time at *Baldwin Hills* magazine.

"So let's get started," Jordan said. Everyone began to leave the office. "Barbara, you stay."

Barbara stopped by the door and let the others out. When everyone had left, she closed the door.

"Is this really true that these brothers are holding these parties?" Jordan asked.

"Jordan, my girlfriends said the after-party was scandalous!"

"Then I want you to find out all you can. Go to the parties and find out what these *Titan* parties are all about. See if you can combine this as an investigative piece and a social piece."

"Ooh, this should be juicy."

"Would your girlfriends be willing to talk about their experience?"

"Not unless we concealed their identity."

"I'm willing to change their names. Get their stories down and check out the four-million-dollar guy. See what he and Steven Cox are all about and how they get these parties going."

"Beautiful! I'll get started today."

"And take a cell phone camera. I want juicy photos, but I want them undercover. I don't even care if they're blurry. We can do some stylistic things with them to illustrate what's going on at these parties."

"Gotcha."

Barbara left and Jordan knew she had a winner on her hands. It might deviate from the subjects *Baldwin Hills* magazine normally covered, but Marcia would see an issue that broke all sales records for the magazine.

CHAPTER 17

"So you're really thinking about leaving Ketchings and moving to a nonprofit?" Carole asked. "What brought that on?"

It was Wednesday and Jason and Carole were having lunch at El Cholo's again. This lunch was part of his "friends with benefits" plan to get Carole into bed and it seemed to be working swimmingly. She remembered all of the things *Titan* said she'd remember about his comments last week.

"I'm feeling fulfilled at Mama's House," he said coyly. "Now I didn't say I wanted to invade your space at Mama's House, but I am interested in finding a nonprofit that gives me that same feeling of 'I helped someone' at the end of the day. I thought about what you said a while back and I guess we lawyers can be just after money, but we can change that if we try. And I'm going to try."

"Now that's what I'm talking about!" Carole said excitedly. "You can be an attorney and do good for the public at the same time."

"I'm beginning to see that," he said. "But what about you? What's going on with you? Did you take my advice? Are you seeing anyone?"

Carole fingered her glass seductively. Jason could tell that his game was working because Carole did one of the things women do when they want to communicate that they dig you. They play with things. Sometimes it's their hair. Sometimes it's their shirt collar.

For Carole, it was her water glass. Each was supposed to say, *I am here if you want me.* And boy, did Jason want her.

"I was going to talk to this one guy who works at the City of Inglewood, but he's boring," Carole said, simulating a yawn. "I'm starting to think that the pickings are slim out there. There are plenty of men in Los Angeles, but not a lot of the right men. I need somebody like you, Jason, someone who is deeper than the car they drive or the job they hold."

"Hey, you dumped me, remember?" Jason said.

"But I was young and impressionable!" Carole said, and laughed.

Here's where Jason played the *Titan* plan to the max. He took his time, looking at Carole as if he was sizing her up.

"No, we wouldn't work," he said finally. "We're friends and friends only mess things up when they get together."

Carole looked a little crestfallen when he said that. But that was how she was supposed to react. Perfect. Jason's cell phone rang at that moment.

"Hello," Jason said, not recognizing the phone number.

"What's up, man, it's Steven."

"Oh, what's up, Steven."

When Carole heard Steven's name, her face immediately turned sour. It surprised him, because he didn't know she disliked Steven that much, but her look told him she did.

"Hey, I'm in the middle of lunch. . . ."

"Cool, do you want to throw another party at your loft?" Steven asked.

"Uh no, not right now, but why don't you do it at your place?"

"I'm getting some static from the loft board about the number of parties I've been having," Steven said. "So your place would have to be it."

"When would you like to do it?" Jason asked, trying to keep the conversation as vague as possible so Carole wouldn't know what they were talking about.

"This Saturday," he said. "I've got some women who'd like to party just like last weekend, if you know what I mean."

"Okay, I'll think about it. I'll get back to you later."

"Great. Get back to me no later than Wednesday. I can contact

people by then. You don't have to worry about the bar and cater-
ing. I'll handle that since you're having it at your loft."

"Cool. I'll talk to you later."

"Later," Steven said.

Jason hung up the phone and turned back to Carole.

"I'm sorry about that."

"No problem."

"No," he said, taking a sip of soda, "I hate when people interrupt my conversation to talk on a cell phone. It's so damn rude.
But back to what we were saying. I would hate to lose a friend like
you and maybe if we dated, that would happen."

"Yeah, maybe you're right," she said. "Well, if you have somebody just like you, let me know because I'd love to meet them."

"You flatter me!" he said, feigning embarrassment.

"You deserve it," Carole said, smiling sweetly. "Okay, I've laid my
life bare for you, but you haven't told me anything about your love
life. Who are you seeing?"

This kind of threw Jason, because *Titan* hadn't said anything
about the woman probing the man. But he decided to wing it.

"Oh, I date from time to time," Jason said, trying not to sound
like a complete loser, "but I haven't found anyone that is completely right. Since I work so much at the law firm, it's always been
an issue with any potential girlfriends. Things get too complicated
before they're supposed to get complicated."

"Uh, I think I know what you mean," Carole said ironically.

They both laughed.

As Jason continued with the conversation, he was happy that his
scheme was working, on the one hand, but on the other hand, he
was wondering if he even needed a scheme to get Carole. She
seemed pretty receptive to his non-advance advances, and she was
becoming a cool person the more he talked to her. Jason was getting confused as to whether Carole was cool because of the advice
from *Titan* or if she just truly liked his conversation. Either way,
things are going well.

"I've got a fund-raising meeting to go to," Carole said as she got
up to leave. "Our main funding source, the Crenshaw Foundation, is
reviewing our work. They've threatened to pull our funding in the
past, but we've been able to stave them off for the past three years."

"How much do they give each year?" he asked while picking up the check.

"Two million dollars."

"Yikes," Jason exclaimed. He didn't know that Mama's House required that kind of funding.

"Good luck," he said as they parted.

"Thanks, and I'll see you on Friday," she said. "You do remember that we have a pizza date, right?"

"I'm looking forward to it," Jason said, smiling.

On her way to the Crenshaw Foundation, Carole smiled to herself. Jason was falling right into her trap, just like *Divas* magazine had said. He was opening up about his likes in a girlfriend, although he had thrown her for a loop when he said they wouldn't work together as a couple.

Jason doesn't know what's going to hit him on Friday, she thought, smiling to herself.

But why in the hell was he friendly with Steven, of all people? They seemed like an odd couple, because Steven didn't have a redeeming bone in his body. Maybe it was something from work, but she would have to watch that.

She pulled into the parking lot of the Crenshaw Foundation, parked her car, and took a deep breath. This was not going to be fun.

The Crenshaw Foundation was named after Barbara Crenshaw, a white socialite who had made her money the old-fashioned way: she'd inherited it. George Crenshaw had been one of the first developers in Los Angeles and the San Fernando Valley and he'd made a mint as an investor in a little area of Los Angeles called Beverly Hills. Feeling guilty that he earned more money in one day than most people would make in a couple of lifetimes, he took some of that money and decided to become a philanthropist. Nearly one hundred years later, the money was still doing good deeds. But the money always came with strings, and today, those strings were being pulled.

Every year, Carole had to run the gauntlet of the Crenshaw Foundation, as they only provided a one-year contract for funding to Mama's House. Each year she had to meet with the board of directors and provide a status report on the direction of Mama's House, and where she saw Mama's House going in the future. It was no small leap to say that Carole's job was on the line each year because Mama's House would do anything to keep the Crenshaw Foundation money, and if that meant firing Carole, then so be it.

"Be cheerful, but forceful," she mumbled to herself as she checked her makeup in her rearview mirror.

Talk about how Mama's House is trying to diversify the people it serves, she thought, trying to think of every angle the board would ask.

"Carole Brantford for James Anderson of the Crenshaw Foundation," Carole told the receptionist.

"He'll be right with you. Please have a seat," she said to Carole.

Carole sat down and looked around the office. Sitting in a reception area had always been nerve-wracking to Carole. She always dreaded the initial meet and greet because she had this feeling that she was going to stand up and trip over her feet, embarrassing her to no end. It may have been an irrational thought, but it was in her head nonetheless.

The worst thing about this visit, Carole thought, was the fact that the Crenshaw Foundation wouldn't reveal its decision for two weeks after this meeting.

No, she thought, I'm mistaken. The worst thing is when they send in people to evaluate us in secret. I hate that.

"Carole, great to see you," said James Anderson, as he came bounding into the reception area.

"Great to see you, too, Mr. Anderson," Carole said, successfully not falling over herself.

James Anderson was a nice enough older gentleman and he did his best to make Carole's visits as painless as possible. He was on her side, but he was only one member of the board.

"Each year you come in, as charming as ever, and each year I have to tell you to call me James," he said, smiling. "Now either call me James or I'm rejecting your funding!"

He laughed, and Carole half laughed. She knew he was joking, but this visit was not about jokes, and certainly not about joking about the future of Mama's House.

They walked to the boardroom, where there were about twelve chairs around a large boardroom table. No one was there yet, but the water and water glasses were already prepped for the drilling.

"Would you like anything?" James said, sitting her at the front of the table. "The rest of the board will be in here in a few minutes."

"No, I'm fine, thank you."

"Great, I'll be back in a minute."

And like that, there was no one in the room. They did this every year, leaving her alone, and Carole wondered if they did it on purpose. It was like icing a kicker before a field goal. Maybe she'd choke if she had enough time to think about it.

Not this sister, Carole thought. This sister doesn't shake. This sister doesn't break.

After about five minutes, the board members all filed into the room and sat down.

"Hello," they said in unison.

"Hello," Carole responded. She looked around the room and saw familiar faces, except for one face. It was a young woman that looked utterly too young to be in the room. She was the unknown and Carole hated the unknown.

"Ladies and gentlemen, as you all know, this is Carole Brantford, the executive director of Mama's House. She's here to reapply for funding, and this is your opportunity to ask her any and all questions," James Anderson said.

And just like that, the meeting was on. The questions came rapid-fire. Carole barely had time to look at the statistics she'd brought in her notes.

"How many women did you serve this year?"

"To date, we have served four hundred and fifty women. That is more than twenty percent more than last year."

"Who are you serving? I mean, what is the demographic?"

"Currently we are serving forty percent Latina, thirty percent African American, fifteen percent Asian, with our outreach effort in the Vietnamese community really showing its effects, and the remaining fifteen percent are white. As you can see, we show a plurality throughout our demographics."

"Did you come in under budget this year?"

"This year, just like the past four years. We at Mama's House believe that we must be fiscally conservative with our spending, so we've implemented a program that requires anyone who receives our help to dedicate at least twenty volunteer hours to Mama's House. We created this requirement last year because we want the single mothers we work with to view Mama's House as not only a place to receive assistance, but also as a place to invest their knowledge for the benefit of other women in need."

"But how do you make sure they are giving good advice?"

Carole was on a roll. These questions weren't going to faze her. She was Carole Brantford!

"We've created a training program for the women," Carole said, speaking quickly. "And also, the women are able to volunteer in a myriad of ways. They can help paint the center, clean up, or help make lunches for our baby's mama lunches. It is really satisfying for them to see that they are not victims, but empowered people."

Everything was going swimmingly, until the very young woman Carole had never met asked a question.

"Are the single mothers at Mama's House getting advice that is consistent with a Christian philosophy and a Christian ethic?" she asked.

Carole paused. This was a question loaded with dynamite because officially Mama's House was nondenominational. But if this woman wanted Mama's House to give out Christian advice, then Carole needed to tread lightly.

"Carole," James said, "please let me introduce you to Amy Crenshaw. She is the great-granddaughter of Barbara Crenshaw and has joined us on the board of directors. Ms. Crenshaw is a student at the University of Southern California Divinity School and is very interested in the spiritual aspect of the charities we fund."

"Very nice to meet you, Ms. Crenshaw," Carole said, nodding nervously in Amy's direction. Amy smiled faintly.

"So with that in mind, you can go ahead and answer her question," Anderson said.

"I would love to," Carole said, still trying to formulate an answer that would satisfy this future minister.

"Ms. Crenshaw, we have a secular mission at Mama's House because of the differing religions our program participants bring to Mama's House. But we do forward our participants to spiritual advisers if they do ask for it."

"But for the most part, your program is devoid of any spiritual basis, and it just gives practical advice?" Amy asked.

Carole didn't like where this was going. The Crenshaw Foundation had never asked these types of questions before.

"Technically no, because we don't want to alienate those participants that aren't Christian," she said.

"But aren't the majority of your participants Christian anyway?"

"I would assume so, but we don't know because we don't keep track of their religion."

Amy was scribbling on a yellow pad furiously, and that was freaking Carole out.

"Perhaps you should," she said. "That's all for now."

All of the other questions the board members asked were normal questions, and soon the grilling was over.

"We'd like to thank Carole for coming in today, and the board will be making their decision in the coming weeks," James said.

After the handshakes, Carole walked to her car, uncertain about the exchange with Amy. Had it been enough to convince her to vote for funding, or did she have her own agenda? Amy made her nervous, not only because of those questions, but also because she was so young.

What did she know about social work? Carole thought. And why, as a divinity student, shouldn't she have tolerance for other religions? Didn't they teach that in divinity school?

As Carole drove away from the Crenshaw Foundation, she felt uncertain about her future.

CHAPTER 18

It was Friday, and strangely, Jason missed his beef Stroganoff. It had been about six weeks since he'd had it, and it was hard to simply go cold turkey after having had the same dish for two years. But more than that, he missed Mrs. Petroff.

I'm going to have to stop by, he thought while showering.

But that was in the future. Tonight, Jason had his "date" with Carole and he was looking to complete the final phase of the "friends with benefits" plan.

Dress casually, he said to himself as he picked up his clothes, but with a little bit of sex appeal. The look he wanted was that he seemed not to have put much thought into his clothing, but really had. So he took a pair of his most expensive Sean John jeans and white silk shirt and he was set. Oh, and a pair of Sketchers slippers, just in case he needed to get out of the shoes really fast.

Jason's cell phone rang just as he was leaving to go to Carole's.

"What's up, man? Do you have the place ready?" Steven asked.

Steven again. Steven was starting to get on Jason's nerves. He kept calling about whether he had his place ready. For the umpteenth time, yes, he had my damn place ready.

"Yeah, man, it's ready."

"Cool! Hey, I've got these women who you are going to—"

"That's great," Jason interrupted. "But I'm on my way out the door. I'll talk to you tomorrow."

"Cool, I'll see you tomorrow," he said. "Hey!"

"What?"

"If you think last week was something, wait until tomorrow."

"I can't wait."

Jason didn't mind having parties at his loft, but prepping for back-to-back parties was pretty taxing. *Titan* said that parties were essential to living the lifestyle, so it had to be done, but he'd just gotten over having a quintetsome so he didn't know if he had the energy to do another one.

That's a lot of sex, and different sex at that, he thought. I don't know. . . .

And there was another thing. He had to admit that he had thoroughly enjoyed the orgy, but afterward he felt strange, sort of like those awkward moments with the women in the morning. He was attracted to the excitement of having phenomenal sex, but the aftermath kind of made him feel cheap. And the more he thought about it, the more he felt uncomfortable. But he was conflicted because he still wanted that sexual excitement. It was addictive.

Jason hung up the phone and ran down to his Hayabusa. Friends with benefits was about to be completed, he thought.

Carole ordered two Round Table pizzas for the night, none with garlic just in case, and got a twelve-pack of beer. *Divas* said that in order to turn a friend into a lover, you have to be honest, but you have to do it systematically. So the come-on had to be so subtle that Jason wouldn't even know it was happening.

Men are so simple anyway, Carole thought, smiling to herself. He'll never figure it out anyway.

She'd decided to wear a sexy but casual outfit that showed off her body, but didn't appear that she was spending a lot of time trying to look good for him. Her pièce de résistance was her perfume. She sprayed a little bit of J-Lo's new perfume just around the crook of her neck. If things we going well, then her neck was going to be a weapon she'd use later in the evening.

Although Carole was scheming to get Jason, she did feel good about herself in one way. Ever since she'd broken up with Sean, or more accurately ever since Sean had broken up with her, she'd been celibate. And yes, she did miss the sex because she loved sex like any other woman, but her mind had gotten clear during this time. She felt less panicky about having just any old boyfriend, but was more confident that she did know what she wanted in a man. It just turned out that the person who had all of those attributes was Jason.

The doorbell rang. Carole did a quick check of her makeup and opened the door.

"Jason!" Is that Sean John he's wearing? she thought.

She said his name with such sunshine that it brought a smile to his face.

"Carole!" Carole was looking absolutely phenomenal, he thought.

They hugged and Jason walked into Carole's apartment.

"Make yourself right at home," she said as she went to the kitchen. "I'll get the beer, and the pizza should be here at any minute."

"Great," Jason said.

He'd never been there before, and he took a quick glance around. As he looked around the apartment, his first instinct said, *Typical girl's apartment.*

Carole had the ubiquitous pictures of her friends and family, along with photos of her sorority sisters. There were elephants on the bookshelves along with other knickknacks. There was one particular photo that caught Jason's eye. In the photo, Carole was completely covered in mud.

"Uh, Carole," Jason yelled to Carole. She was still in the kitchen. "Yes?"

"Do you always get covered in mud?"

Carole walked out of the kitchen with two cold beers.

"Only if you're lucky!" she laughed.

Jason smiled. Carole picked up the picture and took a good look at it.

"Our sorority held a charity mud football game and this is what I looked like after the event," she said while laughing. "It took me three days to get all that mud out of my hair!"

The door buzzed and Carole ran to it. She looked through the peephole and turned back to Jason.

"It's the pizza guy."

She opened the door and the pizza guy had the two pizzas in his hands.

"You ordered two pizzas?" the pizza guy asked.

"Yes, how much?"

"It'll be $25.29."

Carole turned back to Jason.

"Jason, could you please hand me my purse. It's over there by the chair."

Jason walked to the door and pulled out his wallet.

"No need, I've got this," Jason said.

Jason pulled out a hundred-dollar bill and paid the pizza guy.

"Keep the change," he said.

"Thanks!"

As Carole closed the door, she thought that either Jason was trying mighty hard to impress her by paying for the pizza and giving the guy a big tip, or it's what he always did. She suspected that it was what he always did because he didn't act like it was anything out of the ordinary.

"Now we can do this with or without plates," she said.

"Shoot, I'm not worried about plates, just like I don't need a glass to drink my beer," he responded.

"My type of man!" Carole exclaimed. "Let's eat!"

Carole and Jason sat down on the couch and started eating the pizza. Even though Carole kept her figure tight, she was not shy about eating. She liked to eat and she liked men who liked women who ate. Partially it was about not falling into the whole women and eating disorder trap, but the other reason was because she liked food.

"So I didn't see you much this week, you know, after we had lunch. How did the meeting with the foundation go?" Jason asked.

"You mean the Crenshaw Foundation?"

"Yeah, that one. You getting the money?"

"Well, we find out in about a week, but I'm not feeling too confident about it," she said, munching on a slice.

"Why do you say that?"

"Well"—Carole took a sip of beer—"there's a wild card in the mix that I hadn't prepared for. There was a new member on the board, a young Crenshaw I'd never met."

The beers were empty and Carole got up to get another.

"Want another?" she asked.

"Are you trying to get me drunk?" Jason asked.

"If you can get drunk after only one beer, then you're too light-weight to hang with me!" Carole said, and laughed.

"Then bring me two!"

Carole went into the kitchen to get the beer. Now was the time to set the trap, thought Jason.

"I'm going to use your restroom if you don't mind. Where is it?"

"Just go down the hall, it's to your right."

"Thanks!"

Jason got to the bathroom and thought that this was the time to really start working the scheme.

Carole was in a good mood and she had to be impressed by the way he handled the pizza situation, he thought, while looking at himself in the mirror. Big tips impress women, even if it is for plain old pizza. And now, the dog, cleverly disguised as a gentleman, was going to come out. The friends with benefits trap was ready to be sprung.

"Thanks for the beer," he said as he walked back into the living room. "So who is this new Crenshaw?"

"She's different," Carole said as she ate another slice of pizza. Jason liked a sister who ate heartily. He hated going on dates where he'd spend mad loot on dinner, and then the girl picked at the food or ordered some stupid salad.

"Okay, here's the deal," Carole said, sitting cross-legged across from Jason.

"I'm rattling off stats as fast as they can throw questions at me. I'm feeling good; I mean, I'm feeling like our funding is in the bag. I know all of these people in the room, old ladies and gentle-men, because I've pitched Mama's House in front of them many times before. I know what they are looking for in a presentation and I'm giving it to them in spades. And then, here comes Miss Amy Crenshaw, great-granddaughter of Barbara Crenshaw, the moneybags of the whole Crenshaw dynasty and key to my future. She throws me for a loop."

"What? Was she hostile to Mama's House?"

"She wasn't exactly hostile, but she kept asking me questions about whether or not we gave advice under a Christian philosophy and Christian ethic. I was thinking, what the hell does that mean? But then the board president, James Anderson, a cat I really like, explained that she is a divinity student. I was like, 'Oh shit.' Jason, she's about ten years old and making decisions about my life and my community center."

"What is the official policy of Mama's House toward religion?" Jason asked, taking a swig of beer. "I mean, I've never heard anyone even mention religion while I've been there."

"And you won't," she said. "One thing I didn't want was a bunch of people trying to convert people, whether they were Christian, Muslim, or anything else. I had to fire a woman once because she kept giving our single mothers literature on the Jehovah's Witnesses. Now I don't have anything against the Witnesses, but if I allow her to do it, then I have to allow everyone to do it. And I'm not going to do it."

"Did she demand that you preach Christianity to everyone who uses Mama's House?"

"No, she didn't, but . . ." she said, hesitating.

"But what?"

"But I get the feeling that if I don't have some type of religious component, then approval for my funding may get dicey."

"Well, don't worry," Jason said, taking a bite. "God will provide for you!"

Carole laughed. "Well, he better provide for it through the Crenshaw Foundation, or I'm going to be on the unemployment line!"

Carole put down her beer.

Jason decided it was the time to spring the trap. He needed to start "caring."

"Ah, enough about work!" he said, getting up to get her another beer. "One thing has been bothering me."

"What is that?"

"I realized that when I was telling you about what you should do in your next relationship," he said, as he brought the beers back, "I never asked what you look for in a man. So, what do you look for in a man?"

Carole thought for a second.

"I think it would be easy to say I like tall, dark and handsome, but that's too easy. It's more complicated than that. I like comfortability. Is that a word, comfortability?" she laughed.

"It is now," Jason laughed, sipping on his beer. "But I can look at my couch and think, comfortability. What does that really mean with a man?"

"Okay," she said, getting on the couch. "Here's my explanation. If I can take off my makeup in front of you and you don't trip, then that's comfortability. If I can pick my teeth, and this is not to say I'm uncouth or I'm about to do that, but I'm just saying if I can, then that's comfortability."

"How does a brother give you this feeling of comfortability? Isn't that something innate?"

"Yeah, sort of," she responded. "But women can sniff it out. Maybe it's through our female intuition, but we can find it. Men who have comfortability are genuine and aren't trying to run some sort of game on you. They just come to you as they are. See, I look at you, and not saying that we would get together, but I see you and think comfortability. You are nice, genuine, and wouldn't run a game on a girl. I could trust you and I think that the woman would be lucky to have you."

She smiled at Jason so sweetly that he actually felt bad for a second that he *was* running a game on her. But he'd chosen this *Titan* life and he was determined to see if everything they said actually worked.

"Enough about me. We've had tons of conversations about who and what I want. What are you looking for?" she asked. Carole leaned back on the couch. This was her third beer and Jason thought she was feeling a beer buzz because he'd never seen her this loose. It was not like she was doing anything wrong, but she was just really casual.

What I'm looking to do is make love to you, is what Jason wanted to say. But he didn't think that would go over too well.

"I think we have the same type of needs," he said. Subtle, Jason, go subtle, he thought.

"What were your last girlfriends like?"

"What are all exes like? When they are exes, they instantly become heinous people who never deserved you in the first place," Jason said, sort of serious.

"High five on that, Jason," Carole said, throwing her hand up.

"Nah, seriously, they were okay," he continued, "except for the last one. She cheated on me."

"She was a doctor, right," Carole said, remembering. "Marcia told me about her."

"Yep, and she was doing a guy from her hospital."

"What happened?"

"One of my frat brothers is a doctor at King Hospital in Compton."

"Killer King?" Carole said.

"You know its reputation, I see," he said, smiling. "I hadn't seen him in years, and actually lost touch. Well, my girlfriend and he were casual friends and she never told him she had a boyfriend. One evening, he's in an empty hospital room doing her from the back and the next evening my frat and I accidentally run into each other at Jones Café on Santa Monica. We're talking like frat brothers talk, and he mentions that he's over at King and just did this fine new intern."

"Your girlfriend?" Carole asked.

"Exactamundo. It was an awkward moment, to say the least."

Carole's face was all scrunched up in sympathy. She sat her beer down and slid down to the floor where Jason was sitting.

"Oh, you poor dear," she said, giving him a hug.

Oh my goodness, Jason thought. Carole hugging him was delicious. He thought he'd be cool, but he hadn't been this close to her in nearly six years. Everything about her was wonderful. But most of all, she smelled so damn good. She was wearing a perfume on her neck that made it absolutely irresistible.

Jason knew that according to the friends with benefits plan, he was supposed to spring the whole concept on her by passing up opportunities like this, but he couldn't resist the moment. She was just too beautiful.

Carole pulled back from the hug and her face was inches from Jason's. He was so damn nervous when he thought he'd be so much smoother, so much more suave. But Jason took his right hand and caressed her face and kissed her. Her lips melted like soft snow and Jason felt his brain go completely blank. Her head leaned back gently and she closed her eyes. This was a beautiful moment.

But then the article from *Titan* popped back in his brain and he pulled back. According to the article, he had to leave her wanting more, and wanting him on his terms.

"What? What's wrong?" Carole said, exasperated, as Jason pulled back.

"I can't do this because we're friends, and if we do this, then we probably won't end up friends."

"What do you mean? I think we can still be friends if we give it a try."

Jason stood up and tried to gain his composure because he sure didn't want to blow this plan. Because without following the *Titan* plan, he surely loved Carole's lips. But *Titan* said that he had to leave, and leave was what he was going to do. *Titan* hadn't let him down so far, so he was going to keep following its directions.

"Look, let's give ourselves a little time to think about this," Jason said, moving to the door.

Carole seemed desperate for him to stay.

"I think I really need to think about this. I tend to overthink things and that's what's been wrong in the past. I know what I want," Carole said, walking to the door.

"See, that's the thing. I think I want you and you think you want me, but we need to be sure. We both need to know. Maybe we should approach this differently than we've done other relationships?"

Carole looked perplexed.

"What do you mean?"

"I don't know yet, but let me think about it."

Carole looked resigned to let him go.

"Okay, but call me," she said. She then reached up and gave him the best kiss he'd ever been given. Just like Halle Berry and her men troubles, Jason began to wonder why in the world had those other men left Carole when she could kiss like that?

"I will, as soon as I can," Jason said mysteriously.

And like that, he was back on his bike. Little did she know how fast Jason was going to call.

CHAPTER 19

Carole leaned against the door as Jason left. *Divas*'s friends-to-lover plan had worked like a charm throughout the evening, but she didn't understand why Jason had left. Most men would have done anything to stay with her for the night, but Jason acted differently.

I guess that's why I like this man, she thought. He's actually a caring and thinking man, rather than those other losers I've met.

Carole sat on the couch trying to take everything in, when she suddenly had the urge to tell Marcia about her new Jason situation. She knew she was relaxing on some beach in Rio, but maybe her phone was still on.

Carole ran to get her phone.

"Who is this, and it better be good!" Marcia answered. "Hold on!"

Carole could hear Marcia talking in the background. "Yes baby, more baby oil on my back and have one of your friends get me another caipirinha. They taste so good and I just spilled my last one!"

Marcia got back on the phone. "So who is this?"

"How are you liking Rio, girl? And what is a caipirinha?"

"Carole? Girl, you should have come down here with me! The men are all around and they are fine, girl! I'm sitting on the beach now with a man whose only job is to rub my back. It is so beautiful here. By the way, a caipirinha is a drink that puts you on your ass. You can still come, you know, there's plenty of time and plenty of men!"

"No, I think I have found a man right here in Los Angeles."

"Who did you meet?"

"Jason."

There was a slight pause.

"Jason? What the hell are you talking about?"

"Yes, Jason. He just left my apartment."

"Did you break your vow of—"

"No, I'm still celibate, but it is getting harder and harder. Then I saw this article in *Divas* that said you could make a friend your lover if you followed their advice, then—"

"Wait, tell me when I get back. This cell phone bill is going to kill me. Okay, remember my advice. Take it easy and how it comes. Jason is a really sweet guy and I know he wouldn't do anything to hurt you. Don't crowd him, Carole."

"I'm not. He's so sweet. He wanted to think about whether he wanted to risk our friendship before getting involved."

"That sounds just like Jason."

"And he's a great kisser, Marcia," Carole said.

"We'll go over that when I get back. Just take it slow and go with your gut."

"Will do."

"Okay, let me go. Carioca, my Brazilian masseuse, is about to rub my body with oil. It's very good to be a woman in Brazil!"

"Have fun, girl, and use protection."

"I will and have!" Marcia laughed with her trademark gusto.

Carole got off the phone and sat on her couch, doing nothing but letting the evening sink in. The more she thought about Jason, the more she really wanted him. Just like the article had said, the best person for you is a person who is already a friend. And there was just enough mystery about Jason that Carole didn't feel like she knew everything about him.

I wouldn't mind just sitting down and talking to him. Just talking to him and learning about who and what he wants out of life, she thought.

But what Carole really wanted was for Jason to have never left in the first place. She was horny and it took all her energy to not beg him to stay. She didn't think she would feel like that before he came over, but she did now. But he was gone.

"Well, there's always Mr. Chocolate," she said as she made her way to the bedroom.

Jason left Carole just like he was supposed to leave her: with her wanting him with every fiber in her lithe little body. Now was the time to spring the coup de grâce. He rode all the way home, waited about fifteen minutes, and then decided to call her. If this worked, then he knew this would seal the deal.

"Hello," she answered. She sounded sexy as ever.

"Hey, it's Jason."

"I knew it would be you," she cooed.

"What are you doing?"

"Nothing. What are you doing?"

"Nothing."

"Hey, I've been thinking," Jason said coyly.

"What have you been thinking?"

"I want to come back over. Now."

"I thought you needed time to think about it."

"I've thought about it."

"Then get here. Now!"

Snap! The trap had been set, and activated.

And just like that, Jason dropped his phone, kissed his issue of *Titan* and ran down to his Hayabusa.

"I'm going to have sex with Carole! I'm going to have sex with Carole!" he sang to himself as he started up his bike.

Everything in his life had changed, and changed so fast. He was going to have sex with a beautiful woman who had been simply unobtainable only a month before. For these past four weeks, life had been incredible—cash, parties and everything else. But he never would have envisioned that he was going to have sex with Carole!

The streets were a blur as Jason drove as fast as he could to Carole's house. The only thing he wanted to avoid was a ticket. He didn't want anything messing this up. When Jason parked, he didn't even think about locking the Hayabusa. He didn't care.

Jason ran up the stairs and knocked on Carole's door, all while trying to catch his breath, when Carole opened it.

Oh my God! I am the luckiest man in the fucking world!!! he thought.

The lights were off in the apartment and Carole opened the door dressed in the sexiest lingerie Jason had ever seen. She had on a black bra and black panties and nothing else. Her abs were ripped, like Janet Jackson in shape.

Without a word being said, she jumped into Jason's arms, with her legs gripped tightly around his waist.

Jason was hungry for Carole. This was a second chance to make love to her, and it was a chance he never thought he'd get. For Carole, it was a chance at love with a friend, someone she could trust. She wanted Jason. She needed Jason.

They couldn't take off their clothes fast enough as they kissed each other passionately. Stumbling into the bedroom, Jason took off his shirt and Carole seemed surprised by how fit he was.

Thank you, Anderson Recaro, Jason thought as he tried to flex his abs.

Jason had never wanted to have sex more than this moment, but he knew he'd have to follow the dictates of the friends with benefits rules. And he had to do it now, or he'd be on the boyfriend/girlfriend track rather than the *Titan* lifestyle track.

Jason was on top of Carole, their bodies writhing together in perfect rhythm. With dexterous hands, Jason took off Carole's bra and then her panties. He kissed her in the crook of her neck, where he felt drawn for some reason.

"Oooh, oooh, psssst," Carole cooed breathlessly. "That feels so good."

He started kissing her down her chest, and was about to kiss her breasts when he suddenly stopped. They were both breathless, but Jason needed to go over the rules. He hovered over her, looking at her beautiful face.

"Why are you stopping?" Carole said, panic in her voice. She wanted Jason and wanted him now.

"Before we do this, I think we have to establish a few rules."

"A few what?" Carole said breathlessly. "Why? What rules?"

"I thought about this and I want to protect our friendship. So I came up with some rules. Let's go over the rules."

"What rules? Oh, okay!" Panting, she went to the nightstand and pulled out a condom.

"Safe sex, right?"

She put the condom in Jason's hand, and laid back on the bed.

"Yes, safe sex. But those aren't the rules."

"Okay, okay, what are they?"

Jason took a deep breath.

"No sleeping over after sex. We're friends and if we start trying to be boyfriend and girlfriend right off the bat, that might ruin the friendship. Let's take it slow."

"Fine," she said. "I won't be clingy." She started rubbing her nails lightly against his chest. It made it difficult for Jason to concentrate.

"And because if we were to sleep over, that would mean that we have feelings for one another and that there could possibly be love. We don't know that yet. For right now, this is all about sexual lust. I mean, we may develop love for one another, but right now we have to say we are in lust. It's too early for us to say that we are in love."

"Okay, okay, okay!" Carole said, exasperated. "You thought of all this stuff? What else?"

"And lastly, no talking about this to others. This is our agreement. This is just about us. We don't need others to get into our relationship."

"Is that it?"

"Yes, do you think you can handle it?"

"I can handle anything!"

With that, she clicked off the light by throwing a shoe at the switch.

"Now make love to me, you fool," she whispered. Jason smiled and kissed her deeply. Jason took the condom and was about to open it when Carole stopped him.

"Do you want me to put it on?" asked Carole.

"Sure, why not?"

Carole took the condom out of the package and put it in her mouth. What was this with women putting the condom in their mouths? Jason thought. First Vanessa and now Carole. Had there been a secret class on this? She placed her hand on his dick and then said something that made Jason feel proud.

"Oh my God, Jason! You've been hiding this all of this time?" she said, with a little bit of nervousness in her voice. "This is a handful."

If you wanted to stroke Jason's ego, you couldn't have done better than what Carole had just said.

"I'm glad you like it," Jason said proudly.

Carole put her beautiful mouth on Jason's dick and expertly slipped on the condom with her tongue and mouth. It was the sexiest act of safe sex he'd ever seen or felt. She was even better at it than Vanessa.

Jason got back on top of Carole, ready to enter her, when she stopped him.

"It's been a while since I've had sex, so be gentle with me," she said, with her beautiful eyes staring up at him.

"Don't worry, I'll be gentle."

He gently brushed her hair off her cheeks with his hand and entered her. The feeling was beautiful, simply beautiful, as though he should have been there years ago. All of a sudden, pent-up emotions rushed through Jason's body and he realized that he'd been waiting for this moment since college.

He started off slowly, moving his pelvis in concentric circles while kissing Carole on the cheeks, neck and right behind her ear.

"Ahhhhh," Carole moaned as he stroked her slowly.

There was no music. There was no dirty talk. There was no rush. There were just the squeaks of Carole's bed and their comingled moans. They were creating their own sensuous music as they moved in unison. Jason was exploring, probing, as he moved in and out of Carole. When you have a natural rhythm with someone during sex, all you try to do is let your mind go blank and go with it.

"Yes, that feels sooo good," Carole whispered. "Yes, just to the left, okay, straight now. . . ."

This felt so good to Jason that he was breathless. But for some reason, he also remembered what Marcia had said over a month before at G. Garvin's. Marcia had said that Carole complained that too many men had come too soon because of how good her pussy felt. He now knew what those other guys felt and yes, her pussy felt great! He could feel that this was not going to be some hourlong session, because it felt too good.

Plus, no man is a stallion the first time he has sex with a woman, he thought. Right? Right?

"Remember, this is the first time, so I get a do-over," he whispered to Carole.

"This is what . . . shut up and keep going," she growled.

Uh-oh, I had better not come early, he thought. Carole wasn't feeling that at all.

"Oh my . . ." Jason had to really bite his lip to keep control.

"Don't you *dare* come yet!" Carole said, with the exasperation of a person who was used to men coming early.

"Don't move!" Jason said, and when he said don't move, he meant *don't move! Not an inch.* Any movement was going to be a catastrophe for his ego. They were frozen.

"Concrete, Ronald Reagan, television, green grass . . . ," he began muttering to himself.

"What the hell are you doing?" Carole asked. She looked at him as though he'd gone crazy.

"I'm trying to get my mind off how good this feels," Jason said, genuinely trying to take his mind off of his dick and put it on something, anything else. "It's a trick I use."

"It'll feel even better if you start up again. I'm really close," she said, smiling.

"Okay, I'll start up again, but let's go slowly."

The bed began squeaking again.

"Yes, that's it. Keep going!" she said breathily.

"Desks, cars, ugly people—"

"Oh . . . my . . . *God!!!!*"

Carole's body arched as she rode the wave of her orgasm, and they both let out a primordial scream. Yes, they both had an orgasm because there was no way he could hold on once he felt Carole come.

For a minute, Jason just laid on top of Carole, trying to revel in how she felt. He could feel her chest's gentle breathing and he

knew that sex with Carole had been different than with any other
woman. But he had to remind himself that this could not be love.

I'm in this for sex only because I still wanted my freedom, he
thought. I am a *Titan* man. Just a month ago, I would have looked
at Carole as a girlfriend, but now that I had options, I knew I didn't
need to limit myself. Besides, friends with benefits had worked to
perfection, so why do I need to monkey with the results? It's cold,
and I know it's going to appear cold, but I have to follow the rules.

Jason eventually rolled over and they laid there silently. There
wasn't anything awkward about this silence, but he did want to see
if he was disciplined enough to enforce the friends with benefits
rules.

"That was great," he said.

She rolled over and looked at him.

"Yes it was," she said, with eyes that could melt any man.

"You know, this changes our relationship," Jason said.

"I know, but I don't want to think about that now. I just want to
snuggle in your arms."

She put her head right in his chest and it felt so good. Jason
could feel his will faltering. But he had to be strong.

"I'm going to go," Jason said abruptly, getting up from the bed,
looking for his clothes.

"Why?"

"I just want to think about this as much as I can. I'm sorry, but I
just want to make sure I'm not rushing things."

"But we aren't. Or maybe I should say haven't."

She wrapped herself in the sheet and sat up. Jason put on his
pants and his shirt, then leaned over the bed and gave her a
kiss.

"Don't worry, I'm not going to disappear. I'm going out of town
tomorrow, but I'll call you as soon as I can."

"Okay, because I know where you work," she said, smiling.

Jason reached down to kiss her again, but she put her hand on
his mouth.

"You think about it and let me know what you come up with.
After that, you get more kisses," she said, looking so damn good
that he could have committed to her right then and there. But the
Titan lifestyle required discipline.

"Fair enough," Jason said, smiling. "I'll call you."

And with that, Jason left the apartment feeling on top of the world. Mission accomplished.

Meanwhile Carole turned over on the bed, feeling for all the world like a woman fulfilled, finally.

From friends to lovers, she thought while drifting off to sleep, is a beautiful thing.

Friends with benefits, Jason thought while starting his Hayabusa, is a beautiful thing.

CHAPTER 20

Carole! That was one amazing woman. Jason sat in his loft, chilling in his deliciously soft chaise longue, thinking about last night and how beautiful Carole looked. She looked beautiful drinking beer, and eating pizza, and doing everything else she did.

Making love to her was not like having sex with other women, Jason thought, and there was a big difference. Jason respected her, and he didn't think he respected all of the other women he'd had sex with over the past month.

Last night, he'd walked into Carole's bedroom thinking he was going to have sex with just another woman, and left having made love to Carole. It made Jason feel a little bit strange about having manipulated her to get to that point, but he rationalized it by thinking that if he hadn't followed the *Titan* plan, he wouldn't have gotten to sleep with Carole in the first place. So ultimately, the friends with benefits plan worked, so he shouldn't really worry about the fact that it had taken manipulation to do it.

Bzzzzzzzzzz!

It couldn't be anyone else but Steven. He was the only one who'd visited Jason since he'd moved into the loft.

"Hello?" Jason asked through the intercom.

"What's up, man, it's Steven! Let me up!"

Tonight was the party and even though this was only Jason's sec-

ond party at his loft, the party lifestyle was getting a bit tiresome.
Jason wouldn't mind having another after-party like last week's,
but this time, he would like to do it sans Steven. Steven was a little
too into having two men in the bedroom at the same time. Although last weekend had been wild, Jason liked to have his women
to himself. No need for an extra dick in the room.

Jason pressed the button and activated the downstairs door.
Steven came bounding to his door and went straight to the refrigerator.

"Sure, help yourself," Jason said sarcastically.

Steven came back with a cold beer. He had his usual cheese eating grin that three weeks ago had been funny and cool, but now,
for some reason, was starting to aggravate Jason. He didn't know
why it was aggravating him, but it was.

"Guess who's coming to the party tonight?" he said, popping
open the beer.

"I have no idea, who?"

"Miss Blue, and she wants . . . some . . . more . . . dick! Or dicks,
to be more accurate," he said, sipping on the beer.

"Great." Jason didn't say that with the greatest amount of enthusiasm.

Steven looked at Jason curiously.

"What, you didn't like fucking her? I know I did!"

"Nah, that's not it."

"Well then what is it, man? I mean, that was some good pussy.
And there's nothing better than dipping back into some good
pussy."

"Look, I liked her pussy, but you know, I didn't think I'd really
see her again. I thought that was a single instance and if you noticed, I didn't ask for any of their phone numbers."

"What"—he looked at Jason incredulously—"are you embarrassed to see them again? Are you *ashamed* at what you did? Oh, the
horror of fucking three women!"

"No, it's not that," Jason said, feeling uneasy that he had to justify his lack of enthusiasm for some reason. "Whatever, man, just
let's do this party and then the rest of them will be at your loft. I
need a rest."

Steven brightened up.

"Man, I got you. You're just tired. Well rest up buddy boy because you have another big after-party coming. And I do mean coming."

"Yeah, cool."

Steven finished his beer and got up to leave.

"Where are you going?" Jason asked.

"I got to make a run, and then get dressed. I'll be back in about an hour."

"Cool. I'll see you then."

"Later."

And then he was gone.

Jason got up and went to the bedroom. He needed to change the sheets.

Barbara sat at her computer, waiting for Patricia to pick her up. The party was at eight and she didn't want to be late, but she knew that she was hoping in vain. Patricia was always late. But Barbara couldn't go to the party without Patricia. She was the lynchpin of everything she needed to do at this party.

This *Baldwin Hills* article was going to be the juiciest, most scandalous scoop of the year, and she was going to be the writer. She'd heard about these men trying to live a "*Titan* lifestyle" and she'd heard it always involved having sex parties. But she never knew anyone who either gave the parties or participated, until her friend Patricia had given her the scoop. And now, with Patricia's help, she was about to do an exposé on the *Titan* lifestyle.

Jordan wanted the photos and article in by Monday because the magazine was going into production on Tuesday. Marcia was due back on Friday and Jordan wanted to impress her by having the magazine done and in print by the time she got back into the office. To get the photos they needed for the magazine, Jordan had given her the newest cell phone with a camera. It had an extraordinarily high resolution for a cell phone camera, and she was going to take as many pictures of this party as possible.

"Bonk! Bonk!"

Patricia was here and in typical fashion, she decided that she was too good to get out of the car and come up to Barbara's apartment. That was okay because if she did come up, Patricia would probably spend an hour in front of the mirror, making them even later than they already were. Patricia was one of those friends that got on your nerves after about an hour. She was completely self-centered and really didn't let you get a word in edgewise. But she was still pretty cool with Barbara.

Barbara picked up the cell phone camera and ran down to meet Patricia.

"Bonk!"

"Here I come, girl!" Barbara shouted, running out of the apartment building.

Barbara opened the door and caught her breath. And then she lost it again when she saw what Patricia was wearing.

"Damn, girl, what the hell are you wearing?"

"I call it my 'get fucked' outfit," she laughed. "I can almost guarantee it."

"Well I guess!"

Patricia had on a black leather outfit that consisted of a leather bikini top and leather pants with holes down the side. It was obvious that she was either wearing a thong or nothing at all. Barbara didn't ask which.

"So are you sure you're comfortable with this?" Barbara asked. "I mean, if you want to back out, you let me know."

"Girl, please," she said, laughing. "I was going to do this anyway. You are just going to get the added thrill of watching."

Hey, if Patricia was okay with it, then Barbara was. She was about to practice some gonzo journalism, and so she didn't mind a little raunchiness. Patricia was a freak and it didn't bother her that someone was going to see that freakiness. In fact, it probably turned her on. Watching other people have sex wasn't exactly Barbara's bag, but at least she knew it was going to be interesting.

"So who are the men again? Do you have their names and occupations?" Barbara asked.

Patricia gunned the engine and got on the Harbor Freeway going downtown. There wasn't a lot of traffic, so they were making good time.

"The guy's loft we're going to is Jason Richards. He's got a huge dick," Patricia said, using her hands to give Barbara a little too much information. "I don't know what he does, but I do remember hearing that he's worth a few million dollars."

"The other person is Steven Cox, and he's the catalyst for all of these parties. Remember Joy Lofton, the real estate agent?"

Barbara remembered. Joy was one of these typical real estate agents that wore too much makeup and was always trying to sell you a home, even when you'd just moved into a new home. Before she got into real estate, she'd been a bored housewife that drank a bit too much vodka during the day. Her husband was a referee in the NBA, so she had a lot of time alone since he traveled all of the time. Barbara didn't think she spent that time alone.

"Yeah, I remember her. What about her?"

"Well," Patricia said. "She partied with us last week. Girl, she is as freaky as they come, and I *know* freaky! She's actually the one who introduced me to Steven. He was looking for a loft, and she sold him the one he lives in now. As she told me, Steven said that he knew seven men who liked to give parties all week. They were living something called the *Titan* life—you know, basing their lives on what *Titan* magazine said real men should do, and so they tried to be as hedonistic as possible. Joy asked him how hedonistic because, you know, Stewart is always out of town and she wanted some action. Steven said if she played her cards right, she could get invited to the after-party, because that's where the action was. She was intrigued, went to a few, and took so much dick that she became damn near addicted to it."

Patricia turned off the freeway and headed to the industrial part of downtown.

"Last week, she called me," Patricia continued, "and asked if I'd like to go along to one of these parties. Now you know, girl, I love men, so I said great, count me in."

Patricia drove to a parking lot that had a man waving a neon flashlight.

"And the rest is history," she said. "I've been in orgies before, but this was a good orgy. Both men knew what they were doing and did I tell you that Jason has a huge dick?"

"Uh, yes you did," Barbara said.

"Poor Joy!" Patricia said, smiling. "Stewart came home to see her with a bunch of hickeys and has forbidden her from going out. But if she wasn't restricted, she'd be right here with us."

Patricia parked the car and turned off the engine. She looked at Barbara with a gleam in her eye.

"You know, you ought to join me instead of hiding in some closet looking for some compromising pictures. Hell, you should just tell them who you are and what you're doing. I bet they wouldn't mind the publicity. It would fit right into their '*Titan* lifestyle'! Every man likes to be looked at as a stud, and these two are no exception."

"Nah, I better keep it to myself. I don't want to blow this assignment. I could make or break my career at the magazine," Barbara said as they got out of the car. "Anyway, I like my men one at a time, with no extra pussies in the room, thank you."

They began walking to Jason's loft.

"Suit yourself," Patricia said. "But you could have the best of both worlds! And hey, don't knock it if you ain't tried it."

"A man woke up in a hospital after a serious accident," Jason said. "He shouted, 'Doctor, doctor, I can't feel my legs!' The doctor replied, 'I know you can't—I've cut off your arms!' "

About twenty people began laughing hysterically, as though Chris Rock had told the joke instead of Jason.

"That was a good one, Jason, you are so funny!" said someone Jason didn't know. The party had started about an hour ago and Jason swore these were the same people that had come to his house last week. It was almost like they came from central casting of some Los Angeles party emporium. He could imagine Steven going to a store that rented chairs, tables and pretty partygoers.

"Hello!"

"Great to see you!"

Jason repeated these lines over and over, and the novelty was getting old. For the first time in a while, Jason wished he was sitting back in his Gower Gulch apartment, eating some Stroganoff and watching ESPN. The glamour of the party had lost its luster.

At this party, Jason stayed on the fringes, watching people enjoy his loft space. He didn't give a shit about them, but good old Steven was his usual self, kissing the women and acting like he was

a fucking black Hugh Hefner. In less than a week, Steven was starting to get on Jason's last nerve and it wasn't really his fault. But all
of a sudden, the *Titan* lifestyle didn't seem so fantastic, and Steven
was the embodiment of it.

"How have you been?" Jason asked one partygoer.

"Oh my goodness, I'm so glad you came," he told another.

It was all so fake—the people, the reactions, even him. He wasn't
happy to see these people and he didn't care about them. They
were playing a part and he was going along with it. Only a few
weeks ago he'd been awed by the beauty of these people, but now
he started to notice something the more he saw them. He was beginning to notice that they weren't all that beautiful.

Their physical beauty was undeniable. But he didn't see an
inner beauty. It was all very superficial, all very . . . cheap. In any
other circumstance, that could sound like a cliché, but it wasn't.
Jason was starting to really appreciate the inner beauty of, say, a
person like Carole versus these beautiful robots. They were vacant,
insignificant people, and he wondered if they viewed him in the
exact same way.

Jason was moving through the crowd when Patricia and Barbara
walked into the party, and it was in full swing by the time they got
there. They walked over to the bar, ordered a drink, and relaxed
on the same windowsill Patricia and her two other friends had sat
on the week before.

"That's him," Patricia said to Barbara, pointing to Jason.

"So this is the guy who throws parties so that he can have orgies
afterward?" Barbara asked.

"Yep, that's him," Patricia said. "And that's Steven, his cohort."
Steven saw them and waved for them to come over. Jason had
joined Steven and had his back to them as they walked up. It was
then that Barbara's phone rang.

"Hey, Jason, I want you to meet someone," Steven said.

Jason turned around to look and it was Miss Blue and a friend.
The friend was on her cell phone.

"Long time no see, stranger," Miss Blue said, giving a fake kiss.

"Who's your friend?" Jason asked, while Barbara stayed on the
phone.

"I'm Barbara," she said, avoiding Jason's gaze. Barbara held out her hand for Jason to shake, while still having her phone plastered to her ear.

"Glad to meet you," Jason said, not meaning it.

"Yeah," she said, walking away.

"What's up with your friend?" Jason asked Miss Blue.

"Oh, don't mind her. She's got a new phone and she just won't get off that damn thing. Anyway, forget her. I just brought her because she wanted to get out of the house. She's probably going to leave early."

Miss Blue put her lips right in Jason's ear. "But I want to party just like we did the last time."

"Where are your friends Miss Green and Mrs. Brown?"

"Oh, you didn't hear?"

"No, what happened?"

"Well," she started laughing. "Miss Green was so freaked out about last week that she won't answer her phone. And Mrs. Brown . . ."

"She was a freaky married woman, wasn't she?" Jason said.

"Well, very freaky, and you don't know the half of it. Her husband wondered why she was out all night without calling. When he saw all of the hickeys on her body, they had a big blowup. So she won't be going out without him in tow for a long time. So that only leaves me. And I'm not freaked out and I don't have a husband. I just want those two dicks again. You want to oblige?"

"Is your friend Barbara joining us?"

"Barbara? Please! She'll probably be gone before this party is even over. She'll be in a bed, but not ours. So are you down?"

"Yeah, I guess."

"I'll be waiting for the party to end," she said. "Save your energy, big boy. And I do mean big boy!"

She surreptitiously grabbed Jason's dick and he was instantly turned on. But he wasn't thrilled about fucking Miss Blue with Steven. Shit, he thought, does this mean I'm gay if I can feel his dick in her ass when I'm in her pussy? I don't want to have this fool in the bedroom with me, but if she wanted a double penetration, they would give her that.

But Jason had made a vow. This night with Miss Blue was going to be the last one for him. The *Titan* lifestyle was growing old and the excitement had quickly gone. What would have to happen to top what had happened so far? Four women at a time? Or maybe five, six or seven women at once? The one thing *Titan* didn't tell Jason was when enough was enough.

One last sordid fling, Jason thought, sipping on a Maker's Mark and Coke, and then I'm done.

CHAPTER 21

"So when are you going to make your move?" Patricia asked.

Barbara had gone to a corner of the loft, pretending she was on the phone, but really taking pictures of the whole scene.

"I'm about to find a hiding place in the next few minutes," she said. "This party is boring me. All the poseurs, fakers, corporate achievers and the professional partygoers are all here, and if you emptied their brains in a collective bowl, they might equal one intelligent person."

"Oh, you're just bitter that they're not talking to you," said Patricia, laughing. "Look, you can take all the pictures you want, but make sure you find a good hiding place. I really do want to get my freak on, and I don't want anything spoiling it."

"Believe me, I'll be well hidden."

Patricia left and started talking to Steven again, while Barbara slowly began making her way to Jason's bedroom. She felt like a criminal, walking into his bedroom like that, but she had to scope it out. She looked in the mirrored closet and thought about trying to sit in there for a couple of hours, but it didn't seem like she could sit there undetected. The bathroom was another place to hide, but there were reasons to exclude it.

Men always love to take a whiz before they have sex, she thought. So the bathroom was out.

She didn't think there was any place to hide until she looked at the mirrored closet again. And then it dawned on her. She could hide under the bed; Jason had a big four-poster bed with plenty of room underneath. From there, she could focus the camera on the mirrored closet and take perfect pictures of the top of the bed. She could photograph all of the action without being seen.

Perfect! she thought. Absolutely perfect.

And with that, Barbara slid herself under the bed and waited. I wonder if I'll get a raise for this? she thought, smiling to herself.

Jason couldn't stop thinking about Carole. The women at the party were decidedly *not* Carole and for some reason, that was annoying him. Everything about this party was annoying him. But the party was almost over, and he was going to get one more fling with Miss Blue, so he was willing to tolerate their presence.

"He has about four million dollars in the bank," Steven told two women at the party. He'd been working hard to get two more for the orgy. "Maybe he'll share some of it with you if you join us for the after-party."

One of the women left immediately, but the other had something to say.

"I don't care if he's fucking Bill Gates. I'm not a whore and I'm not fucking you or him, no matter how much money he has."

She walked away in a huff.

"Bitch," Steven said under his breath.

The hour was getting late and people started to file out, all of them except for Miss Blue. She looked fantastic in her black leather.

The last couple left the loft, and then the caterers. And Miss Blue sat on the window ledge, just like she had last week. Steven and Jason looked at her and she simply said one thing.

"Gentlemen?"

She then got up and walked to the bedroom.

"Do you want Cristal or something else?" Steven asked as he walked to the kitchen.

"Nothing for me," Jason responded.

"Ah, you just want to concentrate on fucking her!" he said,

laughing. "I can respect that. But I want some bubbly to go with my sex. See you in the bedroom."

Jason walked to his bedroom, where Miss Blue was lying on the bed, looking as sexy as ever. She still had her clothes on, but had taken off her shoes. He moved to turn off the lights and she stopped him.

"No," she said. "I want to see both of you, but mostly you."

Steven walked into the room with two champagne glasses and a bottle of Cristal.

"If you want some Cristal, Jason, feel free to chug from the bottle," he said.

Miss Blue began to get undressed rather matter-of-factly, and for some reason that turned Jason on. Here was a woman who knew what she wanted and held nothing back in reserve. She was going to get fucked by two men, and regardless of any machismo thoughts Steven and Jason may have had, she was in full control.

Wasn't that ironic? Jason thought. The *Titan* lifestyle was all about the man taking control and making women do what they want them to do, but here he was in a situation where it felt like the woman had all of the control.

Steven and Jason took off their clothes and their hands began feeling all over Miss Blue. They were indiscriminant in where they felt her up and how they did it. Steven was concentrating on her legs and thighs, while Jason was up by her neck. Miss Blue had a slow moan that seemed to come from deep within her. As much as Steven and Jason enjoyed double-teaming Miss Blue, Jason thought she enjoyed taking two men more.

Jason took Miss Blue's left side and Steven took her right. She was lying on her back and they were sucking on her breasts. She used both of her hands to begin jacking them off, and Jason was feeling really good, although Steven seemed to have problems getting hard.

"Go down on me," she told Steven.

Steven slid down to Miss Blue's pussy and began licking her. Jason straddled Miss Blue so that his dick was sitting in between her breasts and he started titty-fucking her.

"Fuck those big titties, boy," she said.

She lifted her head and between moans, began sucking his dick.

It felt good, but there was something old hat about all of this for Jason. The excitement level wasn't the same as it had been last week. His dick stayed hard, and yes, he liked getting his dick sucked, but he found his interest was waning fast. Jason never thought he'd ever say this, but this was all boring him.

"Okay, I'm ready!" Miss Blue said breathlessly.

Steven jumped up and went to get the condoms, but Jason knew he didn't want to do this. He'd had enough and he didn't want to have more cheap sex just for the sake of having cheap sex. This had to stop and this had to stop right now.

"Wait," he said as Steven jumped back in the bed.

"What?" Steven said as he tore open the condom with his teeth. Miss Blue lay on the bed masturbating. She was waiting for them to get their condoms on.

"You guys fuck, but I'm out," Jason said. He started looking for his clothes. He didn't know what it was, but something in his conscience just snapped and he suddenly felt as cheap as a two-dollar whore. It was time, definitely time, to go.

"What the fuck are you talking about that you are 'out'?" Steven said angrily. "You can't be out. Miss Blue wants us to fuck her and goddamn it, we are going to fuck her."

"What's going on here?" Miss Blue said, sitting up in the bed.

Click!

"What the fuck was that?" Jason asked, looking around the room.

"What the fuck was what?" Steven asked.

"Didn't you hear that?"

"I didn't hear shit," Steven said. "But I want to know why you don't want to go along with this."

"You don't find me fuckable?" Miss Blue said, taking her hand and rubbing Jason's back.

"Yes . . . no . . . yes," said Jason, slightly confused. "I just don't want to do this anymore."

Steven looked at Jason as though he'd turned into a pumpkin.

"What, you're getting tired of sex? What the fuck are you talking about that you don't want to do this anymore? You never had this much sex before I introduced you to this lifestyle."

"Well you know, I don't want to live it anymore," Jason said, standing on the floor. He started to put on his clothes. Steven sat there with his condom on, but his erection was lost. Miss Blue lay on the bed perplexed, not knowing what to do.

"What the fuck has changed? Just an hour ago, you were all ready to double-team Miss Blue and now you—"

"No, *you* were all excited to do this," he said, pointing at Steven. "I didn't want to have this party and I didn't really want to fuck Miss Blue again. You are the one that wanted all of this."

"I'm out of here," Miss Blue said, sliding off the bed. She went to pick up her leather bikini top from the floor when she tripped. Jason reached to pick her up when he saw a hand.

"What the fuck is it?" he said, looking under the bed. Steven leaped off the bed and they all looked under the bed.

"Who the fuck are you?" Jason screamed as he saw a woman lying there. Barbara had her face covered as though she could hide from them if she just tried hard enough.

She started sliding from under the bed and they all got their first good look at her. As she came out, she was able to put her camera into her pocket without anyone noticing.

"Hey, I know you!" Jason said, completely spooked that someone had hidden under his bed. "You're Miss Blue's friend! What the fuck is going on here?"

Jason looked at Barbara and Miss Blue accusingly. Miss Blue was rapidly getting dressed and Barbara was trying to make her way to the door.

"Steven, were you in on this?"

"Man, I don't know what the fuck is going on," he said. Jason believed him, but then he didn't.

"Okay, nobody is leaving until I get a goddamn explanation about why you were under my bed and what the fuck is going on."

Barbara still hadn't said anything. She just stood there silent.

Finally Miss Blue piped up. "It's not that big a deal, so stop getting your panties into a bunch," she said, putting on her high heels. "I told Barbara that I was going to fuck you guys. She just wanted to see it, but didn't want to fuck because she's too scared. Nothing more, and nothing less."

"Is that true?" Jason asked, getting right in Barbara's face.

"Yes."

This was too damn much for Jason. He felt dirty and soiled, and he just wanted everyone out of his house.

"Get out," he said, taking Steven's clothes and throwing them at him. "Everybody get out!"

Barbara and Miss Blue made a rapid move to the door, while Steven took his time putting his clothes on. Jason followed Barbara and Miss Blue to the door. Miss Blue turned, just as she was about to leave.

"If you want to party without Steven, just let me know."

"That's not going to happen. I'm not partying anymore."

"Patricia, come on!" Barbara said as she walked down the building hallway, trying to get out of the loft building as fast as she could.

"Well, if you change your mind, come to the Bally's gym in Hollywood. That's where I work. I'll get off early for you, but not for him."

And with that, she left.

Jason closed the door and looked for Steven. He was putting on his clothes as though there was no rush, and indeed there was a rush.

"Man, what was the problem?" Steven asked.

"I don't want to talk about it," Jason said, standing by the bedroom door.

"Was it something I did?" he asked, sitting on the bed, putting on his shoes.

"No."

"Then it has to be something."

"Look," Jason said, getting more and more angry that he had to justify himself to Steven. "Maybe this isn't the lifestyle for me."

Steven looked at Jason coolly and stopped putting on his shoes.

"Okay, who is she?"

"What do you mean?"

"You heard me. The only reason a man would get the heebie-jeebies about fucking a woman as beautiful as Miss Blue is if they had another woman on their mind. So who is it?"

Jason flip-flopped in his mind about telling him about who it was. Why did Steven need to know? But then again, why did Jason have to lie?

"Carole."

There was a pause and a silly look on Steven's face when Jason spoke her name.

"Carole?" he said incredulously. He stood up and looked at Jason with a mixture of surprise and anger.

"I thought I fucking told you that Carole was off-limits and that she was mine?"

"What the fuck are you talking about, off-limits?" Jason said, getting more and more pissed as he spoke. "This isn't fucking elementary school, muthafucka, and you don't have claims to anybody. You aren't her boyfriend, and as far as I know, she doesn't even know you exist."

Steven walked up to Jason and started poking him in the chest.

"I told you that she was not a part of this *Titan* lifestyle and that I was going to try to make her my girl. So I made my claim and you should have respected that."

"First of all," Jason said while swiping his finger away from him, "you better stop pointing your finger at me and back the fuck up. Next, I can go after whomever I want. You could fantasize all you want about Carole, but you didn't get her. Too goddamn bad."

Jason was really pissed that this son of a bitch was trying to stake some sort of territorial claim over Carole, as though she was a piece of land. She wasn't, and Jason wanted to make sure he knew it.

Steven went back and put on his shoes, not saying anything. He was steamed, but Jason thought he knew he couldn't beat him in a fight. His shoes on, he stood up and walked past Jason to the door.

"You see all of this?" he said, looking at the loft. "I was the reason you have all of this. But muthafucka, I don't want to hear from you again. When you see me at work, go to your own desk and don't say a damn thing to me. I don't want to know your sorry ass."

"Fine," Jason said with an edge to his voice. "Maybe now I can fuck women without your ass trying to hang on."

They stood there silently, trying to stare each other down. Then Steven backed off and went for the door.

"I'm going to make sure you pay for this, you son of a bitch," he said. And then he left.

Standing there, half naked, yet relieved that everyone had left,

Jason went into the bathroom, turned on the shower so that the steam boiled out of the room, and gave himself a scrubbing. He felt dirty and he wanted to do all he could to get clean. But the dirty was not only on the outside. He needed to be cleaned from the inside out.

CHAPTER 22

"So, how is Sean?" Anna asked.

Carole intended on spending a relaxing Saturday doing nothing but errands, shopping and a little bit of catching up on her e-mails, but first, her mother had called. And that was always an ordeal.

Anna Brantford loved Carole and Carole loved Anna, but she wasn't the most optimistic person in the world. She had a way of looking at the dark side of life, no matter how sunny Carole tried to make it. And that's why Carole made it a point to keep her interaction with her mom to a minimum. Unwanted advice was only a phone call away with Anna, and Carole didn't need it in her life. And issue number one was Carole and her choice of men.

Her mother was getting a manicure and Carole could hear the beauty shop chatter through her cell phone.

"Mom, I'm not with Sean anymore. He decided to move back to Europe and get back with his ex-girlfriend. I haven't seen him in over a month."

"What did you do to him, Carole?"

"Why did I have to do something to him? He made a decision and followed through with it. I had nothing to do with it."

"But weren't you girlfriend and boyfriend? I mean the last time you talked to me, you told me that you guys were on the way to wedded bliss! So something had to have happened that changed his mind."

"I told you. He decided to move back to Europe and get back with his girlfriend. Can we drop this? I'm not thinking about him now anyway."

Anna sighed.

"Okay, who is it now?"

"What do you mean?"

"Well, you're never without a man for long, so I figure you've found another man to fill the void."

"Is that what you think of me? As a woman who just needs a man to get her through her life?"

"No, darling," Anna said. "Hold on."

Carole could hear her mother talking to the manicurist.

"I said I want a deeper red for my toes. Yes, that one. Thanks!" Anna told the manicurist. She then returned to the phone.

"Okay, where were we?"

"I was asking if you thought that I needed a man to get through life."

"No, I don't think that. But even you have to admit that you go through men like J.Lo goes through husbands. You are what *Divas* calls a serial dater. So who is he now?"

Carole thought about telling her mother about Jason, but something stopped her.

What good could come from letting her know about Jason versus the bad advice she could get? she thought. If things worked out, then fine, she'd tell her later. But if things went bad, then no need to pour salt in the wound by having her mother tell her, "I told you so."

"No, I'm not seeing anyone," Carole lied. "I'm just trying to find myself and let life come to me. I think the next man I go out with is going to have to bring me more than a handsome face. He's going to have to be kind, considerate, and wonderful to be with. But you're wrong, Mom, if you think that these men are leaving because of me. They are leaving because of themselves."

"Well, that sounds like a plan, dear. And of course, if you need any type of encouragement for your next relationship, then feel free to—"

"I will, Mom," Carole interrupted. "I've got to go now. I'll call you if anything changes."

"Okay dear, take care!"

Carole got off the phone smiling. She'd beaten her mother at her own game and hadn't let her mother get her down. Jason was going to be something new. He was not going to be burdened with the failures of her past relationships.

This was the new Carole with a new Carole-style relationship, she thought.

For a bit of encouragement instead of discouragement, she decided to give Marcia another call. Yes, she was supposed to keep the whole Jason thing a secret, but she had to tell someone. And Marcia was her best friend.

"Hello." The voice sounded sleepy on the other end.

"Hey, you! How's Rio?"

"Carole, what are you doing? This must be costing you a fortune!"

"Don't worry about it. Did I catch you sleeping?"

"Yeah, I was out last night. But don't worry about it. I needed to get up anyway. What's up?"

Carole could hardly contain her glee.

"I had sex. I had sex!"

"With someone else other than Mr. Chocolate?" Marcia said sleepily.

"Yes, fool! And guess who?"

"It's not Jason, is it? Did you have sex with Jason? Tell me you didn't have sex with Jason."

"Yes I did, girl, and it was not good, but *great*! Why anyone but Jason?"

"Oh Carole, I don't know about this. This could be trouble. Jason is not like the guys you've been dating in the past. He's not a flashy guy, and he's not as sophisticated."

"What do you mean?" Carole said. "He was an absolute gentleman. He was so nice and caring, and he said that he wanted to think about all of this because he didn't want to jeopardize our friendship. Why are you worried?"

"I don't know, Carole," Marcia sighed. "You're my girl and all, but Jason's a really good guy and I would hate for him to get hurt."

"Are you saying that I'm a liability?"

Carole knew that Marcia thought she always sabotaged her relationships, but she didn't think she'd actually be so harsh in her concern about her and Jason.

"No, I think you misunderstand me. Just take things as they come. I think you guys could work out, but you've got to take it slow. So do that, will you? Promise me? Because if it doesn't work, it's going to have an effect on us all. I hate that tension that comes when friends break up and then have to choose which friends to hang out with. You're my girl and he's my boy, and I'd like to have you both around."

"Yeah, I promise you."

"Okay, I'll talk to you when I get back on Sunday. I've got to get another caipirinha. Those things put me on my ass!" She laughed.

"I'll see you this weekend."

"Ciao!'"

Carole hung up the phone and thought about what Marcia had said. She was going to let Jason lead and just take it easy. No pressure and no expectations were going to be the hallmarks of the Carole and Jason relationship, she thought.

"Now, to catch up on those e-mails," she said to herself.

Barbara had gotten to the *Baldwin Hills* office early, and started writing her article. She didn't even take a lunch break because she was late. Finally, Jordan called her into her office.

"So what did you get?" Jordan asked Barbara. The rest of the writers had turned in their assignments for the private party issue, and the only thing remaining was Barbara's.

"Jordan, you don't even know what I had to do to get these photos."

"Don't tell me because I don't think I want to know. But let me see them."

Barbara put the photo disk into the computer and Jordan slowly went through them.

"Wow!" she would say as she perused each of the photos.

"The resolution is great," she said, "but why did you take the photos via reflections through the mirror?"

"Because I was lying under the bed taking photos."

Jordan looked at Barbara strangely.

"I knew I didn't want to know how you got these things," she said, smiling. "Okay, send me your article and we'll be ready to go to press. Nice work, Barbara!"

"Thanks!"

Barbara left Jordan's office and Jordan looked at the calendar. Marcia was due back that weekend, and per her instructions, the magazine should be at the presses by Friday. That was today. She'd gotten permission from Marcia about doing the stories on private parties in L.A., but she hadn't given her specifics about whom they were going to profile.

I've got to shoot this to Marcia, and get her approval by Friday or the issue is going to be late, Jordan thought.

"Your mail is in!" said her computer. Jordan looked at the mail and saw that it was Barbara's article.

> The single American man has always been trying to achieve a nirvana of bachelorhood, and magazines have catered to this dream. Whether it is the Esquire magazine of your grandfather's era, the Playboy magazine of your dad's era, or the Titan magazine of today, the bachelor has forever been on a quest to find the formula that gives him all the trappings of hedonistic pleasure. One group of men, led by Steven Cox and Jason Richards, star lawyers for the Ketchings & Martin law firm, are following the dictates of Titan magazine to the tee, and they are recruiting more men as they go along. They are turning a series of downtown lofts into private pleasure palaces where wild parties are given each and every weekend. And the parties don't end at three in the morning. No, that's when the parties just get started. There's the after-party that consists of multiple-partner orgies . . .

This is juicy! Jordan thought as she continued to read the article.

She finished reading the article and called her copy editor, Monica Paige, into the office.

"Monica, I put all of the articles in your folder. They are ready for copyediting. Let me know when you are done because I've got to get copies to Marcia before she gets on the plane, and then get it to the printer."

Monica looked at Jordan like she was crazy.

"Do you mean we are actually going to get the magazine out on schedule? I think I'm going to turn into a frog!" she said sarcastically.

"Don't be sarcastic," Jordan said, and laughed, "or I'm going to tell Marcia that you talked about her. But yes, we are coming in on time. The advertising is in, and I'm not going to hold it for any latecomers. They can just get on board for the next issue and Marcia can deal with that. So, do you think I can get the copy back in two hours?"

"You got it."

Monica left and Jordan sat back in her chair. All there was left to do was to send it to press.

Not a bad job if I say so myself, she thought. Not a bad job.

CHAPTER 23

"Take the week off?" Jason asked. He was laying in his favorite chaise longue, looking out over the city through his window.

"Jason, you know I can't do that. Mama's House needs me."

"But I need you more and I'm saying that you need to take the week off. I've got something planned for the two of us."

Carole sat on her couch twirling her hair. She hadn't felt so good about talking to a man in so long, and she wanted to savor every word. But she still wanted to take it slow with Jason. There was no need to rush things, and if she remembered all his rules, he wanted to do the same. But still . . .

"I guess I could get Dorothy to watch the center," she said, contemplating her first vacation in three years.

"There you have it. Give her a call right now and tell her that she needs to run the center. You'll be back on Sunday."

"Okay," she said in a girlish voice she didn't even know she had. "Where are we going?"

"Don't worry about it. Just have your passport ready."

"My passport? Jason, you can't afford—"

"You let me figure out what I can afford and what I can't. They pay us pretty well down at Ketchings and Martin, so I'm not hurting."

"Okay, but I at least need to know where we're going so I can know what to pack!"

"No you don't. I'll buy you all the clothes you need when we get there. Just have enough for dinner and possibly to walk around in. That's it. I'll get the rest."

"Jason, you can't afford that. Just let me know . . ."

"Don't worry about it, Carole, I know what's in my bank account and what I can afford. And I can afford to buy you your clothes. So just bring your passport and clothes for when we get there and the next morning I said. I'll pick you up at eight o'clock tonight."

"Okay! I'm excited!"

"You should be. See you at eight."

"Tonight? That's in two hours."

"Yes."

"I'll be waiting."

The blowup with Steven had told Jason that his *Titan* lifestyle had run its course. He was surprised at how fast he'd gotten tired of it, but he had. A *Titan* lifestyle was cool, but it didn't work if you wanted something deeper. And Jason wanted something deeper and was willing to give up immediate pleasure for long-term happiness. The *Titan* life couldn't provide that type of happiness, no matter what Steven said.

So he came up with a plan. He would take Carole out of Los Angeles. Yes, it was impromptu and unexpected, and even a bit premature. But he needed to do something that reflected how he felt, and dinner and a movie just wasn't cutting it. Plus, she could leave the worries of Mama's House and he could get away from Steven and his damn *Titan* lifestyle obsession. But where to go?

He'd wanted something far away, different and exotic. In other words, he wanted the trip of a lifetime that would leave an impression on her. He went online and started scrolling through the possible cities.

London . . . Paris . . . Rome . . . the usual suspects were listed. Then he hit upon a city that he'd thought about visiting in the past, but never really thought he'd visit. Something a little out of the way, and a little unexpected. And when he saw it, he knew that it would be absolutely perfect.

*   *   *

Oh my God! Oh my God, Carole thought as she hung up the phone with Jason. What a surprise! Oh my God! What does this mean? Why are men so damn confusing? I mean, he just left my apartment because he wants to follow some damn rules and now I'm flying off to God knows where with him.

She started walking around her apartment like a chicken with her head cut off. She didn't know which way to go or what to do.

Okay, let me first call Dorothy and tell her that I'm not coming in. Where are we going, I wonder? she thought.

She picked up the phone and began dialing.

"Hello, Dorothy, I need you to do me a huge favor," she said.

"Sure, dear, what is it?"

"I need to go out of town for a week. Could you run the center?"

"Absolutely! Are you going on vacation, because I think you deserve it."

"It's a minivacation. I haven't had one since I came on with Mama's House, so I'm looking forward to it."

"Where are you going?"

"Funny, but I don't know yet. I'm being taken to a mystery place by a young man."

"Ah, young romance and an impromptu trip! How nice it must be to be so young!" Dorothy reminisced. "Have a wonderful time!"

"I will, and thanks again."

Carole sat at the edge of her bed, wondering if she should follow her natural inclinations and let her imagination run wild when it came to her and Jason. It was hard not to.

He'd obviously thought about them and felt there was an us, she mused.

But then she kept hearing the admonitions of everyone who'd given her relationship advice. "Just take it as it comes," they'd all said, and it seemed like as good a piece of advice as anything.

Thank you, *Divas* magazine, she thought. I wouldn't be here without you.

She took out her luggage and packed her toiletries. She was going to follow Jason's advice and not pack anything, but then she remembered those nice pieces she'd picked up at Victoria's Secret. It seemed as though this was as good a time as any to wear them.

Carole sat on her bed again, and sighed to herself. What was going to happen with this? All of a sudden, the excitement turned to nervousness and Carole was unsure of herself. If any of the other fifteen boyfriends had told her they wanted to take her away for the weekend, she would have felt completely confident about the trip. But Jason was different. She really wanted this to work but she didn't want to scare him away.

Take things as they come, she kept telling herself. *Take things as they come.*

"Are you excited?" Jason asked Carole as they made their way to the cab.

"Yes," she said, her face flush with anticipation.

"Good. Now, you have your passport, don't you?"

"Yes, but it was an ordeal to find it," she said. "I normally keep it in my nightstand, but I forgot that I'd decided to hide it, and I ended up hiding it from myself. I was straight panicking."

"LAX, driver," Jason instructed the cab driver.

Carole looked at Jason sweetly. She was so beautiful, Jason thought.

"I think this is so sweet of you, but I don't want you to think that I go away with every man who asks me."

"Of course you don't. I never thought a woman of your sophistication and beauty would ever do something like this," Jason said, smiling. "But then again, you haven't had someone as handsome as me taking you on a trip, so perhaps you haven't truly had the right opportunity to leave everything behind."

"True," she said, going along with the joke. "You are more handsome than all those other boyfriends! But you better watch it. Everyone says I'm clingy, so I could run you away like I did the others."

"Don't worry," he said. "I have balls enough to stand up to you. The others didn't and that's why they didn't hang around."

They were joking around, but there was some truth to their banter. Jason really could stand up to Carole while the others couldn't.

"So where are we going, or are you going to keep that a secret until we get to the airport?" she asked.

"You'll find out soon enough," Jason said.

The taxi pulled into LAX and the cabbie turned to them.

"Which airline?"

"American Airlines."

"Domestic or international?"

"International."

They pulled up to American Airlines and Jason gave the cabbie his fare and a twenty-dollar tip. As they walked into the terminal, Jason looked up at the electric board. Carole squirmed with anticipation. Finally, she couldn't take it anymore.

"Okay, where are we going?" she said, grabbing his arm. "I can't take it anymore!"

Jason smiled and decided to let her off the hook.

"Have you ever been to South Africa?"

"We're going to South Africa?" she said excitedly. "I've been to Nigeria with my parents, but never to South Africa."

"Well, you're going to Cape Town."

"Oh, my!" she said excitedly. "Oh my goodness! I've always heard that it is one of the most beautiful cities in the world. Have you been before? Why did you pick it?"

"I'd always wanted to go, so I made it happen."

"Thank you," she said, looking at Jason with her beautiful eyes.

"You're welcome. We've got to hurry up because our flight leaves in less than an hour."

They literally skipped to the American Airlines kiosk where they got out a boarding pass and went through the security gate.

"Now boarding American Airlines Flight nineteen oh six to Cape Town, South Africa," the gate checker said into the microphone.

It was time to go, so they grabbed their baggage and headed to the front of the line.

"We are now taking our first class passengers."

Carole didn't move, but Jason stood up. She looked at Jason strangely.

"Do you mean we are in first class?" she said incredulously.

"Did you expect us to fly coach?" Jason said, feeling like *the* man.

"Jason, how much are you spending on this trip and can you really afford this?"

"Don't worry about it, I tell you," he said as they made their move to the seats. "I have a little money stashed away for something like this."

"Look, if you say so, I'm not going to complain."

They sat in their seats and began to relax. Jason sat by the window, while Carole sat in the aisle.

"You comfortable?" he asked.

"Yes," she said.

Jason pulled down the shade and turned on the little fan.

"Look, just sit back and enjoy it. You don't have to worry about anything during this trip. You just let me take care of everything."

The airplane took off and they settled in.

It really did feel better to sit in first class than in coach, Jason thought as they flew through the sky. The leg room was plentiful and things were real here. The food came on real china and the wine came in glasses, and not plastic. Little things, but they helped to make the trip a bit more pleasant. It was said that money didn't buy happiness, and that may be true, but it was the decisions you make that create your happiness.

As the hours went by, he looked at Carole as she read her magazines under the soft light of the plane. It was then that it dawned on him that the *Titan* lifestyle had been a fake lifestyle. It didn't really exist because it was a fantasy, and some fantasies are supposed to stay in the mind's eye, and not become reality. And in the end, the *Titan* life hadn't made him happy. What made him happy was happening on that plane. It was Carole beside him, thrilled to be going to a place they'd both never visited, but more importantly, happy to be with him. He didn't need ten women in each city; just one in one city.

A few hours into the flight, Carole nodded off, leaning on his arm as she slept. Jason took the magazine from her hand and drew the blanket over her shoulder. This was Jason's nirvana.

CHAPTER 24

WELCOME TO SOUTH AFRICA, the sign at the airport said.
"I thought we'd get a lei or something as African Americans coming back to the motherland," Jason laughed.

"You're going to figure out very soon that once you're out of America, you're looked at as being very much an American," Carole said, as they walked toward customs. "It was a big shock when I used to go to Nigeria with my parents."

After clearing customs, they retrieved their bags and instantly saw a Cape Town Hilton driver holding a sign with Jason's name on it.

"I'm Jason Richards," he told the man.

"Ah, welcome to Cape Town," he said with a soft South African lilt. "My name is David Mbeki and I'll be your guide during your time here in South Africa."

David took their bags and they walked to a waiting taxi.

"Are you related to the president?"

David smiled.

"No," he said. "If I were, I certainly wouldn't be a driver for the Cape Town Hilton!"

Carole giggled.

"Are you here on a honeymoon?" David asked. He looked back at Jason and Carole, searching for a ring.

"No, we're just here on a minivacation," Carole responded.

"Well you've picked the right place to visit. I'll be happy to show you around my city. Cape Town is beautiful, as you will see, but it is also very dangerous. You really need to have someone who can keep you safe. And I will not charge you much."

"Carole, do you want to have a guide?" Jason asked.

"Sure, it can't hurt."

"How much do you charge for the week?"

"I'll charge you the rand equivalent of about $200 for the week."

"Okay, we have a deal."

They pulled out of the airport and started driving into Cape Town when they saw the most beautiful mountain they'd ever laid eyes on.

"That is our Table Mountain," David said as they stared in awe of its beauty. "We can take a hike to the summit if you like, sometime during your trip."

"That would be wonderful," Carole said. "That mountain is gorgeous."

"You know," Jason said as they drove down the highway, "this reminds me of Santa Barbara. You know, a seaside town where everything is a bit carefree?"

"Yes, but Santa Barbara doesn't have townships," Carole responded, looking out of the car window at the tin roofs and tar paper shacks that seemed to go on as far as the eye could see. "It's the same as in Nigeria. Welcome to Africa."

David turned toward Carole.

"You're Nigerian?" he asked, smiling.

"My parents are from Nigeria," she answered. "I was born in the United States, but we go back and forth all of the time."

"I can also take you into the townships," David said. "That is the township of Khayelitsha, and don't be scared by how it looks on the outside. There's a lot of good people who live there, and I think you'll enjoy yourself. It's where I grew up."

"How are things since apartheid ended?" Jason asked.

David wheeled through traffic as though he was Michael Schumacher, the race car driver.

"Things have gotten better, for the most part, but the whites still have most of the land. We are trying to remain patient because we know there's a lot of things the ANC has to accomplish in a short time, but we are free, so things are better."

They pulled into the Cape Town Hilton and David jumped out to get their bags. Carole pulled out her camera and handed it to David.

"Could you please take a picture of us?"

"Of course!"

After the picture, they walked into the lobby and Jason gave David his tip.

"Thank you, sir," David said. "If you need to contact me"—he wrote his number on a piece of paper, and handed it to Jason— "this is my cell phone number. Call me if you need anything or need to go anywhere. I can tell you which restaurants to go to and also where to go for entertainment. Just let me know and I'll be here in about thirty minutes."

"Thanks," Jason said, and David left.

They checked in and then took the elevator to their room. Upon entering the suite, Carole immediately opened the drapes.

"Jason, this is absolutely breathtaking," Carole said, looking at Cape Town spread out below her.

"Yes it is," Jason said, putting the luggage on the bed. On the bed was a gift basket.

"The Cape Town Hilton would like to welcome you to South Africa with this gift basket," Jason read from the card. "Please enjoy our South African wine, made right here in the Constantia area of Cape Town."

"Do you want a glass of wine?" Jason asked, opening a bottle of white wine.

"Yes, please," Carole said. She opened the French doors, and warm breeze from the Atlantic Ocean blew into the room. It was evening in Cape Town and the sun was slowly setting. Carole walked out onto the balcony and stood there soaking in the view.

"I've never seen something so beautiful in my life," she said with a look in her eyes that said it all. "Thank you, Jason."

He walked over to her and gave her a glass of wine.

"I see this beauty every time I look at you." Those were the perfect words, at the perfect time, from the perfect man, Carole thought. There was only one thing to do—give him a kiss as a reward.

She turned toward him and gave him her best, most sensuous kiss she'd ever given a man.

She took the wine and kissed him. *Screw those damn* Titan *rules, I'm officially in love,* Jason thought.

As Carole kissed Jason, she turned and watched the most beautiful sunset she'd ever seen. How could she make sense of everything that was happening in her life? Just a month ago, Jason was a an ex-boyfriend she'd lost touch with, and still held a grudge against, and now she was in Cape Town, South Africa, completely in love. How had this happened? More importantly, *why* was this happening?

Jason began kissing her neck, but Carole wanted to relax a bit before going any further.

"Later," she said, putting a finger to his lips. "I promise, later."

Carole walked back into the room and lay down on the bed. Jason flopped down beside her.

"So what do you want to do first?" he asked. "We can either do a little exploring by ourselves, or we can call our friend David and he can take us around."

"I know he was saying Cape Town is dangerous, but let's get something to eat ourselves and call David tomorrow when we explore the city. I'm feeling seafood—what about you?"

"Seafood it is," Jason said, jumping off the bed. He got on the phone and asked the front desk about possible restaurants.

"Hello, Mr. Richards, how may I help you?" the concierge asked.

"We're looking for a seafood restaurant within walking distance. What do you recommend?" Jason asked.

"I would recommend Marimba," he said. "They have delicious seafood at great prices."

"Thank you very much."

Jason hung up the phone. "Do you like lobster?"

"Yes, I do."

"Okay, let's go down and get dinner and then come back and rest. I'm feeling tired from the flight anyway, and I bet we'll get jet-lag at some time tonight."

"That sounds good. Plus, I need to get out of these clothes," Carole said.

"Take a shower and I'll sit on the balcony as you get dressed. Then I'll take my shower."

"Sounds like a plan."

Carole got into the shower and thought about what she had to do during dinner. Even though she didn't want to pressure Jason, she was in Africa with a man she only just had sex with a few days before. She'd never even been to his house in Los Angeles, and now she was in a hotel with him in Africa. She was listening to everyone, and was trying to just take things as they came, but she was a little uneasy about knowing where they were as a couple.

Did Jason just want to have sex with her, start a relationship, or take things as they came? *Divas's* friends to lover plan had done a great job in getting Jason to her, but gave her no instructions on what to do when she got him. Tonight, she was on her own, and she was determined to find out where they were going.

Carole walked out of the shower wearing nothing but a towel. As she began putting on her black dress, Jason was amazed at how beautiful she was. He couldn't stop staring.

"Don't watch me get dressed," she said. "A woman needs her privacy as she puts on her face and clothes."

"No problem," he said, and laughed, walking into the bathroom.

Jason took a shower and thought about just coming straight with Carole and letting her know about the money, the loft, and the whole *Titan* lifestyle deal.

But that's a can of worms, he thought. Did he want to risk it? Better to just keep things as they were. He walked out of the bathroom, grabbed his clothes, and was dressed in five minutes flat.

"Ready?" he asked.

Carole took one last look in the mirror.

"Ready!"

"You look gorgeous, by the way," he said.

"Thank you!"

Walking along the beach, they could hear the sound of music coming from the clubs and restaurants. Black faces, white faces, and Asian faces greeted them as they walked. The architecture was also amazing, including beautiful Cape Dutch buildings alongside Muslim mosques.

"Do you smell that?" Carole asked as they passed by restaurant after restaurant.

"Yes," Jason said. "It's like a mixture of salty water and spices and something else I can't figure out."

She stopped and lifted her nose into the air.

"I've got to figure out what that scent is and bottle it."

They turned the corner and saw their restaurant. Marimba was a little seaside restaurant with tables both inside and outside the restaurant. The place was packed with people sitting around tables with little red-and-white checkerboard tablecloths.

"Dinner for two?" a waitress asked. She was a white South African with a Boer accent.

"Yes, please."

"Would you like to eat outside?"

"Yes," they answered.

The waitress gave them menus.

"I'll be back in a second to take your order," she said.

"Look at these prices," Jason said. "I'm not worried about spending money, but a fresh lobster just pulled out of the ocean just shouldn't cost seven dollars. I mean, that's a whole lobster for the price of a Denny's dinner!"

"Hey, with these prices, you can order three lobsters!" Carole said, laughing.

"I think one will do." He smiled. "But order what you want!"

The waitress came back and Jason ordered. Carole ordered a whole lobster and Jason, being greedy, ordered the lobster and prawns.

"Two martinis, one apple and another a straight one," Jason ordered.

"Thank you. I'll be back with your order," she said before leaving with their menus.

They sat there for a second, taking in the sights and sounds of the beach. The South African band that was playing was called Rankin Roger, as in Rankin Roger from the eighties band the English Beat. They were playing old ska tunes, some original and some cover tunes.

The waitress brought the martinis to the table.

"Jason, I don't want to break the mood, but I need to talk to you," Carole said, sipping on her apple martini.

"Sure."

Carole shifted in her chair.

"Before I ask you a question, I just want to tell you that I'm not trying to put any pressure on you. I'm thoroughly enjoying all of this. I mean, look at this!" she said, sweeping her hands from side to side. "I could never imagine myself taking a vacation, moreover one on the other side of the world. But I do need to talk to you first."

"You told me that you needed to think about what happened last week, and so I don't know what to make of all of this," she said. "I just want to get clear about what's happening with us. Again, don't take this wrong, I'm not trying to pressure you."

"I thought about us, and whether we could make it," Jason said, sort of not knowing where to go with this. "Look, I like you and I want to see if this will work, but I don't want to force anything. Now we both know your record with boyfriends . . ."

"Uh, there's no need to bring up my past boyfriends. I told you my experiences as a friend, and they have nothing to do with you. Look, I don't mind having fun and seeing where things go, but I'm not going to get used. I think this is all spectacular and we are going to have a lot of fun, but at some point, we are going to have to talk about what we are looking for in a relationship."

"How about now?"

She looked up from her martini.

"What do you mean, now?" she asked.

"I mean, why don't we talk now?"

"You've got to be kidding."

"Why do you say that?"

"Well, men tend to try to avoid having the 'conversation' as long as they can. I'm just shocked that you want to talk right now."

"Hey, why not? I've got a beautiful setting, a beautiful woman, and a fresh seven-dollar lobster on the way. Why not start talking to get things clear?"

Carole started giggling again. Jason loved her laugh.

"Okay then, Mr. Loquacious," Carole asked. "What do you want out of a girlfriend and in a relationship?"

Jason sat back and thought for a second. Just as he was about to speak, the waitress came back with their orders.

"The lobster for you, miss," she said. "And the lobster and prawns for the gentleman. Enjoy, and if you need anything else, don't hesitate to ask."

"This looks great," Carole said. "Okay, you were about to say something."

"Oh yes, what do I want out of a girlfriend?" he said, breaking the lobster apart. "Well, I think the first thing would be honesty. I got burned by my last girlfriend when I believed she was something she wasn't, and she ended up lying to me. All of us have something to hide, and I'm no exception, but in my next relationship, I'd like there to be honesty within the relationship. I can't survive without it."

"That sounds reasonable," she said, biting into her lobster. "Next question," she said. "Why me?"

"Why you?"

"Yes, why me? I mean we were cool, but I don't think we'd tried to get at each other before, at least not since school. So why did you pick me? It couldn't be that the pizza and beer were so good that you decided to take me to Africa. So yes, why me?"

Jason thought about hemming and hawing, but then he decided to be honest and straight with her. Well, not completely—he wasn't going to tell her about the orgies, but he was going to be as honest as he could be with her.

"Do you know how we didn't really get along at the start?" he started. "Well, it was kind of cool because I didn't have any preconceived notions of trying to talk to you. I wasn't trying to throw lines at you, or trying to run a game at you."

"You mean like your friend Steven?" she said.

That took him aback. "What do you mean? And by the way, Steven is not my friend."

"Steven tried to talk to me every time I saw him. I had to go off on him the last time. I thought he was your buddy because I almost always saw him with you. Anyway, Steven is about as far away from what I want in a man as the moon is from earth. I hate players because I'm not a woman to be played. But I think you're right, it was better that we weren't initially going after each other. We got our faults out before we found the attraction. I hope I don't have too many faults."

"Are you kidding me?" Jason said. "I'm the one trying to not fuck this up."

"Don't worry, you're doing a great job."

"Fucking it up?"

"No, not fucking it up."

Jason ate a prawn and turned to Carole. "Okay, I have a question."

"This lobster is great," she said, smiling. "But jetlag is kicking my behind. I feel like a weight is on my shoulders. I'm so tired, I don't know if I can answer any questions."

"Oh no, turnabout is fair play, and you're not getting out of it claiming jetlag," he said. "Why are you sitting here with me?"

She dipped a piece of lobster into her butter.

"Besides the free trip to Africa, a seven-dollar lobster, and the offer to buy me clothes, I couldn't think of any reason to turn you down," she said, laughing.

"No, I like you and I think I misjudged you," she continued. "When I first saw you as an adult, I just saw another lawyer. To me you were just somebody who was out to use people for their own gain. That's what lawyers do. But then, when you started working at Mama's House, I began seeing a person that was human and caring. You weren't out to manipulate people for your own personal interest. I saw that you really did want to be a lawyer to help people. In other words, I began taking a second look at you and I liked what I saw. And I like what I see here."

"I know what you're thinking, though." Jason said, finishing his prawns.

"What am I thinking?"

"Are we going to make it as a relationship and what are we now?"

"Ooh, you are a mind reader."

"Well," Jason said, finishing his martini, "if you'll have me, I'd like to be your boyfriend. And that obviously means that I'd like to have you as my girlfriend. But that doesn't mean that we immediately have to add pressure to this budding relationship. We can just take it slowly, get over the bumps and bad moments, and not take anything for granted. So it's a combination of taking things easy and the formality of knowing that we are exclusive. Just forgive my mistakes and I'll forgive yours. Does that work for you?"

She looked at Jason with her beautiful brown eyes.

"It works for me. But I do have one question. You laid down a whole bunch of rules before we, you know, did it. Do those rules still apply? Must we not sleep over? Is this simply lust and not love?"

Those damn Titan *rules!* Jason thought. He'd almost forgotten that he'd said them in the first place.

"Fuck those rules," he said. "Plus, love has no rules. Isn't that how the saying goes?"

She smiled. He'd said the right thing.

"Here's to no rules," she said. They clinked glasses, toasting their new relationship.

"Oh, and did I tell you that the other reason I picked you is because you are beautiful and great in bed?" he said with a grin.

"I didn't hear that in your initial explanation, Mr. Attorney, but I'm glad that you included it in your closing arguments."

Jason leaned over to give her a kiss, and this time the garlic from the lobster overwhelmed everything.

"Ooh, perhaps we should get a mint and kiss again?" he said smiling.

"I think a better idea is that we go back to the hotel," she whispered, "and see how the little black thing I bought from Victoria's Secret looks in the Cape Town moonlight."

Jason smiled.

"Check, please!" Jason shouted at the waitress.

CHAPTER 25

"What do you want to do?" Monica asked. The *Baldwin Hills* staff was all standing up, looking at Jordan, and Jordan looked right back at them. She was unsure about what to do, but didn't want her first issue to be dead on arrival because she was indecisive. It was decision time, and she was going to get this issue out, no matter what.

"Call her one more time," she told Monica.

Monica got back on the phone and turned the speaker up.

"You have reached Marcia Cambridge. I'm currently out of the country. Please leave a message and I'll get back to you as soon as possible."

Monica hung up the phone. "It's been like that for the past three days. She hasn't responded to the phone messages or any e-mails. But we don't have time to wait. What do you want to do, Jordan?"

Jordan moved uneasily in her shoes. Where the hell was Marcia? It was a big decision to go to print without Marcia's final approval, but they'd run out of time.

"Send it to the printer and I'll deal with the consequences later when she gets back," Jordan said. "She should have answered her messages."

And with that, *Baldwin Hills* magazine was going to press.

* * *

"Would you like a beverage, miss?" the flight attendant asked.

"No, thank you," Marcia said, reclining in her chair. "I've had enough beverages during my vacation."

When Marcia got on the Air Brazil plane back to Los Angeles, she felt refreshed and reenergized. The mission for her trip to Rio had been to forget about *Baldwin Hills* magazine for two weeks, sit on the beach with a sugary drink in hand, dance at a new club each night and hopefully wake up next to some fine Brazilian man that spoke no English, but spoke the language of sweat, and guttural, base sex. She wasn't looking for love, but pure pleasure. Mission accomplished on all ends.

Over the past week, she'd even met a man who'd taken her into the favelas, where she'd completely cut herself off from the outside world. As far as she knew, *Baldwin Hills had* burned down.

But now was a dash back to reality. She had to get her mind thinking about her magazine, and hopefully things hadn't fallen apart in her absence. Jordan had e-mailed her about the topic of the magazine, and it seemed cool. It was an exposé of private parties in Los Angeles. She'd wanted to do something like that in October 2001, but the World Trade Center tragedy had interrupted that issue. She'd subsequently forgotten about it, so she was happy Jordan had taken the initiative to do the issue.

If she does a good job, I think I'm going to have Jordan run a new Bay Area edition of the magazine, she thought. She hadn't seen the final edit for this edition, but she trusted that Jordan would hold the issue until she got back.

"Would you like a pillow and a blanket, miss?" the flight attendant asked.

"Yes, please."

Marcia took the pillow and blanket and settled down for the flight. She felt like she could sleep for days, and it was nice that the flight was nearly half full and no one was next to her. She could stretch out and sleep without anyone bothering her.

"I'll turn this light off for you," the flight attendant said, switching off the dome light. "Have a nice sleep."

* * *

"Here's the issue, Barbara. How do you like it?" Jordan asked, holding it up. The printer had just made the delivery of the new *Baldwin Hills* issue and Jordan was justifiably proud of it. She'd proven that she could handle the magazine while Marcia was gone. Not only that, but this was the most provocative issue she'd seen since she'd been at *Baldwin Hills* magazine.

"So I get a cover?" Barbara said excitedly as Jordan handed her the new issue.

"Your article makes the issue, so it deserves it."

"Thanks for letting me do it. A lot of editors would have cut it, especially since I got such explicit photos."

"Well," Jordan said, looking at the photos, "how many reporters would have hidden under a bed to get the photos? Hunter Thompson, eat your heart out! Little old *Baldwin Hills* magazine is getting scandalous!"

The topic of this month's magazine was THE SECRET TO L.A.'S BLACK PRIVATE PARTIES and had a blurred photo of Jason, Steven and Miss Blue. INSIDE THE WORLD OF THE *TITAN* PARTY: SINGLE MEN, MULTIPLE WOMEN, WE HAVE PICTURES! read the sub headline.

Over the years, Marcia had understood that you either make the reader angry or happy, but never ambivalent. Jordan knew that angry letters from subscribers would come pouring in once they saw the cover. Christian subscribers would call the article immoral and swear they were going to unsubscribe, but they never did. The feminists would talk about how these men were the scum of the earth and the women were being duped. And the others would tell all their friends about it. All together, that meant sales, sales, sales!

"I wonder what Marcia is going to think about the issue?" Barbara said. "I don't think we've ever had an issue this racy."

"It's too late now. The subscriber issues have already gone out and the newsstand copies are about to be mailed. Marcia is coming in this afternoon, so we'll know soon enough," Jordan said.

Barbara kept reading her article and started walking to her desk. She was proud of her work, but still worried about what Marcia would say.

"Well, you're the managing editor. If she yells at somebody, then let it be you!" Barbara said, half kidding. "I'll be running in the opposite direction."

"Thanks for the confidence boost!" Jordan said, throwing the magazine on her desk.

Marcia's plane landed in Los Angeles, and not a minute too soon. Marcia knew she could never ride on the space shuttle, because a plane was too damn confining for her spirit, and she needed to be able to walk around whenever she wanted.

With her typical brass flourish, Marcia swept through the terminal to the baggage area. Marcia was the type who could will things to happen, and she willed her baggage to be the first one out the shoot. It was ten o'clock on Friday morning and Marcia could have gone home and gone to the office on Monday, but she wanted to see the new issue.

Marcia got into her car and started toward her office. But she didn't feel that she should surprise them. Things might have gotten sloppy, so she wanted them to have a chance to get their act together.

"Jordan, this is Marcia. Hey, I'm on my way back to the office."

"You've already landed?" Jordan asked nervously.

"Yes, I've landed and I'm in the car on my way. So if folks have their feet on their desks, or if they've taken residence in my office, tell them to stop it because Marcia is back. Okay, I'll see you in about ten minutes."

"Will do," Jordan said. "See you here."

Marcia then dialed Carole to let her know she was back in town and to see if she wanted to go out for drinks after work. She couldn't wait to tell her about her time in Rio.

"Mama's House, may I help you?"

"Hello, may I speak to Carole, please?"

"Carole's not in this week. Can I take a message?"

"Not in for the week? Is she sick?" Marcia asked. "Who is this?"

"This is Dorothy."

"Hello Dorothy, this is Marcia."

"Oh hi, Marcia!" Dorothy exclaimed. "I'm running the office for the week."

"Carole not in for the week? When has that ever happened?" Marcia asked.

"She actually decided to take a week vacation. She mentioned something about going off with some guy. I don't know where they went, and that's unusual because I thought she'd have called to check into the office. But she hasn't called once. I guess she's like 'Mama's House will still be here when she gets back on Monday, so why worry about it.'"

"Some guy, huh?" Marcia said as she drove into the *Baldwin Hills* magazine parking lot. "Have you seen Jason around the office lately? I heard that he was spending a month of pro bono work at the center."

"Now that you ask, I haven't seen him. I thought he was working at the law firm this week. Wait, Marcia, you don't think—"

"Don't know, but I suspect. I'll try to hit her on the cell phone later. But don't tell her I asked," Marcia said, getting to the front door of the office. "I wouldn't want her thinking I was trying to get into her business."

"My lips are sealed," Dorothy said. "But make sure to let me know if it's true. This is gossip that's too good not to know!"

"Will do. Gotta go."

"Oh wait, Marcia. I haven't received my issue of *Baldwin Hills* in the last two months. Can you check on my subscription?"

"I'll do it right now. Ciao!"

"Bye!"

Marcia walked into the office and stood looking over everyone.

"Hello, everybody!" she yelled. "Get ready to work, because the bitch is back!"

"Welcome back," they all said in unison. Marcia walked into her office.

"Welcome back, Marcia," Jordan said, walking into Marcia's office. Jordan was nervous about how she would like the magazine.

"The sunshine and white sands must have agreed with you. How was Rio?"

Marcia was back behind her desk, shuffling through the mail that had accumulated during her vacation.

"Rio was fabulous! If you ever decide to go there, you've got to stay in Copacabana and just lie on the beach. Some of the most beautiful men in the world will just come up to you and proposition you. It is wonderful. But enough of that," she said, looking up from her pile of mail.

"Where are the blue lines for the magazine?" she asked. "Did you tell the printer that we were going to be delayed?"

Jordan rocked in her heels, her heart sinking into her stomach.

"We tried to get in touch with you," she started, "but you never answered."

Marcia stared at Jordan.

"Okay, but so what? Just bring me the blue lines and we'll get the magazine out."

Jordan was really nervous now. "I thought you wanted me to take care of things, so I decided to go ahead with taking the magazine to the printer."

Marcia stood up angrily. "You did what?" she shouted. "You did fucking what?"

"Marcia, you told me this was my issue and that you wanted me to take control. And that's what I did."

Marcia walked around the desk and stood in front of Jordan. She was extremely angry.

"I gave you room to do the damn magazine, but I'm the publisher, dammit!" Marcia said. "The managing editor should never decide to take a magazine to press without the approval of the publisher. That is simply unacceptable!"

Marcia walked back to her desk. "So where's the magazine, anyway?"

Jordan held the magazine nervously behind her back. Here was the moment that was going to either make or break her career.

"Here you go!" she said, producing the magazine slowly.

Marcia took the magazine and looked at it carefully.

"Production did a bang-up job on the cover," she said.

Jordan stifled a grin. At least the first hurdle had been successfully traversed.

"Who is this on the cover?" Marcia said, staring at the cover.

"That's our scoop of the month," Jordan said, sitting down. "Barbara was able to find a secret, informal men's club that followed the hedonistic dictates of *Titan* magazine. So they held these parties where they invited all these beautiful women and then tried to have orgies with them afterward."

Marcia was turning the pages of the magazine, looking at the layout for any visible mistakes, and listening to Jordan explain the story.

"That sounds good. I hate *Titan* magazine and its juvenile attitude. They treat women like playthings and objects, and not as human beings," she said, continuing to flip through the magazine. Marcia started reading the *Titan* article.

"You won't believe what Barbara had to do to get some photos," Jordan said as Marcia continued to read. "She hid under the bed and waited until the men were going to have sex with this one woman, and took pictures. . . ."

"Oh, shit!" Marcia said, staring at the page.

"What's wrong?" Jordan said. "Did we do something wrong? Is there a mistake?"

Jordan saw her life flash before her eyes. What did she do wrong?

Marcia closed the magazine and looked at Jordan with a troubled look in her eyes.

"Close the door. Close it right now!"

Jordan got up and closed the door to the office.

"What is it Marcia, you're giving me a heart attack!"

"Jason Richards, the center of this story?" she said, pointing to the magazine.

"Yes?"

"He's a good friend of mine. In fact, I would say he is one of the best male friends I have."

Marcia was completely petrified. She stood up and began pacing around the office, reading the article as she paced.

"Oh my God, Marcia, we didn't know," Jordan said, seeing her career slipping down the drain because of some friend of Marcia's.

"I know you didn't know but this is bad, very, very bad!"

Marcia put the magazine down and turned to Jordan.

"Did the subscriber issues go out already?" she asked.

"They went out yesterday."

Marcia sat back down and put her face in her hands.

"This is going to destroy me and my friends in so many ways."

Jordan felt like crawling under a rock.

"Look, this isn't your fault," Marcia said. "This is my problem and I need to fix this as fast as I can."

"I'm so sorry, Marcia."

"No, don't be. You did a great job. You should be proud."

Jordan stood up to leave. She'd walked into the office feeling that she'd done the best job she could have for the magazine, and now, despite Marcia's protestations to the contrary, she felt that this issue would always tainted. Damn, damn, damn!

"Thanks, Marcia. If I can do anything to mitigate the damage, just let me know and I'll do it."

"Thanks Jordan, but this is my job. I've got to get this thing fixed, and fast."

Marcia continued to read the article, but every sentence was digging a deeper hole. She was petrified that Jason was the topic of this article, but she was even more shocked that Jason was even a part of this. And even though Jordan had blurred the photo, it was clear that it was Steven and Jason on top of that woman. Steven! She knew that he was behind this whole thing. She needed to come up with a plan because the minute Carole saw this issue, it was all going to be over been Jason and Carole.

Damn you, Jason! Marcia thought. *What the fuck were you thinking?*

During their week in South Africa, Carole and Jason did all of the tourist things. David had done a wonderful job of showing them the sites, taking them on a cable car to Table Mountain, where it seemed like you could see forever. They stayed at a bed-and-breakfast run by a nice Afrikaner family. It was strange staying with people who only a decade before were more than likely complicit in suppressing and brutalizing people who looked just like them, Jason thought, but they were extremely nice.

They took a quick trip to Durban and experienced the wonderful markets, with their Indian influence. They also visited a Zulu kraal in the countryside, and participated in a Zulu ceremony.

But now it was time to go back to the States. They'd had their fun, and this had been the trip of a lifetime. Nothing could spoil it, and Jason thought this was going to be the catalyst for everything they wanted to do when they got back.

"Did you pack up everything?" Carole said as she tried to squeeze her African outfit into a bulging suitcase.

"Yes, I've packed everything. You know that men pack faster than women because we don't worry about whether the stuff is crumpled when we get home."

Carole walked over to Jason and planted one of her wonderful kisses on him.

"That's for giving me the vacation of a lifetime. I'll never forget this."

"You won't because we are going to visit every few years."

Carole beamed. He was making plans for the future and she was a part of it, she thought.

"Let's go before I turn in my passport and decide to stay," she said.

"I'm with you. I've got to go back to Ketchings and Martin on Monday, and I'm not too happy about it."

"Oh baby," Carole said, placing her hand on his cheek. "I'm going to lose you!"

"Yeah. Ketchings and Martin has this curious thing. They want their lawyers to actually work in the office on lawsuits and things. Imagine that? The bastards!" Jason laughed.

"Did you give any thought to actually leaving the firm? I mean, you were saying that."

"Yes, and I meant it. I really do like helping people, but I've got to admit that consumer law still holds an attraction for me. I'm helping people who are powerless in that capacity, and sticking it to corporations at the same time. I like that."

"Well, you do what you think is best," she said. "I'll support you."

There was a knock on the hotel door. It was David.

"Mr. Richards, are you ready to go down to the airport?"

Jason brought over the bags.

"Can you take down our bags, David? We'll meet you downstairs in a second."

"No problem, sir."

David took the bags and left.

Jason took Carole's hand and they went back to the balcony and stared out over the Atlantic Ocean. Boats were sailing on the ocean, while surfers were catching waves. This was a scene they'd been awed by when they first arrived and he wanted their last vision of Africa to be that same view.

"Take a long look at this," he told Carole. "We will come back here one day. But remember this as being the start of something wonderful. And if I ever mess up, I want you to think back to this happy time and forgive me. Deal?"

"Deal."

She turned and kissed him.

"Now, let's go home," she said.

CHAPTER 26

"What do you mean, I'm in your magazine?" Steven said, drinking his ice tea. Marcia had called him and suggested they meet at Roscoe's Chicken and Waffles for lunch, but he was swamped at work, so he'd initially declined. But when she'd insisted, he knew something was up.

"You're not just in the magazine," Marcia said, pulling the magazine out of her briefcase, "but on the cover too."

Marcia thought about what she should say to both Carole and Jason, but couldn't come up with the right words. This was so wrong in so many ways, but then again, it wasn't her fault that Jason was having these sex parties. Her reporter was only doing what a good reporter should do: finding the story and then reporting on it. But she was still surprised. Steven, she could have guessed, but Jason struck her as being levelheaded and not a dog at all. And what the hell was this about Jason having millions of dollars? He'd never mentioned any of that. She had a lot of questions that needed to be answered, and Marcia knew that when Carole got home and opened her magazine, she'd hit the roof.

So when Jordan had left her office, Marcia sat thinking. What to do? If Jason and Carole had gone away for a week, things must have been going well. She didn't want that messed up, but she couldn't figure out a way to make this bombshell better. But there was one wild card that could at least help. So Marcia had picked up the phone.

"Where the fuck did you get this?" Steven said angrily. He was trying to keep his voice down, but was having trouble. "You put me having sex on your fucking cover?"

"Remember that woman that was under Jason's bed? She took photos of what you were going to do with that girl you had in there."

"So?" he said. "First of all, I can sue you for defamation. I didn't give her permission to take photos of me, so you'd better watch out. I'll own *Baldwin Hills* magazine faster than you can eat those damn waffles."

"I have my own attorneys, Steven, so if you want to get into a pissing contest, then go ahead," Marcia said, giving Steven an icy stare. "But realize that if we do that, the amount of people who know your freakiness is going to move from a limited circulation of around fifty thousand people, most of whom you'll never meet, to millions nationwide. After that type of publicity, you won't be able to get a job representing anywhere in this country. So stop with the goddamn threats and get real."

Steven smoldered. "So what the fuck did you invite me here for?"

"I need a favor," Marcia said, crunching on some ice.

"Wait, you mean to tell me that you're screwing me and now you want something from me? Hell, why don't you simply ask for a reach around?"

"You would know, wouldn't you?" Marcia said caustically. "Yes, I need a favor, and you're going to help. I know you and I know Jason, and I'm betting that you got Jason into this whole *Titan* lifestyle."

"Whoa, whoa there," Steven said. "I didn't have to twist his arm to get him to join in fucking beautiful women."

Steven drank from his glass and then looked up at Marcia.

"You want me to help Jason with Carole because she's going to find out that he's a freak?" Steven said. "Well fuck him, Marcia! He's a big boy and he knew what he was doing when he got involved in the *Titan* lifestyle. Yeah, I got him involved, but his sorry ass decided he wanted out. Then, to make matters worse, he stabbed me in the back. I told him that I wanted to talk to Carole and he basically did what he wanted. So fuck him now," Steven said.

"Look Steven, you never had a chance with Carole, and I don't think Jason even knew that he was going to fall for Carole."

"He did when he followed *Titan's* advice."

"What do you mean?"

"Look, Carole is nothing but another piece of ass for Jason. Nothing more and nothing less."

"Stop hating, Steven," Marcia said. "You're the shallow one in this conversation, not Jason."

"Sure, go ahead and believe that. But before you finalize that conclusion, go pick up the last issue of *Titan*. They have an article called "Friends with Benefits" that I think you'll find interesting. Call me back when you read it and then tell me if your sweet Jason is as pure as you think."

"Look, I don't know what the hell is in that magazine, but you're going to do something for me. I believe that Jason does care for Carole, and I need you to say that this was all your fault and not his."

"Hell, no!"

"Look, muthafucka," Marcia screamed at Steven. The other patrons at Roscoe's were beginning to turn their way. "You fucking better do what the fuck I just said, or you're going to find out that Los Angeles is a mighty tough place to be when the biggest bitch in the city has put out the blackball on your ass."

"You ain't got that clout."

"Muthafucka, try me." Marcia was now pointing her finger in Steven's chest. "I've got more clout than you ever thought you had."

Marcia stood up straight and looked at all of the people staring at them.

"How many of you read *Baldwin Hills*?" she asked everyone. "Raise your hands if you subscribe."

Nearly everyone in the restaurant raised their hands. "Thank you," Marcia said. She sat back down and looked at Steven, her eyes boring through him.

"Just fucking try me," she said. "You're going to fucking cop to

this shit, or feel my muthafuckin' wrath. Don't make me get nig-
gerish on you."

Steven simply stared back at Marcia, unblinking.

"Are you going to call me tonight?" Carole asked, as she got out
of the cab. The flight from Cape Town to LAX had been tiring and
she was going straight to sleep when she got into her apartment. It
was ten o'clock in the evening and Carole had to get back to
Mama's House early the next morning. As soon as the wheels of
the plane touched down, all of the trials and tribulations of Mama's
House came rushing back.

"Why don't you get some sleep," Jason said, taking her bags to
the front door. "I'll call you in the morning."

"Okay," she said quietly. "Now remember, tomorrow I make my
first visit to your apartment. You should have told me that you have
a loft. I love lofts. Imagine that? We've traveled over ten thousand
miles before I have traveled across town to your home. We've got
to remedy that, don't we?"

"Yes we do. I'll help you take your stuff up inside and—"

"No," she said. "I've got it. You're tired. Get in bed and think of
me."

Jason kissed her and then got in the cab.

"Call you tomorrow," he said.

"Good night."

Carole took her bags to her apartment and just laid them
against the wall. She'd left instructions with her postman to bundle her mail outside her door, and he'd done as instructed. He'd
even bound all of the mail together with string so that she could
pick everything up at once. Carole picked up the bundle along
with her bags and threw everything on her couch.

Oh, the new *Baldwin Hills* issue is out, she thought. She could
just barely see the *Baldwin Hills* masthead through the rest of the
mail. She thought about reading it, but was too tired to do it.

I'll check messages and mail tomorrow, she thought.

And with that, Carole collapsed in her bed, completely exhausted.

Jason walked into his loft and it smelled like something had
died.

"What the hell?" he said, walking to the kitchen. Somehow, the milk had turned to cheese in a week, and it was stinking up the place.

Life was good and he didn't think things could get any better. He turned on the television and picked up the mail off the floor. Jason's postal slot was situated so that the mail fell directly into a basket. And with a week away, there was a lot of mail. Jason was too amped to go directly asleep, so he picked up his mail and grabbed his phone to check messages.

"Thank you for calling," the voice mail voice said. "Please dial your password and press pound."

Bills, bills, bills, he thought, sorting though the mail.

"You have one message," the voice mail voice said.

He pressed pound and it was Marcia.

"Jason, this is Marcia. Please give me a call as soon as you get back in. It is very, very, important that you call me and don't worry about the time. Peace."

What is that all about, he thought, continuing to shuffle through his mail. Then he came across *Baldwin Hills* magazine and saw it: INSIDE THE WORLD OF THE *TITAN* PARTY: SINGLE MEN AND MULTIPLE WOMEN!

"What the fuck? What the fuck?" Jason said. He damn near tore open the magazine trying to get to the article, and there it was. *Baldwin Hills* magazine had uncovered him and Steven and that damn *Titan* lifestyle. They had a picture of them together, fuzzed up, but looking like they were double-teaming Miss Blue on the bed. They *were* double-teaming her.

Oh shit, oh shit! he thought. How could Marcia do this to me? And what the hell is Carole going to say about this?

His head was spinning. He picked up the phone and then put it back down again. Carole would never speak to him again once she saw this.

I have to compose myself, he thought. I am angry, and I want to blame someone. But what was Marcia thinking when she put me out there like that?

He grabbed the phone again and dialed Marcia's phone number.

"Hello."

"Marcia, this is Jason. What the fuck is this article in your magazine? How could you put me out there like that? This is completely fucked up! This article is going to ruin me if anyone at the firm found out about this, and someone is bound to blab. I could fucking *kill* Steven! This reporter detailed everything that Steven had told me, and a whole bunch of stuff that I didn't know. I didn't know that he had a bunch of guys doing this, and I didn't know that Steven had organized this so he would be able to live off of us. As it turned out, the first party I'd gone to, someone else had paid for it."

"First of all, Jason, you need to calm down and stop cursing, because no man curses at me," she said with not a little bit of attitude. "Second, I was in Brazil when my managing editor decided to write this article, and it was too late to do anything about it when I got back. Anyway, why the hell were you involved in this *Titan* lifestyle in the first place? I'm surprised at you!"

This was devastating, absolutely devastating.

"I just don't know. I got caught up in this because Steven made it seem so damn cool and exciting. I made some money from a lawsuit, about four million dollars. And all of a sudden, I was a playboy and playa. Steven's plan made me feel that women wanted me, and I had all the power that comes with a man with a lot of money. So I got the women and the flossy pad, and I got caught up in the lifestyle. But he didn't make me go down the road I went. I made that choice. Jesus, Marcia, what am I going to do? This is going to ruin me both professionally and personally. And I fell in love with Carole and she'll never forgive me for this."

"I don't know what to do, Jason," Marcia said, her voice softened. "I've been thinking about this for the past three days, trying to figure out a way to make this all right, but I don't know what to do. I heard you went on a vacation with Carole. How are things going on that end?"

"That's what I'm talking about. We are doing wonderfully and this is going to destroy that. I took her on a trip to Cape Town, South Africa, and Marcia, it was so beautiful. Do you know how beautiful she is? Do you? I mean she's just a person who radiates beauty both inside and outside. And I'm going to fucking lose it because I made mistakes."

There was silence on the line as he could tell that Marcia felt sorry for him. Jason felt like he'd sunk into a deep, dark hole and there was no way out. He wanted Marcia to tell him that she could make things better, but she couldn't do that. No one could do that. Jason knew that Carole was going to read this thing and never speak to him again. He had been so damn close to finding love that he couldn't imagine losing it, not this way.

"Does Carole have a subscription, Marcia?"

"Yes she does, and, unfortunately, she should have received it by now."

"Then I'm sunk."

"Jason, I'm so sorry. Maybe things can be rebuilt between you and Carole once this blows over? I have faith in things like this, Jason, and sometimes I think you just have to hope that she sees who you really are, and at the same time, you come completely clean with her. There are no guarantees, but at least you can find out if what you have is truly love, or if it isn't."

"I guess you're right, but that doesn't really help me now. Should I call her and come clean before she reads it?"

"I don't know, Jason. Look," she said. "Go to sleep and get some rest. The shit is going to hit the fan tomorrow morning and you can't do a thing about it. My advice? Call her in the afternoon and try to explain yourself as best you can, and then wait. That's all you can do. But I have one question, Jason, and you have to be honest with me on this. I talked to Steven and he told me that you only got with Carole because you were following a *Titan* article called "Friends with Benefits." I bought that issue and read it. Now be honest, were you trying to scam Carole and if so, are you still trying to?"

Jason paused. He could lie, but too much was riding on this. He didn't want to have anything to do with the *Titan* lifestyle and everything it could provide. But if he wanted an honest life, without manipulation, then he was going to have to start that night.

"Yes, I initially followed the rules of the article because I loved the power of feeling I could sleep with anyone I wanted. Again, I was caught up in this whole *Titan* lifestyle. But when I started to think about it, I began to realize that it wasn't the sex I wanted, it was Carole. I wanted her to realize that I was the man for her and she was the woman for me. She's perfect, Marcia, and I don't want to lose her."

Marcia was silent for a few seconds.

"Look, I'm going to be honest. I don't like that you tried to manipulate my girl. I trusted you when I told you that she needed an honest ear, and I thought you'd be the person to give it to her."

She paused. "But I can hear the pain in your voice, and I think you're being honest with me. Okay, I have some ideas about how to fix this. But I'm going to need you to be completely honest from this point forward. Do you understand?"

"Yes. Please help me, Marcia. I'll do anything to keep her. I just . . ."

"Get some rest. I'll call you tomorrow."

"Okay, thanks, Marcia."

"Hey, don't thank me yet. You're not out of the woods yet. Get some rest."

"Peace."

"Peace."

Jason hung up the phone and sank into his chaise longue. All of a sudden, Jason hated everything around him. He hated the loft, his chaise longue, everything that surrounded him. It was someone else's lifestyle and he didn't want it. Just like he had felt dirty when Miss Blue wanted him and Steven to fuck her, he felt dirty now. Thirty minutes ago, he felt as good as he'd ever felt. Now, he was in a big heap of shit and he didn't know how to get out of it.

CHAPTER 27

"Welcome back, Carole!" the staff shouted.

Carole smiled.

"Well it's not like I've been gone for months, guys!" she said, taking the kisses from the staff.

"We missed you anyway," Dorothy said as Carole entered her office. She placed her mail in the chair next to her desk. She'd brought the bundle from home.

"Well, I missed you all. Thanks, everybody!"

Carole turned on her computer as Dorothy closed the door.

"Do you mind if I ask you where you went on vacation?" she asked. "It sounded so mysterious and exciting."

Carole looked up.

"You'll never guess," Carole said. "We went to Cape Town, South Africa."

"Girl, you went to Africa? *You went to Africa?* My goodness, I thought you went to some place like Mexico. You went on the other side of the world. South Africa! How was that? How were the people?"

"Just gorgeous. Jason—"

Carole stopped. She had slipped. She hadn't meant to let people in the office know that she was dating Jason, but now the cat was out of the bag.

"We thought it was Jason!" Dorothy said with a big smile. "Now, we didn't mean to get into your business, but we all agreed that you two would make a great couple. I'm so glad to hear that you're dating."

Carole couldn't hide her delight. Jason was special and she didn't mind people knowing now that she'd let it slip. But she didn't want him to feel pressured when he came into the center.

"I'm glad people think that, but let's try to keep it so he doesn't feel like he's being stared at when he gets here."

"Gotcha."

Dorothy got up to leave and then she stopped. "Oh, I forgot to tell you. This is important. Ms. Amy Crenshaw from the Crenshaw Foundation is coming in today to take a look at the center."

"Wait," Carole said, suddenly looking up. "When did she call and why is she coming over?"

"She said that the board is still contemplating the funding and she wanted to see Mama's House for herself before making the final decision."

"What time is she coming?"

"One o'clock."

"Great."

"Thanks for the heads-up, Dorothy," Carole said.

Dorothy left and Carole sat back in her chair.

One o'clock, Carole thought. Okay, that gives me a few hours to prepare. The first thing I need to do is prep the staff.

She walked out into the main office and cleared her throat.

"Excuse me, everyone," she said. All of the faces looked up.

"In a few hours, one of the most important people associated with Mama's House, a Ms. Amy Crenshaw, is going to make an appearance here. She's one of the people who decides whether to fund us through her Crenshaw Foundation. The impression we give her may be the make or break on whether or not our doors stay open. So with that said, just do what you normally do. I have faith in what you do and how we service our clients. And if she has any sense, she'll think the same thing and give us our money!"

They all laughed and Carole went back into her office.

For the next two hours, Carole met with single women and caught up with her e-mails. Soon it was noon and Carole decided to take her break.

"Dorothy," she said on the phone, "I'm going on break."

"Great, I'll hold your calls."

"Thanks!"

Carole went over to the chair and retrieved her mail. She clipped the burlap string that held everything together.

Hmm. She sighed. *Bills, bills and more bills.*

And then she got to the *Baldwin Hills* magazine.

Who the hell is this? she thought, looking at the cover.

INSIDE THE WORLD OF THE *TITAN* PARTY: SINGLE MEN AND MULTIPLE WOMEN! she read. Marcia was starting to get scandalous.

She strummed through the magazine to get to the article when Dorothy entered her office.

"Carole, I'm sorry to interrupt your lunch, but Ms. Crenshaw called to say that she's going to be early and that she's on her way."

"Shit. Just let me know when she gets here."

"Will do."

Dorothy left the office and Carole turned back to the magazine.

> *The single American man has always been trying to achieve a nirvana of bachelorhood and magazines have catered to this dream. Whether it is the* Esquire *magazine of your grandfather's era, the* Playboy *magazine of your dad's era, or the* Titan *magazine of today, the bachelor has forever been on a quest to find the formula that gives him all the trappings of hedonistic pleasure. One group of men, led by Steven Cox and Jason Richards, star lawyers for the Ketchings & Martin law firm, are following the dictates of* Titan *magazine to the tee, and they are recruiting more men as they go along. They are turning a series of downtown lofts into private pleasure palaces where wild parties are given each and every day. And the parties don't end at three in the morning. No, that's when the parties just get started. There's the after-party that consists of multiple-partner orgies . . .*

Carole closed the magazine and sat still, as though frozen in time and space. Her brain blanked, and suddenly she didn't know what was real and what was fantasy. Her eyes couldn't focus and the office began swirling around her. She forced herself to open the magazine up again and continue reading. When she got to a blurred photo of Jason and Steven on top of Miss Blue, it was too much for her.

Covering her mouth with her hand, she ran out of the office, bumping into Dorothy.

"Carole," Dorothy said. "Ms. Crenshaw is here."

Carole barely heard her and ran into the office bathroom, where she threw up. She hugged the toilet, trying to throw up everything her brain had just taken in. And when she couldn't do anything but dry heave, she collapsed in a heap in the corner of the bathroom where she started sobbing uncontrollably. Dorothy ran into the bathroom.

"Carole, what happened? Are you okay?"

Carole couldn't talk. She was inconsolable.

Dorothy bent down and touched Carole on the shoulder. She'd *never* seen Carole in such a state.

"Please tell me, Carole," she said tenderly. "Did someone in your family pass?"

Carole lifted her tear-streaked face up to Dorothy. At first she was going to say something, but she couldn't. Words had escaped her because her dreams had come crashing down right on top of her. How could her Jason do this to her?

"Baby, let me help you up," Dorothy said. She put her hand under Carole's arm and lifted her up.

"Thank you, Dorothy, I'm okay," Carole said, looking at herself in the mirror. But she wasn't okay and she looked it. Her mascara had run and she looked like someone had broken her heart. But she had to compose herself.

"Baby, Ms. Crenshaw is in the foyer waiting."

"Okay, I'm okay. Could you do me a favor? Could you go into my office and get my purse? I need to do my makeup. Just tell Ms. Crenshaw that I'll be out in a second."

"Sure darling, sure."

Dorothy left the bathroom and Carole got some tissue and wiped her face. She didn't know what to think, but she had to get through this interview with Ms. Crenshaw. Carole steeled herself and put the whole Jason fiasco in a separate part of her brain. She'd deal with that later.

Dorothy came back into the bathroom with her purse and Carole began reapplying her makeup.

"I told Ms. Crenshaw that you'd be ready in a second, but she was really uptight. She said she didn't think the main donor to Mama's House should ever have to wait."

Carole stopped putting on her makeup and looked at Dorothy through blurry red eyes.

"Well, the bitch is going to have to wait today."

Dorothy stood in the bathroom knowing that this meeting between Carole and Ms. Crenshaw was not going to go well. She could feel it in her bones.

"Carole, I know you're upset, but please, make sure you don't take it out on Ms. Crenshaw. Remember that you have the lives of others who are depending on you."

Carole finished her makeup, took a good look and was disgusted by what she saw.

"Lousy," she muttered. "I know, Dorothy. Let's just get this over with."

Carole and Dorothy walked out of the bathroom and turned to see Ms. Crenshaw standing at Carole's office door.

"Ms. Brantford, I am not accustomed to waiting," Ms. Crenshaw said, her face scrunched in disapproval.

Carole was in no mood to take shit from anyone, especially some young millionaire who'd inherited her money instead of earned it. But she had to hold her tongue and emotions.

"I'm sorry, Ms. Crenshaw, I wasn't feeling well," Carole said, escorting Ms. Crenshaw into her office.

"Fine, but next time I expect you to receive me promptly. Do I need to remind you that we provide most of the money for Mama's House? I should be received with that in mind."

"Of course. Would you take a seat?"

Ms. Crenshaw sat down and Carole closed the magazine that was lying open on her desk. It made her nauseous just seeing it.

"The purpose of my visit is to see your facilities, how you work with your clients and what part religion plays in your counseling. I think religion is something that should be a part of the spiritual development of how your clients recover and grow as people."

"Do you have a particular religion we should use?"

"Excuse me?"

"I asked, is there a particular religion I should tell my counselors to use as they counsel our clients?"

Ms. Crenshaw looked at Carole quizzically.

"Christianity, of course," she said. "You believe in our Lord, Jesus Christ, don't you, Ms. Brantford?"

Carole's nerves were on edge already and she was about to snap. But she tried to take the edge out of her voice as she talked to Ms. Crenshaw.

"Ms. Crenshaw, I don't mean to offend you, but I feel that religion has no place in Mama's House. It is a private matter, just like whether I worship Jesus, Muhammad, or Buddha. We can certainly point women to a spiritual advisor, but we don't dispense religious advice. You are free to watch our staff work and you'll see how wonderful they are with our clients. You'll see the hope that comes on the faces of our clients as they see their lives reborn. And it is that light that keeps us going. If you'd like to see that, then feel free to stay here all day. But if you are looking for a bunch of Bible-thumping, fire-breathing, closed-minded Christian evangelists, then you've come to the wrong place. I won't tolerate that at Mama's House, and if you think that your money buys something like that, then you are dead wrong. But you are still welcome to watch us work and change lives."

Carole didn't know it, but by now she was nearly shouting, and she was pounding on her desk. This money was going out the window and she knew it.

"There's no need," Ms. Crenshaw said, rising from her chair. "I will be sending you the final decision of the board about your future funding."

She walked to the door and turned back to Carole. "Perhaps you should have chosen your words more carefully. I am the deciding vote about whether you get funding or not. You'll know my decision soon enough. Good day."

And with that, she turned and left the office.

That was too much for Carole to take. She quickly gathered her stuff and left the office.

"Dorothy, I'm leaving for the day," she said, not stopping to listen to Dorothy's answer.

Carole jumped into her car and drove as fast as she could to her apartment.

Carole rammed her car into her parking spot and ran up to her apartment. For a second, she just stood there, unable to understand what had happened to her life in less than six hours. So she just went to her couch and collapsed.

CHAPTER 28

Jason arrived in the law offices just in time for the weekly Ketchings & Martin walk-through, but this time they threw him for a loop. Instead of just making their obligatory walk-through, they stopped at his desk.

"Hello, Jason, how was your time at Mama's House?" Mr. Ketchings asked. Jason was so unnerved by his presence that he started stuttering.

"It was fine, sir," he stammered.

"Great. That's just great. Well, if you need anything, just let me know. We're glad to have you back."

"Glad to be back, sir."

And like that, they were gone. The other lawyers looked at Jason as though he'd performed some sort of miracle. Before this weekend, Jason would have cared a lot about this little visit, but today he didn't. Who gave a damn that they'd spoken to him when his love might be gone from his life forever.

Jason found his old desk just like he'd left it. Steven hadn't come in yet, so Jason didn't have to deal with him, but it was the first thing he had to confront. But first, he wanted to call Carole again. She hadn't returned a single call since this morning. He guessed that Carole had seen the magazine.

"Carole, please answer my call. I know you're upset, but please let me explain," Jason said into his cell phone. "Just give me a call . . ."

Just at that time, Steven walked in and sat down at his desk. Jason stopped talking into the phone and looked at Steven. Steven turned on his computer, and didn't even look at Jason. Jason wanted to punch the shit out of him, but he knew he couldn't. Not now and not today. This was not the time or place. Finally, Steven turned to Jason.

"I heard you were in a bit of trouble," Steven said with a smirk on his face. "Marcia called me to tell me that we're in her latest magazine. That doesn't bother me a bit, but I bet it's giving Carole a bit of indigestion as she finds out that her love is a *Titan* boy."

Jason scooted his chair right up to Steven's desk.

"It's taking every fiber of my body to not beat the shit out of you right here, and right now," Jason said, whispering. "How fucked up are you? To make up for your tiny-ass dick, you need other men to be in the bedroom with you. *Titan* man, my ass. You're nothing but a bitch with a tiny dick, and you know what? I'll get Carole back, but you'll always be a tiny dick muthafucka."

That wiped the smirk off of Steven's face. The slow burn that had been building between the two had turned into a brushfire. Steven stood up and looked down at Jason.

"You feeling froggy muthafucka, then jump!" Steven said loudly. Other attorneys began looking and Jason knew now that this was indeed the time and place.

Jason stood up and they were now face-to-face, nose to nose. Now everyone in the office was looking at them and something had to give. Out of the corner of his eye, Jason could see the partners stopping their work and looking through their windows to see what was going on in the main office. But he didn't have time to worry about that. He had a score to settle.

"I didn't think you were brave enough to hit me, you bitch," Steven said under his breath. "I gave you the guts you thought you had, and I'll take them back. I hold your balls like the bitch you are."

Then he did it.

"Plus, I'll be up in Carole's pussy probably by the end of the week anyway," he said. "You wouldn't know how to handle a piece of ass like that. Don't worry, I'll give her back to you once she's been fucked correctly."

From that moment on, life became a blur. Jason remembered hitting him with the first thing that he grabbed, which was the telephone, and Steven was knocked down. He hit Jason in the stomach and then Jason tried to club him on the back of the head, but missed. Steven then tried to bum rush Jason into one of the cubicles, but Jason sidestepped and tripped him. Suddenly Jason was on top of Steven using both of his fists to hit Steven as hard as he could.

"You son of a bitch!" Jason said, throwing blows as fast and as hard as he could. "You got me into this shit and ruined my life."

By now, the partners had run out of their offices and other lawyers were dragging Jason away from Steven. Jason had bloodied Steven's nose and Steven had torn Jason's suit.

"Steven Cox! Jason Richards! What the hell is going on here?" shouted Peter Ketchings. He was angrier than Jason had ever seen him.

Steven and Jason looked at each other.

"Nothing, sir, a personal dispute that got out of control," Jason said.

"Well I won't stand for that in my office! Both of you are suspended until further notice. I want you both out of here immediately. I'll contact you separately about what further action I'm going to take."

With that, Ketchings walked back to his office.

Someone had given Steven a handkerchief to stop his nose from bleeding and Jason tried to gather his shirt, which had been ripped. He walked back to his desk because he wasn't done with Steven yet.

"Let me tell you something," Jason said. "If you ever say anything about Carole again, I'll fuck you up again. Do you hear me? I will fuck you up worse than you can ever imagine."

Steven didn't say anything. He just kept gathering his things.

Jason walked out without gathering anything. Despite his work on the Burger World suit, Jason had a strong feeling that this was going to be the last time he worked at Ketchings & Martin. You just don't get into a fight at Ketchings & Martin.

For five minutes, Jason sat in his car wondering what to do next. He could go home, but that would just remind him of the *Titan* lifestyle. He could go to a bar and get drunk, but that wasn't an option. Finally, he decided to drive to Mama's House. It was a risk, but he needed to see Carole.

Walking through the Mama's House door was one of the toughest things Jason had done in his life.

"Hello, Jason, how have you been?" Dorothy asked, taking a furtive glance toward Carole's office.

"Fine, Dorothy," Jason said. "Is Carole around?"

"You know, she was here, but she left early," Dorothy said. "Jason, she got upset this afternoon and I'm really worried about her."

"What happened?"

"I don't know. She seemed so happy and then I found her in the bathroom crying her eyes out. She was inconsolable."

"Oh my," Jason said.

"Do me a favor," she asked. "Could you give her a call and see if she's okay? I'm pretty sure she'd like to hear from you."

"Definitely, Dorothy, I'll do that as soon as I get home. Okay, let me go and I'll see you guys later."

"Are you coming back to the center to do your work?" she asked as he walked back to the front door.

"I don't think I'm going to be doing much of any work right now," he said, walking out the door.

Jason sat in the parking lot of Mama's House not knowing what to do. He wanted to go over to Carole's house, but now he wasn't feeling that brave. Not after seeing how Dorothy had looked talking about Carole. But he knew he had to at least leave a message. And that message had to be something different. He couldn't fudge, he couldn't lie, and he couldn't be evasive. He had to be completely honest and put his cards on the table.

Jason dialed Carole's phone number and hoped she wouldn't answer. She didn't.

"Hello, this is Carole. I'm not in right now but please leave a message and I'll get back to you as soon as I can."

Beep!

"Uh, Carole. I love you. I love you, I love you, I love you. By now you've probably seen the article, and it is true. I was trying to live some *Titan* lifestyle. Steven had convinced me that I needed to live this lifestyle after I got a big bonus from the law firm. But I didn't want that. I thought I did, but I didn't. What I wanted was you and I didn't know it at the time. Oh Carole, please forgive me. Okay, I'm going to go now. Please forgive me and please call me. I love you like I've never loved anyone in my life and I don't want to lose you. Okay, I'll talk to you later."

He hung up the phone not knowing what his life, or his future held. For five glorious days, he'd had a heaven. And in less than twenty-four hours, he was now in a living hell.

CHAPTER 29

"Girl, let me in!" Marcia said. "I know you're in there!"
Marcia had been banging on Carole's door for about thirty
minutes with no results. But Marcia was not a person easily de-
terred. She knew Carole was home because she saw her car in her
parking spot.

"Just a second," a sleepy voice answered. Carole opened the
door and she looked a mess.

"Oh girl," Marcia said, hugging Carole. "Oh, my baby."

Carole was in her pajamas even though it was only the early
evening. She was sitting in the dark, with a big bowl of ice cream.
Her cheeks were tear-streaked and she didn't make an attempt to
wipe them.

"Why, Marcia? Why? And why didn't you tell me?"

Marcia walked in and closed the door.

"Because I didn't know. My managing editor found this out and
did the story without letting me know. I was just as much in the
dark as you were."

Carole laid on the couch in a fetal position.

"He was the one, Marcia. He really was the one. But it was all a
lie. It was all a lie."

"Look, dear, I'm going to tell you something that you don't want to hear right now," Marcia said, moving over to the couch. "He is still the one."

"Why are you saying that? Didn't you read that article? Did you see those pictures?"

"Yes I did," she said. "But that wasn't the real Jason. That was a person who was lost and was trying to find out who he was."

Carole looked up at Marcia. "Why are you taking up for him, Marcia? He had orgies—no, he helped organize and then participate in orgies at his home. I was just a part of his whole scheme to get as many women in bed as possible. He didn't mean any of the shit he said. It was all a lie."

"Wait, Miss Sanctimonious," Marcia said. "I know you weren't out having orgies, but didn't you try to trap Jason by following that article in *Divas*? Who was lying to whom?"

Carole didn't say anything. She just breathed slowly, her eyes looking far, far away.

"Look," Marcia continued tenderly. "I'm not here to make up your mind either way. That's up to you to do. But I do know a couple of things. One, this is a man that loves you deeply. I talked to him last night and he's simply devastated. Steven got him into this mess but when Jason found you, he knew that he didn't want to live this so-called *Titan* lifestyle anymore. He was in love and is in love. And he's in love with you. And the other thing I know is that if you let Jason go and don't forgive him, you'll regret that for the rest of your life. He's a good man that simply made a mistake. And if you'd never seen this article, you'd never have thought differently about him. Forgive him and you'll never have a problem with Jason the rest of your life. Don't forgive him and you'll search for a Jason until you die, and you'll never find him."

Carole didn't say anything, but just listened. How could she forgive Jason when she didn't know who he truly was? Was he the player who wanted as many women as he could get, or was he the person she had fallen in love with in Africa? She was confused and it hurt too much to think about it.

"I've got to go, but if you need me, feel free to call me at any time, I don't care how late," Marcia said, rising to leave. "Think about what I said. It's easy to walk away. But think about who you're going to get if you stay. The guy you fell in love with is right there for you. You just have to be brave enough to forgive him."

Marcia left and Carole stayed on the couch. Her phone rang over and over again, but she didn't get up to answer it. It might be Jason and she didn't have the strength to talk to him right now. She had to think and figure this out. She was upset, not only by the article and the photos, but also because Jason hadn't come clean with her about his past. But then she thought about it. What could he have said? *Hey Carole, things are going great. I just want to let you know that I participated in orgies at my loft. Pass the sugar?* No, there really wasn't a scenario that allowed for this type of admission.

I'm so confused, she thought. What should I do?

There was one person she knew she could ask, but did she want the answer? She picked up the phone to dial the number, but the dial tone was buzzing. She had messages. She steeled herself. If it was Jason, then she didn't know if she could listen to the message, but if it wasn't, she didn't know if she could take that he hadn't called. She was damned either way. She pressed pound to listen to the message.

> *Uh, Carole. I love you. I love you, I love you, I love you. By now you've probably seen the article, and it is true. I was trying to live some* Titan *lifestyle. Steven had convinced me that I needed to live this lifestyle after I got a big bonus from the law firm. But I didn't want that. I thought I did, but I didn't. What I wanted was you and I didn't know it at the time. Oh Carole, please forgive me. . . ."*

Tears started flowing again. She quickly stopped the message without listening to the end, and dialed the number.

"Mom, I need to talk to you."

It had been a week since the magazine article had come out. Jason had left tons of messages for Carole, but he still hadn't heard from her. He was still suspended from the law firm and so he just sat in his loft, unshaven and unwashed. What the hell did he need to shave and wash for?

He'd give up everything he'd gained just to have Carole back, he thought. The money? The money had been a curse. He remembered when he was so cocky and thought money brought happiness. Instead, he was sitting there miserable.

"You have no new messages."

Carole didn't want him, he thought. She didn't want him back and who could blame her. But he couldn't just sit here and waste away in this loft. He needed to talk to someone who would give him unconditional love. He needed to talk to Mrs. Petroff.

Driving on his Hayabusa, he made his way back to his old apartment building, good old Gower Gulch. Leaving the austere surroundings of downtown Los Angeles for his old neighborhood was not only comforting, but also brought Jason closer and closer to a reality he'd taken for granted. As he pulled into the apartment driveway, he thought about how he'd wanted to escape his previously boring existence and get some excitement in his life. Now he would trade that excitement in a minute.

It was Friday, so he was hoping Ms. Petroff was in. He used to curse it, but today he could really use a dish of her beef Stroganoff. He buzzed her door.

"Yes?" she said with her thick Russian accent.

"Hello, Mrs. Petroff, it's Jason."

"Jason!" she said. It was like he was the prodigal son coming back, even though he'd only been gone for a month.

"Come on up!"

He walked through the front door, passing by his old apartment 1A, and he saw Mrs. Petroff waiting for him in her doorway.

"It's so good to see you, Jason," she said, pinching his cheeks as always. "Come on in."

"It's good to see you, too, ma'am."

Mrs. Petroff's apartment wasn't your typical old woman's apartment with doilies and out-of-date furniture. It was surprisingly modern, with a modern television and couch and décor. Jason sat on her couch and she took a chair across from him.

"So how have you been, Jason?" She looked at him closely. "You don't look too good."

"Well, I was hoping I could have some of your wonderful beef Stroganoff."

"Say no more," she said, standing up and going into the kitchen.

She opened the refrigerator door and started pulling out ingredients. "I would love to make you a dish of Stroganoff."

She then turned to him, leaning on the kitchen counter.

"But I've known you for two years and I know you aren't here just for my Stroganoff. What's on your mind, Jason?"

Jason didn't know why he felt he could tell a sixty-year-old woman a tale of sex, money, and love, but he did. Jason told her everything and it was the most cathartic hour he'd ever spent. She listened with the patience of a woman who'd experienced life and love and had kept her hope in both.

"You love this Carole?" she said, fixing two plates of Stroganoff.

"Yes, I do. I love her with all my heart and I don't know how to get her back."

She sat down at the dining room table with her plate and looked at Jason intensely.

"Jason, let me tell you a story about my life, if you don't mind. Before I escaped the Soviet Union, I was a chef at a wonderful Moscow restaurant. I was so good that the Soviet premier asked me to cook during state receptions. I was proud of my country and proud of what I was doing. But I wanted more because it seemed like life in the Soviet Union was less free than in the West."

She stopped and had a faraway look in her eyes, as though she was being transported to another time when she had been young and carefree.

"I met this man, an American man named Thomas Gary. He was a diplomat with the U.S. embassy in Moscow and at first, our relationship was nothing but a pure one. He loved my food and I loved his tales of life in America. He'd come to the kitchen and watch me cook. But soon our relationship became more and we became lovers. I loved him with all my heart.

"You see, it was like he listened to me as though he knew me. And no Russian man had ever done this. But that also meant I was vulnerable. And soon Thomas was asking me to get information from the Soviet premier. I would listen to the conversation at the dinners I cooked for and then I would come back to Thomas. But then the KGB, the Soviet secret service, were tipped off about my spying and they came to my apartment one time looking for me. Luckily I wasn't in and Thomas sent me underground. Eventually I made my way out of the Soviet Union and landed in West Germany, and then later I was able to get to the United States.

"When I got here, I met Thomas again and I thought our love affair would continue, but I found out that he was married. He said his marriage was headed for divorce, but I couldn't forgive him for manipulating me and changing my life while lying to me about his love. But a funny thing happened. He never stopped saying that he loved me, even when I made it clear that I was not going to wait for him. He died last year and his wife sent me a note."

Mrs. Petroff got up and walked to the closet. She slowly reached high for a shoe box and pulled it down. She returned to the table and shuffled through the papers until she found an envelope. She opened the note and handed it to Jason.

"Read it."

Jason started reading the scraggly handwriting.

> *Mrs. Olga Petroff, I'm writing to inform you that my husband, Thomas Gary, has died. You may remember him as the American diplomat that helped you get out of the Soviet Union about forty years ago. I hope that all is well with you as I felt that Thomas's passing was a good enough excuse to finally contact you after all these years. Thomas mentioned you often and as I'm not stupid, I gather that you and my husband had a lovers' relationship while in the Soviet Union. While I was initially pained to realize this, I also know that in this life, love is something that is fleeting and wonderful, and if you and my husband truly shared love, then I cannot and will not be angry at you. And I know that he truly did love you. He had a diary that he kept and after he passed, I sat to read it. His words speak of a man who felt conflicted by his country, his love for you, and his desire to stay loyal to his family. He knew he couldn't have everything, but at least he'd lived a life that had a bit of each. I hope you find comfort in knowing that although Thomas loved his country, he loved you equally. God bless and I wish you nothing but happiness.*

"Jason," she said as she took the letter back, "I sit here regretting that I didn't go with my heart and wait for Thomas. Right or wrong, he was the only man I've ever loved, and every other man has always come up short. If you truly love Carole, then you need to fight for her. Be honest with her and love her with all your heart. And if it's meant to be, then you will get her in the end."

"Thank you, ma'am. I'm going to do just that. I'm going to fight for her."

"That's a good boy. Now finish your Stroganoff."

Everything had gone downhill for Carole since the Jason story had broken. She'd resisted Jason's calls because she didn't know if she wanted to speak to him again. Everything in her fiber told her that she still wanted him, but she just couldn't get the image of him with all these women out of her head. But her mother, of all people, had given her the best advice she could possibly have received.

"Carole, you have gone through boyfriends like Elizabeth Taylor goes through husbands. But I think this one is different," she said.

"Why do you think that, Mom?"

"Well for one, you are asking me for advice. You would never do that with a boyfriend you didn't care about. Think about it. If you are desperate enough to call me for advice, then you are willing to do anything to keep him. Am I wrong?"

"No, so help me, please. I think I love him."

"Then take a week to think about it and him. Is your love deep enough that you can both forget and forgive what he's done and only judge him by how he treats you? Because if you can't, leave now. It wouldn't be fair for either him or you."

"I just don't know if I can forgive and forget."

"Well now you are seeing the back side of love. Love is not always the flowers and candy. Love sometimes means that you must depend on it even when it seems as though it is not enough to hold on to. I'm not talking about being stupid, but about allowing yourself to fall in love for as many times as you can. Carole, this is your man. If you want him and not regret that you lost him, then fight for him. Allow him back in your life."

It had been almost a week since that conversation and Carole was no closer to the answer. Would she, or could she, take Jason back? Or would she just go on with her life? Work at Mama's

House, which used to be her respite from anything going on in her personal life, was now in limbo too. It didn't help that she thought that everyone in the office knew her boyfriend had been having orgies.

"Here's your mail," Dorothy said, dropping the mail on her desk. "How are you feeling, Carole?"

"A little better," she said. "No, that's a lie. I still feel lousy. But I'll get over it."

"Look," Dorothy started. "This is completely out of bounds, but go get your man."

"You are right," Carole responded. "You are completely out of bounds. But thanks."

Dorothy left the office a little depressed. Carole hadn't been the same since the article, and it had made Dorothy sad. While she liked Jason, she was shocked that the nice boy who helped so many people would be so decadent. On the other hand, she thought he was perfect for Carole. But unless something happened drastically, it wasn't going to happen.

Carole looked through the mail. And there it was, the letter from the Crenshaw Foundation that would either sink or save Mama's House. She opened it with trepidation and a certain bit of resignation. Her heart sank when she read the words.

"We regret to inform you that the Crenshaw Foundation is no longer able to fund Mama's House during this fiscal year. We, however, invite you to request for more funding in the following years as we evaluate and renew funding commitments on a year-to-year basis. Signed, Amy Crenshaw."

So that was that. Carole's life was officially a disaster. No man, no Mama's House, and no life. It had all fallen like a house of cards in just a week.

Well, they had about two weeks' worth of funds, and then she'd have to start laying people off, she thought. But she wasn't going to do anything until she was certain that Mama's House was definitely going to have to close.

It was the end of the day anyway and she was meeting Marcia for drinks. Carole didn't like mixing sorrow with alcohol, but what the hell? How worse could things get anyway?

She gathered her purse and made her way out of the office.

"Good night, Dorothy," she said. "Please lock up after you leave."

"Have a great night."

Carole got into her car and then made her way to Chi, the new happening place Marcia was checking out. She turned on her stereo and that African band Rankin Roger began playing again. Carole immediately turned it off because it reminded her of Jason.

When she pulled up to Chi, Marcia was already outside the door. It was happy hour and there was a line running as far as the eye could see. This club was hot, but Marcia of course had the hookup, and they were able to walk straight in.

"Two apple martinis," Marcia said, ordering. "How are things?"

The noise level in the place was deafening, so Carole had to shout at Marcia.

"Not good, but what else is new," she said, taking one of the martinis off of the server tray. "I just found out that we're not getting funding from our biggest donor, so Mama's House is going to close."

"Oh my goodness, that's terrible, Carole!" Marcia said. "Any chance of getting funding from another source?"

"Not at this late date. I've got funds for about two or three weeks and then that's it."

"I know this is a touchy subject, but what about Jason? Have you heard from him or talked to him lately? Where are you with that?"

"I'm still trying to figure that out. I don't know what I'm going to do yet."

"Marcia! Marcia! Over here, Marcia!"

A large woman wearing a blue satin suit came bounding toward Marcia. She was as loud and gregarious as Marcia.

"Girl, your last issue was off the chain!" she said, laughing. "Where did you find those *Titan* brothers? Talk about freaky!"

"But maybe you can hook me up with their numbers because," she said in an exaggerated whisper, "a sister gets a little hankering for some freakiness from time to time, and they'll do in a pinch."

Marcia looked uncomfortable, and finally the woman caught someone else's attention and left the table. Carole gathered her things to leave.

"See, that's what I'm talking about. I don't know if I could be with Jason knowing that everyone will think of him in those terms."

"Carole, don't leave," Marcia said, placing her hand on Carole's. "Stay and have some drinks."

"Yes Carole, don't leave," a male voice said.

But Carole and Marcia looked up to see Steven standing next to them.

"What the fuck are you doing over here?" Carole said.

He had a big bandage on his nose as though it was broken.

"You've got some damn balls to think that you can—"

"Wait, just hear me out and you don't ever have to see me again," he interrupted. Carole stopped and looked at Steven.

"What happened to your nose?"

"Jason broke it when we fought at work."

"Why did you fight at work?" Carole asked.

Steven lowered his head.

"That's not important. But I have to come clean with one thing. I got Jason into all of this. I was enamored with this whole *Titan* lifestyle and I kind of set him up with it. He didn't have a clue and honestly, without me goading him on, I doubt that he would have even been involved."

"Why are you coming to me now?" she asked suspiciously.

"Because . . . ," he started. "Just figure it out for yourself. I've told you the truth and if you don't believe it, then that's on you."

And just like that, Steven walked away. Carole looked at Marcia and didn't say anything. Marcia just kept drinking her apple martini.

"I love him, you know," Carole said to her.

"I know you do."

"I want him, you know."

"I know you do."

"I've got to go. I've got to go get my man," Carole said, grabbing her purse.

Carole ran out of Chi and hopped into her car. She looked in her purse to get her cell phone, but she'd left it at the office. She was going to go home, call Jason and tell him how much she loved him and that she forgave him. She did love him and she did forgive him. She'd work on the forgetting part later.

Thundering down the streets of Los Angeles, Carole drove like she'd never driven before. Finally, she got to her parking space and ran up the apartment building stairs, grabbing for the keys in her purse. She'd been so focused on getting to her apartment that she failed to notice the Hayabusa outside her building, and the man standing with flowers in front of her door, until she almost bumped into him. It was Jason. He'd taken a risk, but Carole was worth it.

When their eyes met, they stood there unsure of each other, not knowing how the other was going to react. Then Carole slapped him. Jason took the blow and stood there silently.

"When you said you loved me in your message, did you mean it?" Carole asked softly, her head lowered.

"Yes."

"How do you know?"

"Because I miss you when you aren't around," Jason said, lifting her head. "I want to hear you laugh, to hear you talk, and I wanted to be near you."

Jason moved closer to Carole.

"I want to love you, and now I am in love with you. I've probably lost my job because of you and I don't regret it a second. I'm willing to do anything to be with you, to love you, and to adore you. And I'll never leave you."

Carole took a step toward Jason, and was right in his face.

"Then you either have to choose a life with me, or the *Titan* life you had. But you can't have both."

"I want you."

"Then prove it."

Jason leaned in and kissed Carole with the most passionate kiss they'd both ever had. Suddenly Jason pulled back.

Carole smiled and looked into Jason's eyes.

"We must be breaking the rules, my friend. You are now getting a girlfriend with all of the benefits."

They've been together since that day. Jason moved out of the loft, because of too many *Titan* life memories, and he didn't want anything to mess up the karma he had with Carole. Funny as it seemed, his old apartment 1A hadn't been rented yet, and it was so perfect that they decided to live together in it. Ketchings & Martin did ask him to resign, but he got the balance of his money from them, so Jason was rolling in cash. And that was good because he was the largest contributor to the new Mama's House Foundation. Jason donated one million dollars to the center, and now he went around the country asking for money, while Carole ran the center. Jason had never been happier and he'd learned one crucial lesson from this whole experience. Love is beautiful and deep when you appreciate it. And with Carole, he found the love that he was after. He did indeed have a friend with benefits.

FRIENDS WITH BENEFITS

LAWRENCE ROSS

ABOUT THIS GUIDE

The suggested questions are intended to
enhance your group's reading of
Lawrence Ross's novel,
FRIENDS WITH BENEFITS.

DISCUSSION QUESTIONS

1. *Friends with Benefits* is Lawrence Ross's first novel. He is best known for his book *The Divine Nine: The History of African American Fraternities and Sororities*. In what ways do you think his background as a journalist and historian influenced his writing as a novelist?

2. When Olga Petroff appears at the beginning of the novel, whom does she represent to Jason? Why is she important to Jason's overall view of women?

3. Throughout the novel, Jason is presented with choices, whether by the law firm, Steven, or *Titan* magazine. Is Jason strong or weak when making these decisions?

4. Carole seems to repeat the same mistakes in every relationship. Do you think she is representative of most women? Why did she choose celibacy as a solution?

5. Marcia seems a direct contrast to Carole when it comes to being comfortable sexually and in relationships. Is Marcia's life more desirable than Carole's?

6. What do you think of the novel's sex scenes? Do they, in your opinion, have literary significance (for example, do they tie into the plot or play upon any themes), or are they more or less intended to titillate?

7. Have you ever had a friend with benefits? Is it possible to follow friends with benefits' rules and not have an emotional connection with your sexual partner? Have you ever done so? What other rules would you add? What rules would you change?

8. In *Friends with Benefits*, Steven is fixated on having group sex. What was your reaction to the group sex scenes? Are men more attracted to group sex, or are women?

9. Are there secret sex parties going on in your social circles?

10. Are men and women overly influenced by men and women's magazines like *Titan* and *Divas*?

11. Which character did you enjoy the most and why?

12. If you were a female, would you go to a *Titan* party and participate in the after-party? If you were a male, would you hold those types of parties?

13. If you were Carole, would you have taken Jason back? If you were Jason, what would you have done to get Carole back?

14. Do you think Carole will trust Jason, even after they've moved in together?